精選生活情境單字，要學就要學最實用的！

八大類項╳互動對話╳外師錄音

快速掌握生活英語

本書使用方式

Step 1　精選生活情境單字，要學就要學最實用的！

本書依生活中的「食、衣、住、交通、教育、娛樂、家庭與社會、各種狀態」將單字分為八個類項，並精選最常用的1800個生活情境單字，一網打盡所有出現頻率最高的實用單字！單字背得多，不如只背最實用的！跟著本書學習，讓你短時間內提升英文實力，快速開口說英文。

Contents 目錄

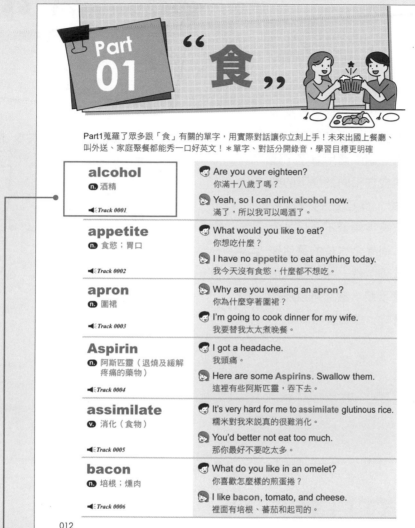

Part 01 "食"

Part1蒐羅了眾多跟「食」有關的單字，用實際對話讓你立刻上手！未來出國上餐廳、叫外送、家庭聚餐都能秀一口好英文！＊單字、對話分開錄音，學習目標更明確

單字	對話
alcohol n. 酒精 ◀ Track 0001	Are you over eighteen? 你滿十八歲了嗎？ Yeah, so I can drink **alcohol** now. 滿了，所以我可以喝酒了。
appetite n. 食慾；胃口 ◀ Track 0002	What would you like to eat? 你想吃什麼？ I have no **appetite** to eat anything today. 我今天沒有食慾，什麼都不想吃。
apron n. 圍裙 ◀ Track 0003	Why are you wearing an **apron**? 你為什麼穿著圍裙？ I'm going to cook dinner for my wife. 我要替我太太煮晚餐。
Aspirin n. 阿斯匹靈（退燒及緩解疼痛的藥物） ◀ Track 0004	I got a headache. 我頭痛。 Here are some **Aspirins**. Swallow them. 這裡有些阿斯匹靈，吞下去。
assimilate v. 消化（食物） ◀ Track 0005	It's very hard for me to **assimilate** glutinous rice. 糯米對我來說真的很難消化。 You'd better not eat too much. 那你最好不要吃太多。
bacon n. 培根；燻肉 ◀ Track 0006	What do you like in an omelet? 你喜歡怎麼樣的煎蛋捲？ I like **bacon**, tomato, and cheese. 裡面有培根、蕃茄和起司的。

bake
v. 烘；烤
◀ Track 0007

bakery
n. 麵包店
◀ Track 0008

banque
n. 宴會
◀ Track 0009

**barbec
BBQ**
n. 烤肉（燒烤派對）
v. 烤肉
◀ Track 0010

bean
n. 豆子
◀ Track 0011

beef
n. 牛肉
◀ Track 0012

Step2 用聽力背單字，打造直覺式單字記憶法！

任何語言的學習，都要從聽力開始。本書所有單字與例句都有專業外師錄製的教學音檔，單字與例句分為兩個音檔，音檔數字編碼相同，讓你可以邊聽邊讀，分別練習單字與對話。學會正確發音的同時，還可以利用聽力，潛移默化學會自然發音法，讓你聽到單字就會拼寫，不用刻意背就能輕鬆累積單字量！

Step 3

情境互動對話，學會單字的道地用法！

每個單字都有搭配示範一組情境互動對話，透過對話示範，不僅可以清楚看到如何在日常對話中活用單字，還可以學會在相同情境下的應答方式。真正達到學以致用，讓單字學習不再只是會拼寫，而是全方位的靈活運用！此外，每一組對話也都有音檔示範，讓你可以邊聽邊跟著唸，練成道地口語！

Step 4

補充相關單字，釐清字義及易混淆單字！

適時補充常見「同義字」、「反義字」、「相關單字」、「易混淆字」等等，讓單字學習更加全面，並對單字的涵義及用法有更深刻的理解。如此一來就可以避免錯誤使用單字，讓你不僅學得快，更學得正確又全面！

Part 02

" 衣

在國外才發現需要購買衣物，卻不知道怎麼~
人是怎麼說的！＊單字、對話分開錄音，學習

accessory
n. 配件

🙂 I don't
dress.
我沒有什

🙂 I can le
我可以

◀ *Track 0158*

beard
n. 鬍子

🙂 You sh
你該刮

🙂 Is it to
對你死

◀ *Track 0159*

belt
n. 皮帶

🙂 Did y
你有

🙂 It's r
就在

◀ *Track 0160*

blonde
n. 金髮的人

🙂 Do
like
你知

🙂 Of
當

◀ *Track 0161*

boot
n. 長靴

🙂 A
啊

🙂 D
別

◀ *Track 0162*

044

字和對答，馬上知道外國

...cessory to go with my

...記我的衣服。

...ur beard.

...？

...t? I can't find it anywhere.
...？我到處都找不到。

...pants.

blonde over there? She's

...的人是誰嗎？她真是位天使！

...my little sister.
...妹妹。

...ake in my **boot**.
...一條蛇。

...me handle it.

brassiere
n. 內衣

同義字
▶ **bra** 胸罩

🔊 *Track 0163*

🗨 Which **brassiere** do you prefer, th...
or the blue one?
你比較喜歡哪一套內衣？粉紅色還是藍...

🗨 I prefer the blue one. I like lace.
我比較喜歡藍色的，我喜歡蕾絲。

button
n. 鈕子

🔊 *Track 0164*

🗨 Please give me a star-shaped bu...
請給我一個星星形狀的鈕扣。

🗨 Sorry, we are out of the one you...
抱歉，你要的已經賣完了。

charm
n. 魅力
v. 吸引；（使著迷）

同義字
▶ **attractiveness**
吸引力

🔊 *Track 0165*

🗨 Peter is really a boy with great...
彼得真是一位有魅力的男孩。

🗨 Yeah, everyone likes to mak...
him.
對呀，大家都喜歡跟他做朋友。

這裡使用的...

clothes
n. 衣服

🔊 *Track 0166*

🗨 You should wear more clothe...
你應該多穿點衣服。

🗨 But I like the cold weather ou...
但我喜歡外面的冷天氣。

coarse
adj. 粗糙的

反義字
▶ **delicate** 精緻的

🔊 *Track 0167*

🗨 The surface of this piece of...
這件衣服好粗糙。

🗨 We should replace it.
我們應該把它換掉。

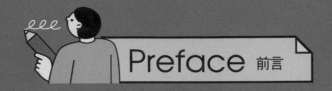

Preface 前言

　　英文作為目前國際間最被廣泛使用的語言，一直是非英語母語者學習外語的首選。良好的英文能力不僅可以消除我們與多數人間的語言隔閡，也能讓我們能有相對多的管道獲取各種資訊。因此，英語一直是備受關注的學科，相關的學習課程與教材都十分豐富。

　　然而，在英語學習上的疑難雜症也是層出不窮。其中，單字作為英語學習的基礎，更是許多人在學習之初就遇到的難題。雖然說單字是只要肯投入時間與心力，就一定可以得到收穫的基礎學習，只是速度快慢的差別。但是這種土法煉鋼的學習方式，在收效不佳的情況下，往往會對學習信心造成打擊，進而影響繼續學習的意願。此外，許多人在剛開始學習單字的時候，會有想要一口氣學會7000單字的迷思，認為單字量越多越好，會的單字越冷僻越厲害。其實，我們在生活中最常使用到的單字量並沒有到那麼多，更不會用到那些看起來好像很厲害的冷僻字詞。真正能使我們快速提升英語實力的，是那些頻繁使用的常用字。

　　看到許多人都沒有認知到優先掌握常用字可以為自己帶來的優勢，更甚者被單字學習迷思所困，我決定要將最萬用的單字學習方法編寫成書，遂有了本書的誕生。

　　本書依生活中的「食、衣、住、交通、教育、娛樂、家庭與社會、各種狀態」將單字分為八個類項，並精選最常用的1800個生活情境單字，一網打盡所有出現頻率最高的實用單字。正所謂「背得多，不如背得巧」！此外，全書皆有專業外師錄製音檔，學會正確發音的同時，利用聽力記憶單字，潛移默化學會自然發音法，聽到單字就會拼寫，不用刻意背就能輕鬆累積單字量！最後再配合對話示範，不僅可以清楚看到如何在日常對話中活用單字，還可以學會在相同情境下的應答方式。

　　相信只要跟著本書，用對方法、背對單字，就一定可以讓英語實力突飛猛進！

Contents 目錄

Part
01

Part1蒐羅了眾多跟「食」有關的單字,用實際對話讓你立刻上手!未來出國上餐廳、叫外送、家庭聚餐都能秀一口好英文!＊單字、對話分開錄音,學習目標更明確

alcohol **n.** 酒精 ◀ *Track 0001*	Are you over eighteen? 你滿十八歲了嗎? Yeah, so I can drink **alcohol** now. 滿了,所以我可以喝酒了。
appetite **n.** 食慾;胃口 ◀ *Track 0002*	What would you like to eat? 你想吃什麼? I have no **appetite** to eat anything today. 我今天沒有食慾,什麼都不想吃。
apron **n.** 圍裙 ◀ *Track 0003*	Why are you wearing an **apron**? 你為什麼穿著圍裙? I'm going to cook dinner for my wife. 我要替我太太煮晚餐。
Aspirin **n.** 阿斯匹靈(退燒及緩解疼痛的藥物) ◀ *Track 0004*	I got a headache. 我頭痛。 Here are some **Aspirins**. Swallow them. 這裡有些阿斯匹靈,吞下去。
assimilate **v.** 消化(食物) ◀ *Track 0005*	It's very hard for me to **assimilate** glutinous rice. 糯米對我來說真的很難消化。 You'd better not eat too much. 那你最好不要吃太多。
bacon **n.** 培根;燻肉 ◀ *Track 0006*	What do you like in an omelet? 你喜歡怎麼樣的煎蛋捲? I like **bacon**, tomato, and cheese. 裡面有培根、蕃茄和起司的。

bake
v. 烘；烤

🔊 *Track 0007*

Would you please teach me how to **bake** a cake?
你可以教我怎麼烤蛋糕嗎？

Sure, let's do it now.
當然，現在就來做吧。

---

bakery
n. 麵包店

🔊 *Track 0008*

The toast of that **bakery** is very delicious.
那間麵包店的吐司很好吃。

Oh, why not buy some for breakfast?
哇，那我們為什麼不買點當早餐呢？

---

banquet
n. 宴會

🔊 *Track 0009*

Can I invite my ex-girlfriend to our wedding **banquet**?
我可以邀請我的前女友來我們的婚宴嗎？

Don't even think about it!
你想都別想！

---

barbecue / BBQ
n. 烤肉（燒烤；戶外燒烤派對）
v. 烤肉

🔊 *Track 0010*

We will go to a **barbecue** party next weekend.
我們下個週末要去烤肉派對。

Sounds cool. Can I go with you?
聽起來很酷。我可以跟你們一起去嗎？

> 這裡使用的是名詞喔！

---

bean
n. 豆子

🔊 *Track 0011*

My mother is good at cooking **bean** soup.
我媽媽很會煮豆子湯。

I agree. I love her **bean** soup very much.
我同意。我好愛她的豆子湯。

---

beef
n. 牛肉

🔊 *Track 0012*

Would you like some **beef** steak?
你要來點牛排嗎？

No thanks. I don't eat **beef**.
不了，謝謝。我不吃牛肉。

beer
n. 啤酒

Track 0013

I like to drink **beer** after work.
我喜歡在工作後喝啤酒。

Me too. It's really joyful.
我也是。那真的很痛快。

beet
n. 甜菜（根）

Track 0014

My neighbor gave me some **beets**, but I don't know how to cook it.
我鄰居給了我一些甜菜，可是我不知道怎麼料理。

You can cook **beet** soup, hot or cold.
你可以拿來煮湯，熱的冷的都可以。

biscuit
n. 餅乾；小甜麵包

Track 0015

What do we have for tea time?
我們的下午茶有什麼？

Coffee and **biscuits**.
咖啡和小甜麵包。

bite
n. 咬；一口；（咬傷）
v. 咬；（叮咬；蟄傷）

Track 0016

I was **bitten** by a stray dog.
我被一隻流浪狗咬了。

Oh my goodness! Take care of your wound!
天啊！好好照顧你的傷口！

這裡使用的是動詞喔！

bitter
n. 苦啤酒
adj. 苦的；（怨恨的；使人痛苦的）

Track 0017

Can I take a sip of your beer?
我可以喝一口你的啤酒嗎？

Are you sure? It's very **bitter**.
你確定嗎？這很苦哦。

這裡使用的是形容詞喔！

breakfast
n. 早餐

相關單字
▶ **lunch** 午餐
▶ **dinner** 晚餐

Track 0018

I always get up early and prepare **breakfast** for my family.
我都很早起床替家人準備早餐。

How nice of you!
你人真好！

bread
n. 麵包

🔊 *Track 0019*

👦 Can you buy some **bread** on your way home?
你回來時能順便買些麵包嗎？

👧 No problem. What kind of **bread** do you want?
當然可以。你想要什麼種類的麵包？

broil
v. 烤；炙

🔊 *Track 0020*

👦 I went fishing this afternoon.
我今天下午去釣魚。

👧 So, can we **broil** fish tonight?
所以晚上我們可以吃烤魚囉？

broth
n. 湯；清湯

🔊 *Track 0021*

👦 I don't feel well and have no appetite.
我很不舒服，而且也沒有胃口。

👧 Eat some **broth** and you will feel better.
喝一點清湯，你就會感覺好一點了。

brunch
n. 早午餐

🔊 *Track 0022*

👦 I got up late and missed breakfast.
我起的太晚所以錯過早餐了。

👧 It's OK. We can have **brunch** instead.
沒關係，我們可以改吃早午餐了。

buffet
n. 自助餐

🔊 *Track 0023*

👦 If you girls win the game, what do you want as a reward?
如果妳們贏了這場比賽，想要什麼獎賞？

👧 Treat us to a luxury **buffet**!
請我們去吃高級自助餐！

butter
n. 奶油

🔊 *Track 0024*

👦 Do you want me to smear **butter** or peanut **butter** on your toast?
你想要我塗奶油還是花生醬在吐司上面？

👧 I want both combined. Thanks.
我兩個都想要。謝謝。

cabbage

n. 甘藍菜

◀ Track 0025

What do you plant in the vegetable farm?
你種了什麼在菜園裡？

Only **cabbages**. It's very tasty and very cheap.
只有種甘藍菜，它好吃又便宜。

carrot

n. 胡蘿蔔

相關字
▶ **radish** 白蘿蔔

◀ Track 0026

I only feed my rabbit with **carrots**.
我只用胡蘿蔔餵我的兔子

Do you know it's bad for rabbits?
你知道這樣對牠不好嗎？

carve

v. 切；切成薄片（雕刻）

同義字
▶ **cut** 切

◀ Track 0027

I bought a big potato in the market.
我在市場買了個大馬鈴薯。

Good, we can **carve** it and make some potato chips.
很好，我們可以切成薄片，然後做些薯片了。

catering

n. 承辦酒席；（餐飲業；準備或提供食物的工作）

◀ Track 0028

Who's **catering** your wedding?
誰幫妳承辦婚禮的酒席？

I have no idea. My husband handled everything by himself.
我也不知道，我老公自己處理所有的事情了。

cereal

n. 穀類作物；（麥片）

◀ Track 0029

Cereal with milk can bring the perfect flavor!
麥片配牛奶真是絕配！

I don't think so. Juice is better.
我不覺得耶。果汁比較好。

champagne
n. 香檳

Track 0030

How about buying **champagne** to celebrate Mother's Day?
要不要買香檳慶祝母親節？

Good idea, she would be very glad.
好主意，她應該會很高興。

cheese
n. 乳酪

Track 0031

Who bit my **cheese**?
誰咬了我的乳酪？

You should ask your doggy.
你該去問問你的狗兒。

chew
v. 咀嚼

同義字
▶ **munch** 用力咀嚼

Track 0032

Hey, **chew** slower, or you'll have hard digestion.
喂，你要嚼慢一點，不然會消化不良。

But I am in a hurry, I have no choice.
但我在趕時間，我也沒辦法。

chopstick(s)
n. 筷子

Track 0033

I am not used to using forks.
我還不習慣用叉子。

You can ask the waiter to serve you **chopsticks**.
你可以叫服務生給你筷子。

cigarette
n. 香菸

Track 0034

Can I buy some foreign **cigarettes** for dad?
我可以買些外國香菸給老爸嗎？

No way! He's quit smoking for several years!
當然不行！他已經戒菸好多年了！

cocktail
n. 雞尾酒

Track 0035

Don't you serve **cocktail** in this restaurant?
你們這間餐廳沒有賣雞尾酒嗎？

I'm sorry, we only serve alcohol-free drinks.
不好意思，我們這裡只賣無酒精飲料。

cocoa
n. 可可亞（粉或飲料）

🔊 Track 0036

Whenever winter comes, I want to drink **cocoa** in particular.
每次冬天到了，我就會特別想喝可可亞。

So do I. It can warm both our body and mind.
我也是，它可以溫暖我們的身體和心靈。

coconut
n. 椰子（椰子肉）

🔊 Track 0037

It's so hot today, I want to drink something cool.
今天好熱，我想喝點涼的。

Coconut water can make you feel cooler.
椰子汁可以讓你清涼一點。

consume
v. （尤指大量地）消耗（花費；吃或喝）

反義字
▶ **produce** 製造

🔊 Track 0038

There are five kids in my family.
我家有五個小孩。

Wow, they must **consume** a great amount of food everyday.
哇，那他們每天應該消耗掉很多食物。

cook
n. 廚師
v. （做飯）烹調

🔊 Track 0039

Why are you in a hurry to go home?
你為什麼這麼趕著回家？

It's time to **cook** dinner!
該回家煮晚餐了！

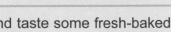
這裡使用的是動詞喔！

cookie
n. 餅乾

同義字
▶ **biscuit** 餅乾

🔊 Track 0040

Everyone, come and taste some fresh-baked **cookies**.
大家過來嚐嚐剛出爐的餅乾吧！

Hurrah! Thank you boss.
萬歲！謝啦老闆。

cream
n. 乳酪；奶油；乳製品

🔊 *Track 0041*

👦 I'm getting fatter and fatter recently.
我最近變得越來越胖了。

👧 Then you should not eat **cream** anymore.
那你就別再吃乳製品了吧。

crisp/crispy
adj. 鬆脆的、易裂的

🔊 *Track 0042*

👦 This cookie is not **crispy** anymore.
這塊餅乾已經不脆了。

👧 It was exposed to the air for too long.
它曝露在空氣裡面太久了。

cucumber
n. 小黃瓜

🔊 *Track 0043*

👦 What are you going to do with these **cucumber** slices?
你要拿這些小黃瓜片做什麼？

👧 I'm going to make a face mask.
我要拿來做面膜。

cuisine
n. 烹調；烹飪；菜餚

🔊 *Track 0044*

👦 I love Japanese **cuisine**.
我真的很愛日本菜。

👧 I know a nice Japanese restaurant nearby. Would you like to go?
我知道附近有一間不錯的日本料理店。你想要去嗎？

curry
n. 咖哩

🔊 *Track 0045*

👦 I'm tired of eating the same meal everyday.
每天都吃一樣的東西，我已經煩了。

👧 Alright, alright, let's have **curry** today.
好啦好啦，我們今天吃咖哩。

delicious
adj. 美味的

反義字
▶ **distasteful**
難吃的

🔊 *Track 0046*

👦 This apple pie is extremely **delicious**! I want one more!
這個蘋果派真的太美味了！我還要一塊！

👧 Watch your weight!
注意你的體重！

dessert

n. 餐後點心；甜點

易混淆字

▶ **desert** 沙漠

 Track 0047

What's up? Why don't you eat **dessert**?
怎麼了？你怎麼不吃飯後甜點？

I'm too full to eat anymore!
我再也吃不下任何東西了！

---

diet

n. 飲食；節食

 Track 0048

I don't eat chocolate and dairy products now.
我現在不吃巧克力和乳製品了。

Why? Are you on a **diet**?
為什麼？你在減肥嗎？

---

dish

n. 盛食物的盤、碟（餐盤；菜餚）

 Track 0049

Would you please give me a **dish**?
你可以給我一個餐盤嗎？

No problem, momma.
沒問題，媽媽。

---

donut

n. 甜甜圈

 Track 0050

Finally, it's the end of the day!
一天終於結束了！

What I want the most is some **donuts** and a cup of tea!
我現在最需要的就是一些甜甜圈跟一杯茶！

---

drink

n. 飲料
v. 喝

同義字

▶ **beverage**
飲料

 Track 0051

The shop sold out the **drink** we want.
這間店賣完了我們想喝的飲料。

Let's go to check the next shop.
我們去下一間看看吧。

這裡使用的是名詞喔！

020

drunk
n. 醉鬼；（酗酒者）
adj. 酒醉的；著迷的

What's that smell?
那是什麼味道？

There's a **drunk** man walking by.
有個喝醉的男人走了過去。

這裡使用的是形容詞喔！

Track 0052

egg
n. 蛋

To make an egg roll, you need sugar, butter, flour…
做蛋捲會需要糖、奶油、麵粉……

And most important of all, **eggs**.
還有最重要的，就是蛋。

Track 0053

empty
adj. 空的

The classroom is **empty**. Where are the students?
教室是空的，學生都去哪了？

They are taking PE class.
他們去上體育課了。

Track 0054

enjoy
v. 享受；欣賞

Thank you for inviting me to this private party.
謝謝你邀請我參加這個私人派對。

You're welcome. **Enjoy** yourself.
不客氣。祝你玩的開心。

Track 0055

famine
n. 饑荒

同義字
▶ **starvation**
饑荒

Did you hear the news of **famine** in Africa?
你知道非洲饑荒的新聞嗎？

Yeah, I've donated some money to help them.
知道，我已經有捐些錢去幫他們了。

Track 0056

feast

n. 盛宴；（感官享受）
v. 宴請；使⋯⋯享受；
（參加宴會；享受）

◀︎ *Track 0057*

What do you intend to **feast** your professor?
你打算宴請你們教授什麼？

I've reserved seats at Wang-steak restaurant.
我已經訂了王品牛排的位子了。

這裡使用的是動詞喔！

feed

v. 餵（養）；（供給；從
某事物中得到滋養）

◀︎ *Track 0058*

Remember to **feed** your son on time.
記得要準時餵你兒子吃飯。

Yes, my dear wife!
好的，老婆大人！

flavor

n. 味道；（韻味）
v. 調味；（給⋯⋯增添風
趣）

同義字
▶ **relish** 滋味

◀︎ *Track 0059*

The **flavor** of the soup is awful.
這個湯的味道真糟。

It's stored in refrigerator for three weeks!
它放在冰箱三個禮拜了！

這裡使用的是名詞喔！

flour

n. 麵粉

◀︎ *Track 0060*

Why does my dough feel so sticky?
為什麼我的麵團會這麼黏？

Perhaps you put too less **flour**.
你大概放太少麵粉了。

food

n. 食物

◀︎ *Track 0061*

The shelter is now lack of **food** and water.
收容所現在缺乏食物跟水。

Alright, I'll ask for help from the government.
好，我會跟政府請求協助。

fork
n. 叉子

🧒 It's so hard to eat spaghetti with chopsticks.
用筷子吃義大利麵好不方便。

👩 Why don't you use a **fork**?
那你為什麼不用叉子呢？

🔊 *Track 0062*

fry
v. 油炸；炸

🧒 What do we have for midnight snacks?
我們宵夜吃什麼？

👩 I've **fried** some chicken, and you can buy some salad to go with it.
我做了一些炸雞，你可以去買沙拉來配。

🔊 *Track 0063*

garlic
n. 蒜

🧒 You have bad breath!
你有口臭！

👩 Oh, I just ate **garlic** bread.
噢，我剛剛吃了大蒜麵包。

🔊 *Track 0064*

glass
n. 玻璃；玻璃杯；（複數可指眼鏡）

同義字
▶ **cup** 杯子

🧒 Why is your hand bleeding?
你的手怎麼在流血？

👩 I broke a **glass** and the fragments cut my finger.
我打破了玻璃杯，然後碎片弄傷了我的手指。

🔊 *Track 0065*

grain
n. 穀類；穀粒；（細顆粒）

🧒 This year we have a good harvest in **grain**.
今年我們的穀物大豐收。

👩 Congrates! You will have a good time in the rest of the year!
恭喜啊！這一年剩下來的時間你們都能過的很好了！

🔊 *Track 0066*

greasy

adj. 油膩的

Track 0067

I have stomachache because of the **greasy** meat.
那塊油膩膩的肉害我胃痛。

I have some gastric medicine. You want some?
我有胃藥，你要一些嗎？

---

greedy

adj. 貪婪的

反義字
▶ **generous**
　慷慨的

Track 0068

The **greedy** politician is sentenced to jail.
那個貪婪的政客被判入獄了。

He deserves it!
他活該！

---

ham

n. 火腿

Track 0069

Both **ham** and bacon are made from pork.
火腿和培根都是用豬肉做的。

Everybody knows it.
大家都知道啊。

---

hamburger/burger

n. 漢堡

Track 0070

How about having lunch in a fast-food restaurant?
要不要在速食店吃午餐？

Sure, I am a **hamburger** lover!
好啊！我超愛漢堡的！

---

hungry

adj. 飢餓的；（渴求的）

Track 0071

Mother, I am **hungry**.
媽，我餓了。

Eat some cookies, dear. I'm too busy to prepare meal.
親愛的，先吃些餅乾。我現在忙到沒辦法做飯。

indispensable

adj. 不可缺少的

同義字
▶ **necessary**
必要的

◀ Track 0072

You are the most **indispensable** friend to me.
你是我最少不了的朋友。

Come on! That's too mushy!
拜託！這太肉麻了！

ingredient

n. 成分；原料

◀ Track 0073

The **ingredients** of this cocktail is complicated.
這杯雞尾酒的成份很複雜。

I'm curious, can you tell me some?
我很好奇，可以跟我說一些嗎？

jam

n. 果醬；堵塞；（交通堵塞；堵在機器中的東西）
v. （使）堵塞

◀ Track 0074

Excuse me, I want some fresh **jams**.
你好，我想要一些新鮮果醬。

What flavor would you like? Peach or Blueberry?
你想要哪種口味？桃子還是藍莓？

這裡使用的是名詞喔！

jug

n. 帶柄水壺

同義字
▶ **kettle** 水壺

◀ Track 0075

Why did you leave the **jug** in the yard?
你為什麼把帶柄水壺留在院子裡？

I forgot to bring it in.
我忘了帶進來。

juicy

adj. 多汁的

◀ Track 0076

Those apples are in season.
那些蘋果都是當季的。

Then they must be very **juicy**.
那一定很多汁。

ketchup
n. 番茄醬

Track 0077

Don't you put **ketchup** on French fries?
你不淋蕃茄醬在薯條上面嗎？

No, I only eat plain.
不，我吃薯條不加任何東西的。

lemonade
n. 檸檬水

Track 0078

Call the waiter to bring us **lemonade**.
叫服務生給我們檸檬水。

He seems busy now. Wait a second.
他現在看起來很忙，等一下。

lick
v. 舔食；舔

Track 0079

See! Your cat is **licking** my hand!
你看！你的貓在舔我的手！

She likes you, I think.
我想她喜歡妳噢。

liquor
n. 酒；烈酒

Track 0080

Hey, buddy, try this **liquor**!
嘿老兄，試試看這款酒！

I'm glad to, but I need to drive later.
我很樂意，但我等一下得開車。

loaf
數量 一條（麵包）

Track 0081

How many **loaves** of bread do we need?
我們需要幾條麵包？

Let me see...let's take ten loaves.
我看一下……我們要拿十條。

lunch/ luncheon
n. 午餐

Track 0082

I've eaten lots things in brunch.
我早午餐吃了很多東西。

Are you sure you're able to eat **lunch**?
你確定你還能吃中餐嗎？

a
b
c
d
e
f
g
h
i
j
k
l
m
n
o
p
q
r
s
t
u
v
w
x
y
z

mayonnaise
n. 美乃滋；蛋黃醬

🧑 Please don't put **mayonnaise** in my sandwich.
請別在我的三明治裡加美乃滋。

👩 You don't eat **mayonnaise**?
你不吃美乃滋？

🔊 *Track 0083*

---

meal
n. 一餐；餐

🧑 I need to eat several **meals** a day.
我一天要吃好幾餐。

👩 That's alright, you're so slim.
沒關係啊，你這麼瘦。

🔊 *Track 0084*

---

meat
n. （食用）肉

同義字
▶ **flesh** （人或動物的）肉；果肉；蔬菜的可食部分

🧑 I'm a vegetarian.
我是個素食者。

👩 Such a pity! This **meat** is delicious.
好可惜哦，這塊肉很好吃耶。

🔊 *Track 0085*

---

menu
n. 菜單；（電腦螢幕上顯示的功能表）

🧑 Can you give me the **menu**?
可以給我菜單嗎？

👩 We don't have **menu**, you can order whatever you want.
我們這裡沒有菜單，你可以點任何你想吃的東西。

🔊 *Track 0086*

---

microwave
n. 微波爐

🧑 Don't stand in front of the **microwave** while it's working.
微波爐在運作的時候，別站在它前面。

👩 I'll beware of it next time.
我下次會注意的。

🔊 *Track 0087*

milk
n. 牛奶

Track 0088

This **milk** is a little bit sour.
這牛奶有點酸掉了。

Then stop drinking, and throw it away.
那就別喝了，把它倒掉吧。

mug
n. 馬克杯

Track 0089

I got a present from my senior today. It's a **mug**.
我學姐給了我一個禮物，是個馬克杯。

Is it your birthday today?
今天是你的生日嗎？

mushroom
n. 蘑菇

Track 0090

How is my new hairstyle?
我的新髮型怎麼樣？

Very cute, like a **mushroom**.
很可愛，像顆蘑菇。

mutton
n. 羊肉

Track 0091

There's an offensive smell of **mutton**.
羊肉有股討厭的味道。

But some people find it very yummy.
不過對一些人來說，那很美味。

napkin
n. 餐巾紙

Track 0092

Sir, my **napkin** is stained.
先生，我的餐巾紙弄髒了。

Please wait a minute, I'll give you another one.
請等一下，我給你一條新的。

noodle
n. 麵條

Track 0093

I've prepared some **noodles** for dinner.
我晚餐準備了些麵條。

Noodle again? Can we eat something else?
又是麵？我們可以吃些別的嗎？

nutritious

adj. 營養的

反義字
▶ **innutritious**
不營養的

◀ *Track 0094*

Son, eat up the soup. It's very **nutritious**.
兒子，把湯喝光，那很營養的。

Are you killing me? It's disgusting!
妳要殺了我？它很噁心耶！

odor

n. 氣味

◀ *Track 0095*

The **odor** seems to come from the corner of the room.
這味道好像從房間角落傳出來的。

Nonsense. It's from your bag.
才不是，是從你的包包傳出來的。

offer

n. 提議；折扣；（主動幫忙）
v. 提議；提供

同義字
▶ **serve** 供應

◀ *Track 0096*

The hotel **offers** room services, like free dinner and free wi-fi .
這旅館有很多客房服務，比如免費的晚餐和無線網路。

And it just cost 1000 dollars a night?
這樣一晚才1000塊？

這裡使用的是動詞喔！

oven

n. 爐子；烤箱

◀ *Track 0097*

It smells like something is burning.
好像什麼東西燒焦了。

Oh no! I forgot to turn off the **oven**!
完蛋了！我忘了關烤箱！

pack
n. 背包
v. 打包
數量 一包（盒，箱，袋）

同義字
▶ **package**
包；包裹

🔊 *Track 0098*

🗣 There're several **packs** piling by the door.
有好幾袋東西堆在門口。

🗣 Let's remove them.
我們把它們移開吧。

這裡使用的是名詞喔！

---

pan
n. 平底鍋

🔊 *Track 0099*

🗣 I'm going to make fried rice with my new **pan**.
我要用新買的的平底鍋來做炒飯。

🗣 Wow, I can't wait!
哇，我等不及要嚐嚐看了。

---

pasta
n. 麵團；義大利麵

🔊 *Track 0100*

🗣 I suddenly feel like eating **pasta**!
我突然很想吃義大利麵耶！

🗣 Action speaks louder than words.
想吃就去吃吧。

---

picnic
n. 野餐
v. 野餐

🔊 *Track 0101*

🗣 My family is craving **picnics**.
我的家人很熱愛野餐。

🗣 Do you mind if my family go with yours next time?
那你介意下次我們家人也一起去嗎？

這裡使用的是名詞喔！

---

pie
n. 派；餡餅

🔊 *Track 0102*

🗣 Where is the apple **pie** I just baked?
我剛烤好的蘋果派去哪了？

🗣 Ha! It's in my stomach now!
哈，都在我的肚子裡了！

pizza
n. 披薩

Track 0103

Hello, this is **Pizza** Hut.
你好，這裡是必勝客。

Hi, I would like to order some **pizzas**.
嗨，我想要訂披薩。

plate
n. 盤子

Track 0104

The **plates** are very fragile, watch your step.
那些盤子很容易碎哦，要小心。

Don't talk to me now!
現在別跟我説話啦！

popcorn
n. 爆米花

Track 0105

Whenever I watch movies, I eat **popcorn**.
我每次看電影的時候都要吃爆米花。

Me too. Do you eat salty or sweet?
我也是。你吃鹹的還是甜的？

pork
n. 豬肉

Track 0106

Muslims can't eat **pork** or drink wine.
穆斯林不能吃豬肉也不喝酒。

Then I think I'll never be a Muslim.
那我想我一輩子都不會當穆斯林了。

pot
n. 鍋；壺

Track 0107

Can I use this **pot**?
我可以用這個鍋子嗎？

Be careful, I just boiled water and it's very hot now.
小心點，我剛剛煮了開水，它現在很燙。

pour
v. 澆；倒；（使傾瀉）

Track 0108

I'm so sorry about **pouring** your wine out.
我真的很抱歉把你的酒倒掉了。

Never mind. You didn't mean it, did you?
別介意，你又不是故意的，不是嗎？

pub
n. 酒館

🔊 *Track 0109*

🗨️ I met a cute boy in a **pub** last night.
我昨天在酒吧認識了一個可愛男生。

🗨️ You did? Did you get his cell phone number?
真的？那你有要到他的手機號碼嗎？

pudding
n. 布丁

🔊 *Track 0110*

🗨️ I can make **puddings** by myself!
我會自己做布丁哦。

🗨️ That's nothing.
那沒什麼了不起的啊。

raisin
n. 葡萄乾

🔊 *Track 0111*

🗨️ You've eaten too many **raisins**.
你已經吃太多葡萄乾了。

🗨️ But **raisins** are good for our health!
但葡萄乾對身體很好啊！

recipe
n. 食譜；秘訣

🔊 *Track 0112*

🗨️ The chocolate cake you made is so delicious. May I borrow your **recipe**?
你做的巧克力蛋糕好好吃喔，我可以跟你借食譜嗎？

🗨️ Well… actually I don't have a **recipe**.
這個嘛……其實我沒有食譜。

require
v. 需要；（有賴於；要求；規定）

🔊 *Track 0113*

🗨️ My class teacher **requires** us to hand in the assignment before noon.
我的導師要我們在中午之前交作業。

🗨️ You'd better start to work on it, then.
那你最好開始做了。

a b c d e f g h i j k l m n o p q r s t u v w x y z

restaurant
n. 餐廳

🧑 There is a new Indian **restaurant** on the corner of the street. Do you want to give it a try?
轉角那裡開了一家新的印度餐廳。你想不想去試試看？

👩 Nah. I'm not a fan of spicy food.
不了，我不喜歡辣的食物。

🔊 *Track 0114*

rice
n. 稻米；米飯

🧑 I prefer noodles to **rice**.
我比較喜歡麵不喜歡飯。

👩 But we only have **rice** for dinner.
但我們晚餐只有飯。

🔊 *Track 0115*

roast
v. 烘烤

同義字
▶ **grill** 烤

🧑 We are planning to **roast** a turkey on Thanksgiving Day. Do you want to join us?
我們準備在感恩節那天烤一隻火雞，你要加入我們嗎？

👩 Sounds great. Count me in.
聽起來很棒，算我一份。

🔊 *Track 0116*

salad
n. 生菜食品、沙拉

🧑 Do you want some **salad**?
你要吃一點沙拉嗎？

👩 No, thanks. I don't like vegetable at all.
不了謝謝，我一點都不喜歡蔬菜。

🔊 *Track 0117*

salt
n. 鹽

🧑 Why does this pork taste flavorless?
為什麼這塊豬肉沒什麼味道？

👩 Oops. I forgot to add some **salt**.
喔，我忘了加鹽。

🔊 *Track 0118*

salty
adj. 鹹的

Track 0119

The soup is too **salty**.
這湯太鹹了。

I'm sorry. I dropped the salt bottle while I was cooking the soup.
抱歉，我在煮湯的時候不小心將鹽罐掉下去了。

sandwich
n. 三明治

Track 0120

What are you going to bring for picnic?
你野餐要準備什麼？

Sandwich! I am crazy for **sandwich**.
三明治！我超愛三明治。

sauce
n. 醬料

Track 0121

Where should I add the **sauce**?
我應該把這醬料加在哪裡？

Mix it with the spaghetti.
和義大利麵拌一拌。

sausage
n. 臘腸；香腸

Track 0122

Want some **sausage**?
要吃一點香腸嗎？

No, thanks. **Sausage** is not good for our health.
不用了謝謝，香腸對健康不好。

seasoning
n. 調味料

同義字
▶ **flavoring**
調味料

Track 0123

Oh-Oh. I forgot to mix the **seasoning** and the salmon together.
喔喔，我忘記將鮭魚和調味料拌在一起了。

That's okay. I can do it myself.
沒關係，我可以自己來。

a b c d e f g h i j k l m n o p q r s t u v w x y z

serving

n. 服務；（供一人食用的一份）

adj. （尤指）現役的

🔊 *Track 0124*

The **serving** of this restaurant is pretty good.
這家餐廳的服務挺好的。

Yeah. I think I will come here again.
對呀，我想我還會再來一次。

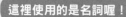
這裡使用的是名詞喔！

---

slice

n. 片；薄的切片

v. 切片

🔊 *Track 0125*

What did you have for breakfast?
你早餐吃什麼？

Only a **slice** of bread and a cup of milk.
只有一片吐司和一杯牛奶。

這裡使用的是名詞喔！

---

snack

n. 小吃；點心

易混淆字
▶ **snake** 蛇

🔊 *Track 0126*

My mom doesn't allow me to eat any **snack**.
我媽媽不准我吃任何點心。

Why? **Snack** is my second life.
為什麼？點心是我的第二生命！

---

soda

n. 汽水；蘇打

🔊 *Track 0127*

Want some **soda**?
要喝一點汽水嗎？

Sure. The weather is extremely hot.
好啊，這天氣真是熱翻了。

---

soup

n. 湯

🔊 *Track 0128*

This corn **soup** is excellent. Did you make it yourself?
這個玉米湯太棒了，你自己做的嗎？

No. I bought it from the convenience store.
不是耶，我在便利商店買的。

sour

adj. 酸的

同義字
▶ **acid** 酸的

◀ *Track 0129*

This apple juice is too **sour**.
這個蘋果汁太酸了。

Do you want to add some sugar?
你要加一點糖嗎？

spaghetti

n. 義大利麵

同義字
▶ **pasta** 義大利麵

◀ *Track 0130*

What do we have for dinner?
晚餐吃什麼？

The same, **spaghetti**.
一樣，義大利麵。

spicy

adj. 辛辣的；加香料的

◀ *Track 0131*

The curry is too **spicy** for me.
咖哩對我來說太辣了。

Do you want some water?
你要喝一點水嗎？

spoon

n. 湯匙、調羹

◀ *Track 0132*

Use your spoon to eat the soup.
用你的湯匙喝湯。

Do I really have to do that?
我一定要這樣做嗎？

sprinkle

v. 撒；灑；噴淋

◀ *Track 0133*

Let's sprinkle some chocolate chips on the ice cream.
我們來灑一些巧克力碎片在冰淇淋上面。

Great! I'm a chocoholic!
太棒了！我超愛吃巧克力！

a
b
c
d
e
f
g
h
i
j
k
l
m
n
o
p
q
r
s
t
u
v
w
x
y
z

stale
adj. 不新鮮的

反義字
▶ **fresh** 新鮮的

◀ *Track 0134*

The guava is **stale**.
這個芭樂不新鮮。

Just put it in the trash can.
那就把它丟到垃圾桶吧。

starve
v. （使）飢餓；（使）餓死

同義字
▶ **hungry** 飢餓的

◀ *Track 0135*

Oh, I'm **starving**. Do you have anything to ear right now?
喔我快餓死了，你有什麼東西可以吃嗎？

Let me see. Here. I've got a chocolate bar.
讓我看看，諾，我有巧克力棒。

steak
n. 牛排

◀ *Track 0136*

How would you like your **steak**?
你的牛排要幾分熟？

Medium, please.
五分，謝謝。

stir
v. 攪拌

反義字
▶ **still** 靜止

◀ *Track 0137*

How to make a cup of banana milkshake?
怎麼做香蕉奶昔？

Add some banana and milk, and then **stir** them.
加一些香蕉跟牛奶，然後攪拌。

stomach
n. 胃

◀ *Track 0138*

Oh, a butterfly is in my **stomach**.
哦，我現在好緊張。

Take it easy. It's not the end of the world.
別緊張，又不是世界末日。

straw
n. 吸管

◀⟪Track 0139

- Why do you need a big **straw**?
  為什麼你要大吸管？
- Because I'm drinking pearl milk tea.
  因為我要喝珍珠奶茶。

---

strawberry
n. 草莓

◀⟪Track 0140

- Let's go to the **strawberry** ranch on Sunday.
  我們週日去草莓農場吧。
- Oh, I can't wait!
  噢，我已經等不急了！

---

suck
v. 吸；（令人厭惡）

◀⟪Track 0141

- Oh, no. Baby John is **sucking** father's pipe.
  不好了，小約翰在吸爸爸的煙斗。
- Stop him! And take that away!
  阻止他！然後把煙斗拿走！

---

sugar
n. 糖

◀⟪Track 0142

- I like to put a lot of **sugar** into coffee.
  我喜歡加很多砂糖的咖啡。
- It must be so sweet.
  那一定很甜吧。

---

supper
n. 晚餐；晚飯

◀⟪Track 0143

- Why don't we go out for **supper**?
  要出去吃晚餐嗎？
- Yes, we can call Lily to come with us.
  好，我們也可以叫莉莉一起去。

---

sweet
n. 甜食；（甜點）
adj. 甜的；（愉快的；討人喜歡的；甜美的）

同義字
▶ **sugary** 甘甜的

◀⟪Track 0144

- I have a **sweet** tooth.
  我熱愛甜食。
- So you must know where to buy nice desserts.
  那你一定知道哪裡買的到好吃的點心。

這裡使用的是形容詞喔！

tableware
n. 餐具

🔊 *Track 0145*

👦 I want to buy a set of silver **tableware**.
我想買一套銀餐具。

👧 Will it be expensive?
那會很貴嗎？

takeout
n. 外賣

🔊 *Track 0146*

👦 Are you using the phone now?
你在講電話嗎？

👧 Yeah, I'm ordering **takeout**.
對，我在訂外賣。

taste
n. 味道；（嚐；（個人的）愛好；品味）
v. 品嚐

🔊 *Track 0147*

👦 Would you like to **taste** some handmade pancake?
要嚐嚐手工煎餅嗎？

👧 Nice. They make my mouth water.
好啊，他們讓我垂涎三尺。

> 這裡使用的是動詞喔！

tasty
adj. 好吃的

同義字
▶ **yummy** 美味的

🔊 *Track 0148*

👦 The cake is so **tasty**.
這蛋糕很好吃。

👧 Sure. My mom is a good baker.
當然，我媽是個厲害的烘焙師。

tea
n. 茶水；茶

🔊 *Track 0149*

👦 May I drink **tea**? I feel sleepy.
我可以喝茶嗎？我好想睡覺。

👧 Help yourself.
請自取。

thirsty
adj. 口渴的；（渴求的）

🔊 *Track 0150*

👦 I'm so **thirsty** after playing basketball.
打完籃球之後，我很渴。

👧 Let's buy a bottle of water.
那我們去買瓶水吧。

toast
n. 吐司麵包

Mary. Go to the supermarket and get some **toast**.
瑪莉，去超級市場買些吐司。

Mom, sorry, I'm late for a date and I have to go now.
媽，對不起，我約會已經遲到了，現在要出門了。

◀ *Track 0151*

tobacco
n. 菸草

同義字
▶ **baccy** 菸草

Do you have **tobacco**?
你有菸嗎？

No, I don't. I quit already.
沒有，我戒了。

◀ *Track 0152*

tofu
n. 豆腐

It tastes so special.
這個味道很特別。

Yes, it's **tofu** cheese cake, a new flavor.
對，這是豆腐起司蛋糕，新口味。

◀ *Track 0153*

tomato
n. 番茄

Tomato is rich in different types of vitamins.
蕃茄有各式各樣豐富的維他命。

Then why do you never eat it?
那你為什麼從來都不吃？

◀ *Track 0154*

vanilla
n. 香草

Which flavor ice cream do you like?
你喜歡什麼口味的冰淇淋？

I like **vanilla**.
我喜歡香草。

◀ *Track 0155*

vegetable
n. 蔬菜

同義字
▶ **veggie** 蔬菜

🔊 *Track 0156*

😀 Eat more **vegetable** is good for health.
多吃蔬菜有益健康。

😊 And, you should do more exercise.
還有，你也應該多運動。

yogurt
n. 優酪乳

🔊 *Track 0157*

😀 Mom, can I have **yogurt** after dinner?
媽，我晚飯後可以吃優酪乳嗎？

😊 Of course honey.
當然好啊親愛的。

It tastes so special.

Part

02

在國外才發現需要購買衣物，卻不知道怎麼辦嗎？看以下單字和對答，馬上知道外國人是怎麼説的！＊單字、對話分開錄音，學習目標更明確

---

accessory

n. 配件

Track 0158

I don't have any **accessory** to go with my dress.
我沒有任何配件可以搭配我的衣服。

I can lend you some.
我可以借你一些。

---

beard

n. 鬍子

Track 0159

You should shave your **beard**.
你該刮鬍子了。

Is it too long for you?
對你來説太長了嗎？

---

belt

n. 皮帶

Track 0160

Did you see my **belt**? I can't find it anywhere.
你有看見我的皮帶嗎？我到處都找不到。

It's right under your pants.
就在你的長褲下。

---

blonde

n. 金髮的人

Track 0161

Do you know the **blonde** over there? She's like an angel.
你知道那邊那個金髮的人是誰嗎？她真是位天使！

Of course. She is my little sister.
當然，她是我的小妹妹。

---

boot

n. 長靴

Track 0162

Ah! There's a snake in my **boot**.
啊！我的靴子裡有一條蛇。

Don't move! Let me handle it.
別動！讓我處理。

---

a
b
c
d
e
f
g
h
i
j
k
l
m
n
o
p
q
r
s
t
u
v
w
x
y
z

brassiere
n. 內衣

同義字
▶ **bra** 胸罩

◀ *Track 0163*

> Which **brassiere** do you prefer, the pink one or the blue one?
> 你比較喜歡哪一套內衣？粉紅色還是藍色？

> I prefer the blue one. I like lace.
> 我比較喜歡藍色的，我喜歡蕾絲。

button
n. 釦子

◀ *Track 0164*

> Please give me a star-shaped button.
> 請給我一個星星形狀的鈕扣。

> Sorry, we are out of the one you want.
> 抱歉，你要的已經賣完了。

charm
n. 魅力
v. 吸引；（使著迷）

同義字
▶ **attractiveness**
吸引力

◀ *Track 0165*

> Peter is really a boy with great **charm**.
> 彼得真是一位有魅力的男孩。

> Yeah, everyone likes to make friends with him.
> 對呀，大家都喜歡跟他做朋友。

這裡使用的是名詞喔！

clothes
n. 衣服

◀ *Track 0166*

> You should wear more **clothes**.
> 你應該多穿點衣服。

> But I like the cold weather outside.
> 但我喜歡外面的冷天氣。

coarse
adj. 粗糙的

反義字
▶ **delicate** 精緻的

◀ *Track 0167*

> The surface of this piece of clothes is **coarse**.
> 這件衣服好粗糙。

> We should replace it.
> 我們應該把它換掉。

coat
n. 外套

Put on your **coat** or you will catch a cold. The wind is getting stronger.
穿上外套，不然會感冒。外面的風越來越強了。

Don't worry. I am pretty healthy.
別擔心。我很健康。

Track 0168

comb
n. 梳子

I need a new **comb**.
我需要一把新梳子。

Try this wooden one.
試試這把木製的。

Track 0169

conventional
adj. 傳統的；古板的

My father is really **conventional**.
我爸好老古板。

Why? He didn't let you go to the party?
怎麼說？他不讓你去舞會嗎？

Track 0170

cosmetics
n. 化妝品

This kind of **cosmetics** is on sale now.
這種化妝品現在在特價。

Wow! I like this brand. Tell me where I can get it.
哇！我喜歡這個牌子。告訴我哪裡可以買到。

Track 0171

costume
n. 服裝；服飾；劇裝

Do you have any **costume** for Halloween?
你有適合萬聖節的服裝嗎？

No, but I will rent one.
沒有，但我會去租一套。

Track 0172

cotton
n. 棉花

The pillow is so soft.
這個枕頭好軟。

I stuffed much **cotton** in it.
我塞了很多棉花進去。

Track 0173

curl

n. 捲髮；（捲曲物；螺旋狀物）

v. （使）捲曲；（使彎曲）

反義字
▶ **straight** 筆直的

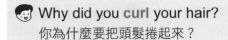

🎧 *Track 0174*

🧑 Why did you **curl** your hair?
你為什麼要把頭髮捲起來？

👩 It's too long for me to do the housework.
它太長了，我不好做家事。

> 這裡使用的是動詞喔！

---

dress

n. 洋裝

v. 穿衣服；（給小孩穿衣服）

🎧 *Track 0175*

🧑 What did your boyfriend give you on Valentine's Day?
你男朋友送你什麼情人節禮物？

👩 He gave me a pink **dress**.
他送我一件粉紅色洋裝。

> 這裡使用的是名詞喔！

---

drop

v. 掉落；（丟下；捎某人至某地）

n. 滴

🎧 *Track 0176*

🧑 Be careful not to **drop** the painting on the floor.
小心不要將畫掉到地板上。

👩 Don't worry. I will handle it with care.
別擔心。我會小心拿它。

> 這裡使用的是動詞喔！

---

durable

adj. 耐穿的；耐磨的

🎧 *Track 0177*

🧑 I want something **durable** to wear. Could you show me some?
我想要找耐穿的衣服。你可以拿一些給我看看嗎？

👩 Sure. How about this pair of jeans?
當然。這條牛仔褲如何？

---

dye

v. 染髮；（染色）

n. 染料

🎧 *Track 0178*

🧑 My mom doesn't allow me to **dye** my hair.
我媽不准我染髮。

👩 She's right. It's not good for your health.
她是對的。那對你健康不好。

> 這裡使用的是動詞喔！

earring
n. 耳環

👦 This pair of **earrings** is fabulous. I want to give it to my girlfriend.
這副耳環美極了，我要送給我女朋友。

👧 Are you sure? The quality is not that good.
你確定？它的品質不太好欸。

🔊 *Track 0179*

elegant
adj. 優雅的

👦 Karen always acts like a princess. She is so **elegant**.
凱倫舉手投足都像位公主，她好優雅。

👧 Right. She is also a very kind person.
沒錯，而且她人也好好。

🔊 *Track 0180*

fabric
n. 布料；織物

👦 What kind of **fabric** is this sweater made of?
你知道這件毛衣是什麼材質做的嗎？

👧 It's made of wool.
是羊毛做的。

🔊 *Track 0181*

fashion
n. 時髦；流行

👦 This necklace is out of **fashion**.
這條項鍊好老氣。

👧 I don't think so. The color is great.
哪會。它的顏色很漂亮。

🔊 *Track 0182*

feather
n. 羽毛；裝飾

👦 Excuse me. I want a hat with a **feather** on it.
不好意思，我想要上面有羽毛的帽子。

👧 Sorry. We don't have the one you want.
很抱歉，我們沒有你要的那種。

🔊 *Track 0183*

fold
n. （紙、布的）褶痕
v. 摺疊

反義字
▶ **unfold** 解開

👧 Henry, come here and help me fold those clothes.
亨利，過來幫我摺衣服。

👦 I hate **folding** clothes.
我討厭摺衣服。

這裡使用的是動詞喔！

🔊 *Track 0184*

glove(s)
n. 手套

Track 0185

You had better wear the **gloves**. It is really cold outside.
你最好戴手套，外面很冷。

Okay, then I will put on the scarf too.
好，那我也圍圍巾好了。

gorgeous
adj. 華麗的

同義字
▶ **splendid**
燦爛的

Track 0186

The wedding gown looks **gorgeous**.
這件結婚禮服看起來好華麗啊。

Do you like it? It's my design.
你喜歡嗎？這是我設計的。

hairstyle
n. 髮型

同義字
▶ **hairdo** 髮型

Track 0187

I like your new **hairstyle**.
我喜歡你的新髮型。

Thank you. The hairdresser is quite skillful.
謝謝你，那位設計師技法很純熟。

handsome
adj. 英俊的

Track 0188

Look at the **handsome** guy over there. He is our new chemistry teacher.
快看在那邊那位帥哥，他是我們的新化學老師。

Great! Then I will start to like chemistry.
太棒了！那我要開始喜歡化學了。

hat
n. 帽子

同義字
▶ **cap** 帽子

Track 0189

The **hat** you wore yesterday is really good. Where did you get it?
你昨天戴的帽子好好看，在哪裡買的？

In the supermarket on the corner of the street.
在街角的超級市場。

heel
n. 腳後跟;(鞋跟)

Track 0190

My **heel** hurts a lot.
我的腳跟好痛。

Let me see. You shouldn't wear high-**heels** anymore.
讓我看看。你不該再穿高跟鞋了。

helmet
n. 頭盔;安全帽

Track 0191

The **helmet** with Hello Kitty on it is really cute.
這個 Hello Kitty 安全帽好可愛喔。

The Hello Kitty won't protect you from any danger.
Hello Kitty 不會從危險中保護你。

jacket
n. 夾克;外套

Track 0192

Look! This is the new **jacket** I bought last week.
看!這是我上星期買的新夾克。

I think it is a little bit too big for you.
我覺得對你來說有點太大了。

jeans
n. 牛仔褲

Track 0193

Mandy doesn't like to wear **jeans**.
蔓蒂不喜歡穿牛仔褲。

No wonder she looked unhappy when she saw the **jeans** her friend gave her.
難怪她看到她朋友送給她的牛仔褲時不怎麼開心。

jewel
n. 珠寶

Track 0194

Not every woman likes **jewel**.
不是每個女人都喜歡珠寶。

But I do.
但我喜歡。

lace
n. 花邊;緞帶;(蕾絲;鞋帶)

Track 0195

I don't like any clothes with **lace**.
我不喜歡有花邊的衣服。

Why? **Lace** is so pretty.
為什麼?花邊很漂亮啊。

laundry
n. 洗衣店；送洗的衣服

同義字
▶ **washing**
洗滌；待洗衣物

◀ *Track 0196*

Could you help me do the **laundry**?
你可以幫我洗衣服嗎？

I'd like to. But I should finish my report first.
我很樂意，但是我得先完成我的報告。

leather
n. 皮革

◀ *Track 0197*

How much does the **leather** purse cost?
這個皮製的錢包多少錢？

About $2,000.
大概兩千塊。

loose
adj. 寬鬆的

◀ *Track 0198*

The shirt is too **loose**. You should wear another one.
這件襯衫太鬆了，你應該穿另一件。

But I only have one shirt.
但我只有一件。

make-up
n. 化妝

◀ *Track 0199*

You look great after putting on some **make-up**.
你化妝起來好漂亮。

Really? This is my first time wearing it.
真的嗎？這是我第一次化妝。

mask
n. 面具；（偽裝；口罩）
v. 掩蓋；（掩飾；遮蔽）

◀ *Track 0200*

The man over there is weird.
那邊那個男人好奇怪。

Why? Only because he wears a **mask**?
為什麼？只因為他戴面具嗎？

這裡使用的是名詞喔！

mend
v. 修補

◀ *Track 0201*

There's a hole in your coat.
你的外套上有一個洞。

What? Then I need to ask my mom to **mend** it.
什麼？我要請我媽媽幫我補。

---

modern
adj. 現代的

◀ *Track 0202*

The **modern** art is one of my favorite type of art.
現代藝術是我喜愛的藝術類型之一。

Tell me more about it.
告訴我多一點。

---

necklace
n. 項鍊；項圈

◀ *Track 0203*

My wife keeps asking me to give her a **necklace**.
我太太一直要我送給她一條項鍊。

Then just give her one.
那就送她一條啊。

---

necktie
n. 領帶

◀ *Track 0204*

A **necktie** kills a man.
領帶殺死一個男人。

Don't be angry. I won't ask you to wear it again.
別生氣嘛，我不會再要你打領帶了。

---

nylon
n. 尼龍

◀ *Track 0205*

Is **nylon** made from oil?
尼龍是石油做的嗎？

I'm not sure. Let's check it out.
我不確定欸，來查查看吧。

pajamas
n. 睡衣

同義字
▶ **nightdress**
睡衣

Mommy, where is my **pajamas**? I feel sleepy.
媽咪，我的睡衣在哪哩？我好想睡喔。

Honey, you are wearing your **pajamas**.
親愛的，你正穿著你的睡衣啊。

◀ *Track 0206*

pants
n. 褲子

My **pants** are worn out.
我的褲子穿壞了。

Let's go shopping and get a pair of new one.
那我們去逛街買一條新的吧。

◀ *Track 0207*

perfume
n. 香水

Do you wear **perfume**?
你擦香水？

Yah, do you like it?
對呀，你喜歡嗎？

◀ *Track 0208*

perm
n. 燙頭髮（燙捲）

I want to get a **perm**.
我想燙頭髮。

Great. I look forward to it.
好耶，我很期待。

◀ *Track 0209*

pocket
n. 口袋

What did you put in my **pocket**?
你放什麼在我口袋？

Just some chocolate.
一些巧克力。

◀ *Track 0210*

polish
n. 指甲油；（磨光；精巧；波蘭語）
v. 擦亮；（磨光）
adj. 波蘭的

Wendy has to **polish** her nails every day.
溫蒂每天都要擦指甲油。

No wonder why she is always late for school.
難怪她上學常遲到。

這裡使用的是動詞喔！

◀ *Track 0211*

053

powder
n. 粉

Track 0212

Watch out! There's **powder** on the chair.
小心！椅子上有粉。

Thank you for telling me. I need to be more careful.
謝謝你告訴我，我要小心點才行。

purse
n. （女用）錢包

同義字
▶ **moneybag**
錢袋

Track 0213

Where did you buy the **purse**? I like it a lot.
你的錢包在哪裡買的？我好喜歡。

In the night market.
在夜市。

razor
n. 剃刀；刮鬍刀

Track 0214

May I borrow your **razor**?
我可以跟你借刮鬍刀嗎？

Sorry. You should use your own one.
對不起，你應該用你自己的。

ring
n. 戒指；（圓形的東西；鈴聲；鐘聲）
v. 響起鈴聲；（圍住；繞……畫圓）

Track 0215

I lost my wedding **ring**.
我把結婚戒指搞丟了。

What? How could that happen?
什麼？你怎麼搞的？

這裡使用的是名詞喔！

sandal
n. 涼鞋；便鞋

Track 0216

Wearing **sandals** is not allowed in the museum.
不能穿涼鞋去博物館。

Sorry. I didn't notice that.
抱歉，我沒有注意到。

select
v. 挑選;(選擇)

同義字
▶ **pick** 挑選

◀ *Track 0217*

Let me **select** a fine desk for you.
讓我來幫你挑張好桌子。

I want the one with blue flowers on it.
我想要上面有藍色小花的。

sew
v. 縫;縫上

◀ *Track 0218*

My mother taught me how to **sew** yesterday.
我媽媽昨天教我怎麼縫東西。

It's easy. I can do that too.
很簡單啊,我也會。

shave
n. 刮鬍子
v. 刮鬍子;剃

同義字
▶ **scrape** 刮、擦

◀ *Track 0219*

You have to **shave** now.
你應該刮鬍子了。

No, I think I'm pretty good like this.
不要,我覺得我這樣很好看。

這裡使用的是動詞喔!

shirt
n. 襯衫

◀ *Track 0220*

This blue **shirt** fits you a lot.
你穿那件藍色襯衫很好看。

But I like the black one.
但我比較喜歡黑色的。

shoe(s)
n. 鞋

◀ *Track 0221*

Those **shoes** are so cute.
那些鞋子好可愛。

I want to buy a pair for my nephew.
我想要買一雙給我的姪女。

shorts
n. 短褲

相關單字
▶ **slacks** 長褲

🔊 Track 0222

😃 Don't you know that you can't wear **shorts** to a museum?
你難道不知道你不能穿短褲去博物館嗎？

😊 Really? No one tells me about that.
真的嗎？沒人告訴我啊！

---

silk
n. 絲；綢

🔊 Track 0223

😃 This **silk** gown is perfect.
這件絲製的禮服真完美。

😊 It costs a lot too.
但它很貴。

---

skirt
n. 裙子

🔊 Track 0224

😃 Students nowadays like to wear mini-**skirts**.
現在的學生喜歡穿迷你裙。

😊 I like to wear mini-**skirts**, too. But I am not young anymore.
我也喜歡，但我不再年輕了。

---

slipper(s)
n. 拖鞋

🔊 Track 0225

😃 I don't like to wear **slippers**.
我不喜歡穿拖鞋。

😊 Why? **Slippers** are convenient.
為什麼？拖鞋很方便啊。

---

sneaker(s)
n. 慢跑鞋

🔊 Track 0226

😃 Can a pair of good **sneakers** make you run faster?
一雙好的慢跑鞋會讓你跑快一點嗎？

😊 You can give it a try.
你可以試試看。

---

soak
n. 浸泡
v. 浸泡

同義字
▶ **drench** 浸溼

🔊 Track 0227

😃 Let's **soak** the clothes in the water.
把衣服泡在水裡吧。

😊 Won't **soaking** damage the fabric?
浸泡不會傷材質嗎？

> 這裡soak是動詞，soaking是動名詞喔！

sock(s)
n. 短襪

◀ *Track 0228*

Where are my **socks**?
我的短襪在哪裡？

I throw them in the trash can.
我把它們丟到垃圾桶了。

stocking(s)
n. 長襪

◀ *Track 0229*

Seldom people wear **stockings** now.
現在很少人穿長襪了。

But I do.
但我穿。

stripe
n. 條紋

◀ *Track 0230*

The **stripes** on the T-shirt are too dark.
這件T恤上的條紋太暗了。

But I think they are pretty nice.
但我覺得很好看啊。

stylish
adj. 時髦的

反義字
▶ **old-fashioned**
過時的

◀ *Track 0231*

My English teacher is **stylish**.
我的英文老師很時髦。

True. I never saw her wear the same clothes.
對呀，我從沒看過她穿同樣的衣服。

suit
n. 西裝；（套裝）
v. 適宜；（適合；與……
相稱）

◀ *Track 0232*

You look handsome in that **suit**.
你穿西裝看起來很帥。

Thank you. But I feel uncomfortable in it.
謝謝。但我不太自在。

這裡使用的是名詞喔！

suitcase
n. 手提箱

同義字
▶ **valise** 手提行李袋

🔊 *Track 0233*

My **suitcase** is full. I need to buy another one.
我的手提箱滿了,我需要再買一個。

Did you put a lot of things in it?
你塞很多東西進去嗎?

---

sweater
n. 毛衣;厚運動衫

🔊 *Track 0234*

Wearing a **sweater** on Christmas day is our family's tradition.
聖誕節當天穿毛衣是我們家的傳統。

It's so nice.
很好耶。

---

tie
n. 領帶;領結
v. 打結

🔊 *Track 0235*

The **tie** makes me breathless.
領帶讓我無法呼吸。

Just take it off.
那就拿下來啊。

這裡使用的是名詞喔!

---

tight
adj. 緊的;緊密的

🔊 *Track 0236*

These trousers are too **tight**. Can I try another one?
這件長褲太緊了,我可以試另一件嗎?

But I think it quite fits you.
但我覺得剛剛好啊。

---

top
n. 上衣;(頂部)
adj. 頂端的;最好的

🔊 *Track 0237*

I cannot find a **top** that goes well with the skirt.
我找不到可以搭配這條裙子的上衣。

How about the yellow one?
黃色這件如何?

這裡使用的是名詞喔!

trousers
n. 褲；褲子

Jane bought a new pair of **trousers** yesterday.
珍昨天買了一條新褲子。

Really? I thought she wears only skirts.
真的？我以為她只穿裙子。

◀ *Track 0238*

T-shirt
n. 運動衫；T恤

Why do you wear **T-shirt** all the time?
為什麼你總是穿T恤？

It's quite convenient, don't you think so?
你不覺得穿T恤很方便嗎？

◀ *Track 0239*

underwear
n. 內衣

I forgot to wear **underwear** today.
我今天忘了穿內衣了。

My goodness, don't take off your coat till the end of the day.
天啊，今天結束以前都不要脫掉妳的外套！

◀ *Track 0240*

undies
n. 內衣褲

Sweetie, did you see my **undies**?
小甜心，你有看到我的內衣褲嗎？

I am sure it is in the second drawer.
我很確定在第二個抽屜裡。

◀ *Track 0241*

uniform
n. 制服；校服

相關單字
▶ **leisurewear**
便服

Mommy, do I really need to wear **uniform** to school?
媽咪，我一定要穿制服上學嗎？

Sure, honey. But you can wear whatever you want on Wednesday.
當然囉親愛的，但星期三可以穿你想穿的。

◀ *Track 0242*

059

vest
n. 背心；馬甲

Track 0243

The **vest** in the store is fabulous.
那家店裡的背心好好看。

No way. The color is just not right.
不會吧，那顏色不對啊。

warm
adj. 暖和的；溫暖的

反義字
▶ **cold** 寒冷的

Track 0244

The weather is **warm** and nice. Let's go out.
天氣好好又溫暖，我們出去走走吧。

How about having a picnic in the backyard?
在後院野餐如何？

wear
v. 穿；戴；（磨損）

Track 0245

Wow! I never saw you **wear** a skirt. You look gorgeous.
哇，我沒有看過你穿裙子，你看起來超美的。

Thank you. I think it's time to give it a try.
謝謝你，我想是時候穿穿看了。

wool
n. 羊毛

Track 0246

Your sweater feels soft.
你的毛衣感覺好軟。

Of course. It's made of **wool**.
當然，它是羊毛製的。

zipper
n. 拉鍊

Track 0247

Oops. The **zipper** of my pants is broken.
糟糕，我褲子的拉鍊壞了。

There is no time for you to fix it. Just put on another pair of pants.
沒有時間讓你修它了，直接換一條吧。

NOTE

Part

03

Part 03 "住"

在國外需要住宿，應該說些什麼好？看以下單字和對答，馬上知道外國人是怎麼說的！＊單字、對話分開錄音，學習目標更明確

account
n. 帳目；紀錄

🔊 *Track 0248*

> How much money do you have in the bank?
> 你在銀行裡放了多少錢？

> Let me go to the ATM and check my **account**.
> 我去自動提款機查一下我的帳戶。

apartment
n. 公寓

🔊 *Track 0249*

> I rent an **apartment** near my company.
> 我租了一間公司旁的公寓。

> That's great! Can I go visit you someday?
> 太好了！我改天可以去拜訪你嗎？

appliance
n. 器具；家電用品

🔊 *Track 0250*

> I am tired of doing housework.
> 我厭倦做家事了。

> Let's buy some household **appliance** to make it easier.
> 我們去買一些家電用品來，好讓家事變輕鬆。

architecture
n. 建築物；建築學

同義字
▶ **structure**
建築物

🔊 *Track 0251*

> What's your major in college?
> 你在大學主修什麼？

> I major in **architecture**.
> 我主修建築學。

arrangement
n. 佈置；準備

🗣 Let's make some new **arrangements** for Christmas.
一起來為聖誕節做些新的布置吧。

🗣 Good idea!
好主意！

🔊 *Track 0252*

asleep
adj. 睡著的

🗣 I fell **asleep** in the math class.
我在數學課時睡著了。

🗣 I understand why. The class was too boring.
我可以理解。因為那堂課太無聊了。

反義字
▶ **awake** 清醒的

🔊 *Track 0253*

attic
n. 閣樓；頂樓

🗣 Why did he sleep in the **attic** last night?
為什麼他昨夜睡在閣樓裡面？

🗣 Because he had a quarrel with his mother last night.
因為昨晚他和他媽吵架了。

🔊 *Track 0254*

backyard
n. 後院

🗣 It's such a sunny holiday.
今天真是個天氣很好的假日。

🗣 And we have a good chance to weed in the **backyard**.
那我們有個清除後院雜草的好機會了。

🔊 *Track 0255*

balcony
n. 陽台

🗣 Did you see that beautiful girl standing on the **balcony** next door?
你有看到那個站在隔壁陽台的漂亮女孩嗎？

🗣 Yes, She is my girlfriend.
有，那是我的女朋友。

🔊 *Track 0256*

basement
n. 地下室；地窖

I heard that there's a secret door in the **basement**.
我聽說地下室有一道神祕的門。

Let's go and check it out!
我們快點去瞧瞧吧！

Track 0257

bath
n. 洗澡

同義字
▶ **shower** 淋浴

Do you know who is the guy singing while taking a **bath**?
你知道那個邊洗澡邊唱歌的人是誰嗎？

I want to know, too.
我也想要知道。

Track 0258

bathroom
n. 浴室

You have already stayed in the **bathroom** for one hour.
你已經在浴室待了一個小時。

I know. But I just started to wash my hair.
我知道，但我才剛開始洗頭髮而已。

Track 0259

bathtub
n. 浴缸

Promise me you'll never sleep in the **bathtub** again.
跟我保證你以後絕對不會在浴缸裡睡覺了。

I try my best, mom.
我就盡力，媽。

Track 0260

bedroom
n. 臥房

Could you come out please? Your teacher is here.
你可以出來嗎？你的老師來了。

No, I want to stay in the **bedroom**.
不，我想要待在房間裡。

Track 0261

bench
n. 長凳

🔊 *Track 0262*

😊 Did you see that couple sitting on the **bench**?
你有看到坐在長凳上的那對情侶嗎？

😊 Yes, I did. It's our son and his girlfriend.
有，我有看到，是我們的兒子還有他的女朋友。

bookcase
n. 書櫃；書架

🔊 *Track 0263*

😊 Have your dad read all the books in that **bookcase**?
你爸爸已經把那書架上的書都讀過了嗎？

😊 No, his just put them there as decoration.
沒有，他只是把那些書當成裝飾而已。

bottle
n. 瓶

🔊 *Track 0264*

😊 Did you bring your own water **bottle**?
你有帶自己的水瓶嗎？

😊 No, I didn't. Can I borrow yours?
我沒有，可以和你借嗎？

bubble
n. 泡沫；氣泡

🔊 *Track 0265*

😊 I want to drink **bubble** tea after class.
我下課後想要喝泡沫茶。

😊 Me too. I am so thirsty.
我也是。我很渴。

build
v. 建立；建築

同義字
▶ **construct**
建築

🔊 *Track 0266*

😊 I want to **build** a house for my mom.
我想要蓋一棟房子給媽媽。

😊 That's really nice of you.
你這樣做很好。

building
n. 建築物

🔊 *Track 0267*

😊 Did you see that old **building** on the hill.
你有看到那山丘上的老建築嗎？

😊 I did. It looks haunted.
我有看到，看起來真的很像鬼屋。

buy
v. 買

◀ *Track 0268*

I can't stop myself from **buying** those shoes.
我無法阻止自己買鞋。

Me too. They are so cheap now.
我也是。它們現在實在太便宜了。

cabin
n. 小屋；茅屋

◀ *Track 0269*

Do you know where that old man lives?
你知道那個老人住在哪裡嗎？

He lives in that **cabin** next to the river.
他住在那間河邊的小屋。

cage
n. 籠子；獸籠；鳥籠

◀ *Track 0270*

The two birds are fighting with each other in the **cage**.
這兩隻鳥在籠子裡打架。

Maybe it's because they don't have enough space.
也許是因為空間不夠的關係。

candle
n. 蠟燭；燭光

◀ *Track 0271*

Blow the **candles** on the birthday cake!
吹生日蛋糕上的蠟燭吧！

But I haven't made a wish.
可是我還沒有許願耶。

castle
n. 城堡

同義字
▶ **palace** 宮殿

◀ *Track 0272*

I want to buy a **castle** in the Europe someday.
我將來有一天想要買歐洲的城堡。

You're dreaming.
你做夢！

cave
n. 洞穴

◀ *Track 0273*

Let's go and find out what's in that dark **cave**.
我們一起去看看那個黑暗的洞穴裡有什麼。

I am not going. You can go by yourself.
我不去。你可以自己去。

ceiling
n. 天花板

He is so tall that his head will hit the **ceiling**.
他太高了以至於會撞到天花板。

I don't have that kind of problem. I'm too short.
我沒有這方面的問題。我太矮了。

Track 0274

chair
n. 椅子；主席席位

Do we have enough **chairs** for everybody?
我們有足夠的椅子給所有人嗎？

We need one more.
我們還需要再一張。

Track 0275

chamber
n. 房間；寢室

She stayed in her **chamber** when everybody is out.
當所有人都出去的時候，她留在她的房間。

No wonder I didn't see her.
難怪我沒有看到她。

Track 0276

circulate
v. 傳佈；循環

I feel stuffy with this room.
我覺得這個房間好悶。

Let's open the window to make the air **circulate**.
打開窗戶讓空氣流通吧！

Track 0277

closet
n. 櫥櫃

I need to buy a new **closet** for my clothes.
我需要買個新的櫥櫃來放我的衣服。

Maybe you should stop buying too many clothes.
也許你應該停止買太多衣服。

同義字
▶ **cabinet** 櫥櫃

Track 0278

coffer
n. 保險箱

同義字
▶ **safe** 保險箱;
安全的

◀ *Track 0279*

You'd better not put all your treasures in a **coffer**.
你最好不要把所有貴重物品都放在保險箱裡。

I don't have a **coffer** at all.
我根本沒有保險箱啊。

---

cohabit
v. 同居

◀ *Track 0280*

I didn't let my parents know that I'm **cohabiting** with my boyfriend.
我沒讓我父母知道我現在和男友同居。

But your parents are coming now!
但妳爸媽現在要過來了!

---

comfort
n. 舒適;(慰藉)
v. 安慰;(撫慰)

同義字
▶ **ease** 舒適;悠閒

◀ *Track 0281*

The music brings **comfort** to our lives.
音樂帶給我們慰藉。

That's why I listen to music while I work.
那就是為什麼我邊聽音樂邊工作的原因。

這裡使用的是名詞喔!

---

community
n. 社區;(社群)

◀ *Track 0282*

Why do you know each other?
你們為什麼會彼此認識呢?

Because we used to live in the same **community**.
因為我們曾住在同個社區。

---

condo
n. 公寓;大樓

◀ *Track 0283*

Sooner or later I will have my own **condo**.
總有一天我會擁有自己的公寓大樓。

Before that, you have to stop dreaming and go back to work.
在那之前,你要先停止作夢,然後回來上班。

costly

adj. 價格高的；（昂貴的）

同義字
▶ **expensive**
昂貴的

Track 0284

The houses in Taipei are **costly** for young people.
台北的房子對於年輕人來說很貴。

It sure is. I can't afford to buy one.
真的。我也買不起。

cottage

n. 小屋；別墅

Track 0285

I want to live in the **cottage** next to the sea.
我想要住在海邊的別墅中。

The you can go surfing every day.
那你就可以天天衝浪了。

couch

n. 長沙發；睡椅

Track 0286

He fell asleep on the **couch** as soon as he got home.
他一回家就在沙發上睡著了。

Maybe he's too tired.
也許他太累了。

courtyard

n. 庭院；天井

Track 0287

Who is playing in the **courtyard**?
誰在庭院裡面玩耍呢？

My son and my wife are playing in the **courtyard**.
我的兒子和太太在庭院裡玩耍。

cupboard

n. 櫥櫃

Track 0288

How many cups are there in your **cupboard**?
你的櫥櫃裡面有幾個杯子？

There are fifteen cups in my **cupboard**.
櫥櫃裡面有15個杯子。

curtain
n. 窗簾

同義字
▶ **drape** 窗簾

◀ *Track 0289*

The sun is too bright. Could you put down the **curtain**?
太陽太大了，可以請你把窗簾放下嗎？

Sure. Let me help you.
當然。讓我幫你吧。

---

decorate
v. 裝飾；佈置

◀ *Track 0290*

My mom **decorates** the room with a lot of flowers.
我媽媽用很多花裝飾房間。

It must be beautiful.
那一定很漂亮。

---

decoration
n. 裝飾

同義字
▶ **adornment** 裝飾品

◀ *Track 0291*

What can we buy for the party **decoration**?
我們可以買什麼來裝飾舞會呢？

Maybe we can buy some red roses.
或許我們能買一些紅色的玫瑰。

---

desk
n. 書桌

◀ *Track 0292*

Where do you usually study?
你平常都在哪唸書？

At the **desk** beside the window.
我平常都在窗戶旁的書桌那裡。

---

detergent
n. 清潔劑

◀ *Track 0293*

What kind of detergent do you use?
你用哪種清潔劑？

I usually use natural liquid **detergent**.
我通常用天然清潔劑。

dirty
adj. 髒的

同義字
▶ **grimy** 髒的

◀ *Track 0294*

I haven't washed my hair for two weeks.
我已經兩個星期沒有洗頭了。

It must be very **dirty**.
那頭髮一定很髒了。

disconnect
v. 切斷（電、氣、水等）；（電話）斷線

◀ *Track 0295*

The web service has been **disconnected** since last night.
昨晚開始網路服務就中斷了。

Oh, that's too bad.
哦，那真是太糟糕了。

disorder
n. 無秩序；（混亂）

同義字
▶ **order** 秩序

◀ *Track 0296*

The downtown was totally in **disorder** last night.
昨晚市中心呈現完全無秩序的狀態。

Yeah, I spent 3 hours to get home.
是啊，我花了三小時才到家。

district
n. 區域

◀ *Track 0297*

Which is the most developed **district** in China in the recent 30-year?
近三十年來中國哪個區域發展最好？

I think it must be Shanghai.
我想一定是上海。

dome
n. 穹頂；圓屋頂

◀ *Track 0298*

Why did you not go to the church on Sunday?
你為什麼禮拜天沒有去教堂？

The church was closed because its **dome** is under repair.
教堂因為整修穹頂而關閉了。

door
n. 門

Who is knocking on the **door**?
是誰在敲門？

I think it's the mailman.
我覺得應該是郵差。

Track 0299

doorstep
n. 門階；（門前的階梯）

I am going out now.
我現在要出去了。

Watch out for the **doorsteps**.
請小心門前的臺階。

Track 0300

drag
v. 拖曳

How do I cut this file into another folder?
我要怎麼把這個檔案剪下放到另一個資料夾？

Just **drag** it directly into the folder you want.
只要直接把它拖曳到你想要的資料夾裡面就可以了。

Track 0301

dresser
n. （有鏡子的）梳妝台；（五斗櫃）

Hey, have you seen my wallet?
你有看到我的皮夾嗎？

It's on your **dresser**.
它在你的梳妝台上。

Track 0302

dryer
n. 烘乾機；吹風機

It's been rainy for days. My clothes can't get dry anyway.
已經下雨很多天了，我的衣服都不會乾。

Well, you can use the **dryer** in my house.
好吧，你可以用我家的烘乾機。

Track 0303

dust
n. 灰塵；灰

Oh, there's lots of **dust** on the floor.
地板上有好多灰塵。

Yeah, let's mop it clean.
是啊，一起來把它拖乾淨吧。

Track 0304

dwell
v. 住;居住

🔊 *Track 0305*

👦 Where do you **dwell** in the last two years?
過去兩年你住在哪呢?

👧 Tokyo.
東京。

dwelling
n. 住宅;住處

同義字
▶ **residence**
居住;住所

🔊 *Track 0306*

👦 Welcome to my **dwelling**!
歡迎來到我的住處!

👧 Ah! What a lovely house it is!
噢!多麼可愛的一間房子啊!

echo
n. 回音

🔊 *Track 0307*

👦 I heard some scaring sound last night.
我昨夜聽到了一些可怕的聲音。

👧 Don't worry. That was the **echo** of the rail train.
別擔心,那只是火車的回音。

electric
adj. 電的

同義字
▶ **electrical** 電的

🔊 *Track 0308*

👦 What kind of motorcycle do you have?
你的摩托車是哪一種呢?

👧 I have an **electric** motorcycle.
我有一台電動摩托車。

electricity
n. 電

🔊 *Track 0309*

👦 There will be a restriction of **electricity** use tonight.
今晚會有限電。

👧 That's too bad! I will miss the special TV program tonight.
這真的太糟糕了,這樣我就會錯失今晚的電視特別節目。

elevator
n. 電梯

相關字
▶ **escalator**
手扶梯

◀ *Track 0310*

The **elevator** is broken. We need to climb the stairs.
電梯故障了，我們得爬樓梯了。

You kidding? Our office is on the 17th floor!
你開玩笑嗎？我們辦公室在17樓耶！

environment
n. 環境

◀ *Track 0311*

The protection of our **environment** is the most critical issue.
保護環境是當前最關鍵的議題。

Yeah, and we can start with our daily life.
是啊，我們可以先從日常生活開始。

faucet
n. 水龍頭

同義字
▶ **tap** 水龍頭

◀ *Track 0312*

Remember to turn off the water **faucet** after you leave.
離開的時候記得關閉水龍頭。

OK. I promise.
好的，我保證會。

fax
n. 傳真
v. （發）傳真

◀ *Track 0313*

How can I receive your resume?
我要怎麼拿到你的履歷呢？

I will **fax** it to you before Tuesday.
我禮拜二之前會傳真給你。

這裡使用的是動詞喔！

fence
n. 籬笆；圍牆

◀ *Track 0314*

Who's the boy jumping over the **fence**?
那個跳過籬笆的男孩是誰？

That's the son of my neighbor.
那是我鄰居的兒子。

fireplace

n. 壁爐;火爐

Track 0315

I feel so cold.
我覺得好冷。

Let's stoke fire by the **fireplace** and it will be warm later.
來用壁爐生火吧,等一下就會變暖了。

firm

n. 公司;(商號)
adj. 堅固的;(結實的)

同義字
▶ **fixed** 穩固的

Track 0316

Is this car really safe? It looks so small.
這個車真的安全嗎?他看起來好小。

Don't worry. It's quite **firm**.
別擔心。它很堅固。

這裡使用的是形容詞喔!

flat

n. 平的東西;公寓

Track 0317

Is there any **flat** surface that I can place my notebook?
有任何平坦的東西可以讓我放筆電嗎?

There's a small table over there. You can use it.
那邊有個小桌子。你可以用它。

floor

n. 地板;樓層

Track 0318

How many **floors** are there in this apartment?
這個公寓有幾層樓?

Five **floors**.
五層樓。

furniture

n. 傢俱;設備

Track 0319

I have to rearrange my **furniture** for my new house. Can you help me?
我必須要為我的新家重新擺放傢俱。你可以幫我嗎?

Sure, why not?
當然,為什麼不呢?

garage
n. 車庫

Track 0320

Why do you not park your car into your **garage**?
你為什麼不把車停到你的車庫裡面？

Because there is too much stuff inside.
因為裡面太多雜物了。

garbage
n. 垃圾

同義字
▶ **rubbish** 垃圾

Track 0321

When will the **garbage** truck come? I have lots of **garbage** to throw out.
垃圾車什麼時候要來？我有好多垃圾要丟掉。

Usually at 7 p.m.
通常在晚上七點。

gas
n. 瓦斯；汽油；（氣體；煤氣；天然氣）

Track 0322

Where's the closest **gas** station? My car is out of **gas**.
最近的加油站在哪裡？我的車子沒油了。

There's a **gas** station 3 blocks away.
三個街區外有一個加油站。

gate
n. （大）門；閘門

Track 0323

Where's the **gate** of the exit?
出口的閘門在哪裡？

Over there.
在那裡。

gloom
n. 陰暗；昏暗；（愁悶）

Track 0324

The basement seems filled with **gloom**.
地下室看起來很暗。

Don't worry. I have a flashlight here.
別擔心，我有一支手電筒。

hall
n. （大）廳；（禮）堂；（走廊）

◀ *Track 0325*

Excuse me. Where's the lecture **hall** of this building?
不好意思。請問這棟樓的演講廳在哪裡？

It's on the third floor.
在三樓。

hang
v. 吊；掛

同義字
▶ **suspend** 懸掛

◀ *Track 0326*

Hey, have you seen my jacket?
嘿，你有看到我的夾克嗎？

It's **hanging** on the hook.
它吊在鉤子上。

hide
v. 隱藏

反義字
▶ **expose** 暴露

◀ *Track 0327*

Let's play **hide**-and-seek!
一起來玩躲貓貓吧！

Yeah! Count me in!
好啊，算我一份。

hive
n. 蜂巢；鬧區

◀ *Track 0328*

Where's the **hive** of New York?
哪裡是紐約的鬧區？

Manhattan district.
曼哈頓區。

hometown
n. 家鄉

◀ *Track 0329*

Where did you go in summer vacation?
你暑假去了哪裡？

I went back to my **hometown**.
我回到我的家鄉。

hostel
n. 青年旅舍

▶ *Track 0330*

Why do you not book the **hostel**? It's much cheaper.

你為什麼不訂青年旅舍？它便宜很多。

The **hostel** is currently full and doesn't accept any booking.

青年旅舍已經滿了，而且不再接受任何預約。

hotel
n. 旅館

▶ *Track 0331*

Did you live in a five-star **hotel** before?

你有住過五星級旅館嗎？

Yes, I did. But it was not as good as you think.

是的，我有住過。但它沒有你想像的如此好。

house
n. 房子；住宅

▶ *Track 0332*

The new **houses** of this area are now mushrooming.

這個地區的新房子正在迅速增加中。

Yeah. The government is going to build a new station in this area.

是啊。政府將要在這個區域興建一個新車站。

hut
n. 小屋；茅舍

同義字
▶ **shed** 棚；小屋

▶ *Track 0333*

There was a **hut** here. Where is it?

這裡原有個小屋。它在哪裡？

It was pulled down last year.

它去年被拆除了。

immigrate
v. 遷移；移入

反義字
▶ **emigrate**
移居國外

▶ *Track 0334*

Immigrating into the US has been more and more difficult.

移民到美國已經越來越困難了。

It's because the terrorism attack 10 years ago.

是因為十年前恐怖攻擊的關係。

indoor
adj. 屋內的、室內的

Track 0335

I like to do **indoor** activities.
我喜歡做室內活動。

Me too. It won't get sunburn.
我也是。這樣就不會被曬傷。

inhabit
v. 居住

Track 0336

There were thousands of American buffalos **inhabiting** here.
這裡曾經有數千隻美洲水牛。

But they went extinct after the Indians have guns.
但牠們在印地安人擁有槍之後就滅絕了。

inhabitant
n. 居民

Track 0337

There are only 500 **inhabitants** here.
這裡僅有500個居民。

Oh! That's really a small town.
噢！那還真是個小鎮。

inn
n. 旅社；小酒館

Track 0338

Is there any **inn** in this area?
這附近有旅社嗎？

There's one at the corner.
在轉角有一家。

insomnia
n. 失眠

Track 0339

You have dark under-eye circles.
你有黑眼圈耶。

I had **insomnia** last night.
我昨天晚上失眠了。

island
n. 島；安全島

Track 0340

I want to hold my wedding on an **island**.
我想要在一個島上辦我的婚禮。

How romantic!
多麼浪漫啊！

item
n. 條款；項目

Track 0341

How many **items** do we need to buy at the market?
我們去市場要買幾樣東西呢？

There are six in total.
總共有六項。

kitchen
n. 廚房

Track 0342

I am making chocolate cake in the **kitchen**.
我正在廚房裡做巧克力蛋糕。

I can't wait to try some.
我等不及要試吃了。

ladder
n. 梯子

相關單字
▶ **stairs** 樓梯

Track 0343

Why are you standing on a **ladder**?
你為什麼要站在梯子上？

I'm fixing the light bulb.
我正在修理電燈泡。

lamp
n. 燈

Track 0344

I can barely see what is on the street. It's too dark.
我幾乎看不到路上的東西了。天色太黑了。

Don't worry. The street **lamp** will be turned on later.
別擔心。路燈等一下就會打開了。

landlord
n. 房東

Track 0345

My **landlord** treats me so well!
我房東對我超好的。

I bet he lowered your rent!
他一定降你房租了對不對！

layout

n. 規劃；佈局；（佈置；排列）

Track 0346

 The proposal of his thesis **layout** was rejected by his adviser.
他的論文規劃提案被他的指導教授否決了。

Oh, that's too bad.
噢，那真的太可惜了。

---

leak

n. 漏洞；（洩漏處；漏出物）
v. 洩漏（液體、氣體或機密）

Track 0347

 I found a water **leak** in the bedroom.
我發現臥室會漏水。

Hurry up and find someone to fix it.
快找人來修吧。

> 這裡使用的是名詞喔！

---

light

n. 光；（光線）；燈
v. 點燃；（照亮）
adj. 輕的；（明亮的；顏色淺的；少量的）

反義字
▶ **darkness** 黑暗

Track 0348

 Why are you turning off the **light**?
為什麼你要關燈呢？

I want to go to sleep now.
我現在想要睡覺了。

> 這裡使用的是名詞喔！

---

lobby

n. 休息室；大廳

Track 0349

 The tourists are gathering in the **lobby**.
觀光客在大廳集合。

They are so noisy.
他們好吵。

local
n. 當地人
adj. 當地的

反義字
▶ **exotic** 外來的

◀ *Track 0350*

I want to do language exchange with the **local** students.
我想要和在地的學生語言交換。

I can introduce some of them to you.
我可以介紹一些給你認識。

這裡使用的是形容詞喔！

---

locate
v. 位在……；（發現……的位置）

◀ *Track 0351*

Where is your house?
你家在哪裡？

It **locates** on the small hill.
它位於小山丘上面。

---

lock
n. 鎖；（門鎖）
v. 鎖；（鎖定）

◀ *Track 0352*

I lost the key of this **lock**.
我把這個鎖的鑰匙弄丟了。

That's ok. I have a backup key.
沒關係。我有備份鑰匙。

這裡使用的是名詞喔！

---

lofty
adj. 非常高的；（崇高的；高傲的）

反義字
▶ **low** 低的

◀ *Track 0353*

The trees of this mountain are **lofty**.
這個山上的樹木非常的高聳。

Yeah, I am in awe of them.
是啊，我對它們感到敬畏。

---

mansion
n. 宅邸；大廈

◀ *Track 0354*

Who is living in this great **mansion**?
誰住在這個宅邸裡面？

The man with greatest power of this country.
這個國家最有權力的人。

marble
n. 大理石

Track 0355

What's the material of this monument?
這個紀念碑是什麼材質？

It is the material of **marble**.
它是大理石的材質。

match
n. 比賽；火柴；敵手；
（般配的一對）
v. （和……）相配；（搭配）

Track 0356

The screw doesn't **match** this drilled hole.
這個螺絲和這個鑽孔不合。

Yeah, I think there must be something wrong with this design.
是啊，我覺得這個設計一定有問題。

這裡使用的是動詞喔！

mattress
n. 墊子；（床墊）

Track 0357

Don't keep your money under the **mattress**. It's not safe at all.
不要把你的錢藏在床墊底下。這樣不安全。

But I have no place to keep it.
但是我沒有地方可以放了。

mental
adj. 心理的；心智的；（精神的）

反義字
▶ **physical** 身體的

Track 0358

I have **mental** problems recently.
我最近有一些心理上的問題。

Oh, you'd better go see a psychological doctor right away.
噢，你最好馬上去看心理醫生。

mess
n. 雜亂；（困境；混亂局面）

Track 0359

Oh, your room is totally a **mess**.
噢，你的房間真的是一團混亂。

Yeah, I'm going to clean it up recently.
是啊，我最近就會打掃它了。

metropolitan

n. 都市人

adj. 大都市的

反義字

▶ **rustic** 鄉下人

🔊 *Track 0360*

👦 How many **metropolitans** are there in Hong Kong?

香港有多少都市人口？

👧 Over 7 million.

超過700萬人。

這裡使用的是名詞喔！

---

migrate

v. 遷徙；移居

🔊 *Track 0361*

👦 The global warming is getting severe and the sea level is also rising.

全球暖化越來越嚴重，海平面也持續上升。

👧 So people living near the coast must **migrate** to inland.

所以沿海居民必須往內陸遷移。

---

migration

n. 遷移

🔊 *Track 0362*

👦 There is no one living here anymore.

這裡已經沒有住人了。

👧 It seems that there was a great **migration** before.

看來這裡曾經有一個大遷移。

---

mop

n. 拖把

v. （用拖把）拖地板

🔊 *Track 0363*

👦 Can you **mop** the room with the mop?

你可以用拖把拖一下地板嗎？

👧 I'm exhausted now, can I do that later?

我現在很累，可以晚點再拖嗎？

這裡使用的是動詞喔！

---

motel

n. 汽車旅館

🔊 *Track 0364*

👦 This **motel** seems bad. We should leave and find another one.

這個汽車旅館看起來好糟。我們應該離開去找另外一家。

👧 It's the only one **motel** around here actually.

事實上這是附近唯一的一家。

narrow
adj. 窄的；狹長的

🔊 *Track 0365*

😊 How is that room?
那個房間如何？

😊 It's **narrow** in width.
寬度上很窄。

neat
adj. 整潔的

同義字
▶ **tidy** 整齊的

🔊 *Track 0366*

😊 Please keep your desk **neat**.
請保持你的書桌整潔。

😊 No problem.
沒問題。

neighbor
n. 鄰居

🔊 *Track 0367*

😊 Who is the man washing the car?
那個在洗車的男人是誰？

😊 He's my new **neighbor**, Mr. Huang.
他是我的新鄰居，黃先生。

neighborhood
n. 社區

🔊 *Track 0368*

😊 It there any place for sporting?
有可以運動的地方嗎？

😊 Yes, there's a basketball court in our **neighborhood**.
有，社區裡面有一個籃球場。

ornament
n. 裝飾品

🔊 *Track 0369*

😊 Hey, have you seen my **ornament**?
你有看到我的飾品嗎？

😊 Yes, it's on the desk.
有啊，在桌上。

owner
n. 物主；所有者

同義字
▶ **possessor**
擁有者

◀ *Track 0370*

Who's the **owner** of this dog?
誰是這隻狗的主人？

My son.
我的兒子。

paint
n. 顏料；油漆
v. 刷油漆；繪畫；（塗）

◀ *Track 0371*

What kind of **paint** do you like?
你喜歡什麼顏色的顏料呢？

Black and white
黑色和白色。

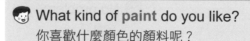
這裡使用的是名詞喔！

penthouse
n. 頂層豪華公寓

◀ *Track 0372*

Wanna spend the night with me? I live in a **penthouse**.
要跟我一起過夜嗎？我住在頂層豪華公寓裡。

No thanks, I have a curfew.
不，謝了，我有門禁。

pillar
n. 樑柱；棟樑

◀ *Track 0373*

How lofty this building is!
這個建築物多麼高啊！

Yeah, it takes lots of **pillars** to support it.
是啊，它需要很多樑柱去支撐。

pillow
n. 枕頭

◀ *Track 0374*

I didn't sleep well last night.
我昨晚睡得不好。

Changing a **pillow** may improve your sleeping quality.
換個枕頭或許可以改善你的睡眠品質。

populate
v. 居住

Track 0375

😊 Hong Kong is really a crowded city.
香港真的是個擁擠的城市。

😊 Yeah, there are 7 million people **populating** in this city.
是啊，有七百萬人居住在這個城市裡面。

porch
n. 玄關；入口處；門廊

Track 0376

😊 Oh, it's raining hard.
噢，雨下得好大。

😊 We can wait in the **porch** until it stops raining.
我們可以在玄關等雨停。

pottery
n. 陶器

Track 0377

😊 What's your interest?
你的興趣是什麼？

😊 Collecting antique, like old potteries.
收集古董，像是舊陶器。

property
n. 財產；（房地產）

Track 0378

😊 The ranking of **property** is different from last year.
資產排行和去年不同。

😊 Yeah, Ms. Wang is the richest person in Taiwan.
是啊，王小姐是台灣最有錢的人。

quilt
n. 棉被

Track 0379

😊 I felt cold last night and I didn't sleep well.
我昨晚覺得好冷，而且也沒睡好。

😊 Maybe your **quilt** is not thick enough to protect you from the cold.
也許是你的被子沒厚到可以讓你保暖。

refrigerator
n. 冰箱

同義字
▶ **fridge** 冰箱

◀ *Track 0380*

Did you see the pie that we ate last night?
你有看到我們昨晚吃的派嗎？

Yes, it is in the **refrigerator**.
有啊，它在冰箱裡面。

---

rent
n. 租金
v. 租用；（出租）

◀ *Track 0381*

How much is the **rent** for this house?
這個房子的房租是多少？

NTD10,000 per month.
每個月 10,000 新台幣。

這裡使用的是名詞喔！

---

residential
adj. 居住的

◀ *Track 0382*

Where's the wild field before?
之前的田野在哪裡呢？

The wild field gradually becomes a **residential** area.
田野逐漸變成了居住區。

---

resident
n. 居民
adj. 定居的

◀ *Track 0383*

The **residents** are protesting against the proposal of the incinerator.
居民正在抗議焚化爐的提議。

Yeah, the house price here will fall down immediately, so they have to do that.
是啊，因為這裡的房價將會一落千丈，所以他們必須這麼做。

這裡使用的是名詞喔！

---

restroom
n. 洗手間

同義字
▶ **washroom**
廁所

◀ *Track 0384*

Excuse me. I have to go to the **restroom** for a while.
不好意思，我必須要去一下廁所。

That's ok. I'll wait here.
沒關係，我會在這裡等。

roof
n. 屋頂；車頂

🔊 *Track 0385*

👦 Who's the boy on the **roof**?
在屋頂上的男孩是誰？

👧 That's my son.
那是我的兒子。

room
n. 房間；空間

🔊 *Track 0386*

👦 Do you have your own **room**?
你有自己的房間嗎？

👧 No, I have to share a room with my brother.
不，我必須和我弟弟共用一個房間。

roommate
n. 室友

🔊 *Track 0387*

👦 Did you meet our new **roommate**?
妳見過我們的新室友了嗎？

👧 Yeah. Her name is Elma, isn't it?
嗯，她名字叫艾爾瑪，對不對？

rug
n. 地毯

同義字
▶ **carpet** 地毯

🔊 *Track 0388*

👦 The **rug** on the floor is dirty.
地板上的地毯髒了。

👧 Yeah, I'm gonna wash it later.
是啊，我準備要洗它了。

scarcely
adv. 勉強地；幾乎不

🔊 *Track 0389*

👧 Sorry, I can **scarcely** remember your name.
對不起，我幾乎想不起來你的名字。

👦 That's ok. Just call me John.
沒關係。叫我約翰就好了。

scrub
v. 擦拭；擦洗

🔊 *Track 0390*

👦 The window is a little dirty.
窗戶有點髒了。

👧 I'm going to **scrub** it.
我正要擦拭它了。

separate

adj. 分開的
v. 分開

🔊 *Track 0391*

There are thousands of **separate** parts of this model. I'm going to assemble it.
這個模型有幾千組個別零件。我要把它組合起來。

Oh, it seems very complicated.
噢，聽起來很複雜呢。

> 這裡使用的是形容詞喔！

shampoo

n. 洗髮精

🔊 *Track 0392*

What's the flavor of your **shampoo**?
你的洗髮精是什麼味道的？

Peach. I love the fragrance.
桃子。我好愛那香味。

sheet

n. 床單；（印有字的紙）

🔊 *Track 0393*

Are you going to wash your **sheet**?
你要洗你的床單了嗎？

No, it's raining today. I'll wash it tomorrow.
不，現在正在下雨。我明天再洗它。

shelf

n. 棚架；架子

🔊 *Track 0394*

Hey, did you see my text book?
嘿，你有看到我的教科書嗎？

Oh, it's on the **shelf**.
噢，它在架子上。

shelter

n. 避難所；庇護所
v. 躲避；遮蔽

🔊 *Track 0395*

What should we do when the earthquake hits?
地震來襲時我們該怎麼辦？

Take shield right away. And go to the **shelter** immediately.
馬上尋找遮蔽。並且馬上前往避難所。

> 這裡使用的是名詞喔！

sink
n. 水槽；洗手台

🔊 *Track 0396*

👩 Why is the **sink** full of bubbles?
為什麼洗手台都是泡泡？

👨 Someone overturned the laundry detergent.
有人打翻了洗衣精。

skyscraper
n. 摩天大樓

🔊 *Track 0397*

👨 When was the **skyscraper** built?
這個摩天大樓是什麼時候蓋起來的？

👩 In year 2005. I guess.
我猜是2005年吧。

soap
n. 肥皂

🔊 *Track 0398*

👨 Hey, did you watch the TV show yesterday?
你有看昨天的電視節目嗎？

👩 No, I don't watch **soap** opera.
沒有，我不看肥皂劇的。

sofa
n. 沙發

🔊 *Track 0399*

👩 Please take a seat on the **sofa**.
請坐在那個沙發上。

👩 Thanks.
謝謝。

solitude
n. 獨處；獨居

🔊 *Track 0400*

👨 The old man lives in **solitude**.
那個老人獨自生活。

👩 How poor he is.
他多可憐啊。

spacious
adj. 寬敞的；寬廣的

同義字
▶ **roomy** 寬敞的

🔊 *Track 0401*

👨 This living room is quite **spacious**.
這個客廳相當寬敞。

👩 Yeah, we can place lots of furniture here.
是啊，我們可以在這裡放很多家具。

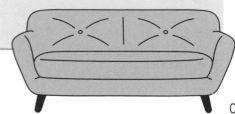

stair
n. 樓梯

Track 0402

👦 Where's the meeting room?
會議室是在哪裡？

👩 Go up the **stairs** and you'll see it.
走上樓，你就會看到了。

steady
adj. 穩固的；穩定的

同義字
▶ **constant**
固定的

Track 0403

👦 Is this table **steady**?
這個桌子穩固嗎？

👩 No, it has some defects.
不，它有一些缺陷。

stink
adj. 惡臭；臭

Track 0404

👦 What's that smell? I smell a **stink** of something rotted.
那是什麼味道？我聞到一個東西腐爛的味道。

👩 It's the smell of a special cheese.
這是一種特殊起士的味道。

suburban
adj. 郊外的；市郊的

Track 0405

👦 Where is your house?
你的房子在哪裡？

👩 It's in the **suburban** area.
在郊區。

suite
n. 套房

Track 0406

👦 How much do you pay to rent your **suite**?
你每個月花多少錢租你的套房？

👩 NTD5,000. Very cheap huh?
新台幣五千元。很便宜吧？

surroundings
n. 環境；周圍

Track 0407

👦 How are the **surroundings** here?
這附近的環境如何？

👩 There are a school, park and subway station here.
這裡有學校、公園和地鐵站。

sweep
v. 掃；打掃

Track 0408

😊 I'm going to **sweep** the house.
我要打掃家裡了。

😊 Let me help you.
讓我來幫你吧。

switch
n. 開關
v. 轉換

Track 0409

😊 Where's the **switch** of the light?
電燈開關在哪裡？

😊 Over there, next to the vase.
在那裡，就在花瓶旁邊。

> 這裡使用的是名詞喔！

tissue
n. 面紙；（細胞組織）

Track 0410

😊 Do you have a **tissue**? I've got a runny nose.
你有面紙嗎？我一直流鼻水。

😊 Here you are, take care of yourself.
給你，好好照顧身體啊。

toilet
n. 洗手間

同義字
▶ **lavatory**
洗手間

Track 0411

😊 Excuse me. I have to go to the **toilet** for a while.
不好意思。我要去洗手間一下。

😊 That's Ok. Go ahead.
沒關係，去吧。

towel
n. 毛巾

Track 0412

😊 Is there any **towel** or tissue? I want to scrub my table.
有任何毛巾或是面紙嗎？我想要擦我的桌子。

😊 Here it is.
在這邊。

trash
n. 垃圾

Track 0413

😊 The carnival created lots of **trash**.
嘉年華製造了超多垃圾。

😊 It will take some time to clean it up.
需要些時間去清理它。

tray
n. 托盤

Please place the **tray** on the bar counter after dining.

請在用餐之後把托盤放到吧台上。

Ok.

好的。

---

unlock
v. 開鎖；揭開

Can you **unlock** this box? I don't have the key.

你可以開一下這個盒子嗎？我沒有鑰匙。

Neither do I. We need a locksmith.

我也沒有，我們該去找個鎖匠來。

---

unpack
v. 解開；卸下；（打開行李）

Please **unpack** your luggage. We have arrived at the hotel.

請打開你的行李，我們已經到達飯店了。

OK. Can you help me to unload them from the car?

好的，你可以幫我把它們從車上卸下來嗎？

---

utilities
n. 水、電等生活必需品

The **utility** fee is a big burden to us now.

水電費現在對我們來說是個大負擔。

We shall not use air conditioner any more.

我們別再開冷氣了。

---

vase
n. 花瓶

Is there anything special about this **vase**?

這個花瓶有什麼特別的嗎？

It is a vase made in Ming, a dynasty of China.

這是一個在明朝製造的花瓶。

---

villa
n. 別墅

Where did you live when you travel in Indonesia?

你之前去印尼玩的時候住在哪裡？

I lived in a **villa** in Bali.

我住在峇里島的一個別墅裡面。

village
n. 村莊

There was a **village** before.
之前在這邊有個村莊。

But it turns into residential area of the near city.
但後來它轉變成了附近城市的居住區。

🔊 *Track 0420*

wake
v. 喚醒；醒

同義字
▶ **rouse** 喚醒

Would you please **wake** me up at 10 p.m.?
你可以在晚上十點叫我起床嗎？

Sure, why not?
好啊，何不呢？

🔊 *Track 0421*

wall
n. 牆壁

When did Berlin **wall** collapse?
柏林圍牆是何時倒塌的？

Let me think…it's 1990, right?
讓我想想…是 1990 年對吧？

🔊 *Track 0422*

wash
v. 洗；洗滌

Who's willing to **wash** dishes?
誰願意去洗盤子呢？

I'll do that, it's my turn today.
我會洗，今天輪到我洗了。

🔊 *Track 0423*

wide
adj. 寬廣的；（寬度為……的）

What's the width of this box?
這個盒子的寬度是多少呢？

This box is 5 meters **wide**.
這個盒子有五公尺寬。

🔊 *Track 0424*

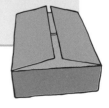

wipe
v. 擦；消除；拭去
n. 紙巾；（抹布）

◀ *Track 0425*

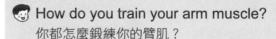 How to **wipe** out the data in the hard disk?
要怎麼抹除硬碟裡面的資料呢？

You can format the disk and the data will be eliminated.
你可以對硬碟格式化然後資料就會被消除。

這裡使用的是動詞喔！

wood
n. 木頭；（木材；樹林）
adj. 木製的

同義字
▶ **timber** 木材

◀ *Track 0426*

How do you train your arm muscle?
你都怎麼鍛練你的臂肌？

I chop **wood** from the morning to the evening everyday.
我每天從早到晚劈木頭。

這裡使用的是名詞喔！

yard
n. 庭院；院子；（碼，約 91.4公分）

◀ *Track 0427*

I planted some trees in the **yard**.
我在庭院裡面種了一些樹。

Yeah, I saw them. It seems good.
是啊，我看到了。看起來不錯呢。

I planted some trees in the yard.

NOTE

Part

04

Part 04 "交通"

在國外旅遊，不論是觀光還是交通出行，都會用到英文。一起看以下單字和對答，學會外國人是怎麼說的！＊單字、對話分開錄音，學習目標更明確

aboard

adv. 船上；登機；火車上
prep. （在）船上；飛機上；火車上

◀ *Track 0428*

> 🧑 Sir, welcome **aboard**! How can I help you?
> 先生，歡迎登機，您有甚麼需要嗎？
>
> 🧑 I'd like a glass of water, please.
> 請給我一杯水。

這裡使用的是副詞喔！

abroad

adv. 到國外；海外

同義詞
▶ **overseas**
到國外；在國外；國外的

◀ *Track 0429*

> 🧑 Have you ever been **abroad**?
> 你有出過國嗎？
>
> 🧑 Yes, I've been to the United States and Australia
> 有的，我去過美國和澳洲。

abut

v. 鄰接；毗連；（相連接）

◀ *Track 0430*

> 🧑 Where do you live?
> 你們住在哪呢？
>
> 🧑 Our house **abuts** Taipei 101!
> 我們的房子緊鄰台北 101。

access

v. 接近（使用）；通道；入口

◀ *Track 0431*

> 🧑 Excuse me! How can I get the **access** to the computer lab?
> 不好意思！請問我要如何進入電腦實驗室？
>
> 🧑 You need to show us your student ID.
> 你需要出示你的學生證。

accident
n. 事故;偶發事件

Track 0432

A terrible **accident** happened yesterday!
昨天發生了一個很糟的意外!

Are you OK? What's wrong?
你還好吧?發生了甚麼事?

accompany
v. 隨行;陪伴;伴隨

Track 0433

Will you **accompany** me to the supermarket?
你會陪我去超市嗎?

Sure! Why not?
當然啦!為什麼不呢?

across
adv. 橫過

Track 0434

Go **across** the street. Then you'll see McDonald's.
過了這條街,你就會看到麥當勞。

Thank you very much! I am so hungry!
謝謝你!我好餓!

address
n. 住址;致詞
v. 處理

Track 0435

Please fill your **address** in this blank.
請將你的住址填在這個空格。

I see. Thank you!
我知道了,謝謝!

這裡使用的是名詞喔!

admission
n. 准許進入;入場費

反義詞
▶ **prohibition**
禁止

Track 0436

You know what? He got the **admission** to Yale.
我跟你說,他獲得進耶魯大學的入學許可了。

Wow! He's amazing!
哇!他真厲害!

advance
v. 前進;(促進;使進步)

Track 0437

The **advance** of technology has brought us a lot of convenience.
科技的進步帶給我們很大的便利。

Yes, especially the Internet!
說的對!特別是網際網路。

adventure
n. 冒險

😊 Have you read the novel "Adventures of Huckleberry Fin"?
你讀過《頑童歷險記》這本小說了嗎？

😊 Not yet. It's still beside my bed.
還沒讀，它還在我的床邊。

airline
n. （飛機）航線；航空公司

😊 There are many **airline** companies in Taiwan.
台灣有很多家航空公司。

😊 Can you name some? I only know EVA Airlines.
你可以列舉一些嗎？我只知道長榮航空。

airplane
n. 飛機

同義詞
▶ **plane** 飛機

😊 Should we take the **airplane** or should we drive?
我們應該要搭飛機還是開車？

😊 Both will do.
兩個都可以。

airport
n. 機場

😊 The **airport** is state-of-the-art.
這個機場設備很新。

😊 I can tell.
看得出來。

aisle
n. 教堂的側廊；通道

😊 Walk down the **aisle** of the church, and you'll see a statue of Cupid.
沿著教堂的側廊走，你會看到邱比特的雕像。

😊 I can't wait to see it.
我等不及要看了。

alley
n. 巷；小徑

🔊 *Track 0443*

Down the **alley**, there are many stray cats.
巷子底有很多流浪貓。

Can we find them homes? They are very cute.
我們可以幫牠們找到家嗎？牠們很可愛。

altitude
n. 高度；海拔

🔊 *Track 0444*

The Jade Mountain is 3997 meters in **altitude**.
玉山海拔高度3997公尺。

It's also the tallest mountain in Taiwan.
它同時也是台灣最高的山脈。

Antarctic
n. 南極洲

🔊 *Track 0445*

Is there any animal living in the **Antarctic**?
有動物住南極嗎？

Yes, penguins.
有，企鵝。

anywhere
adv. 任何地方
pro. （在或去）任何地方

同義詞
▶ **anyplace**
任何地方

🔊 *Track 0446*

I will go **anywhere** with you.
你去哪裡我都跟著你。

Don't worry. I won't leave you alone.
別擔心，我不會把你一個人丟著。

這裡使用的是副詞喔！

apart
adj. 分離的
adv. 分散地；遠離地

同義詞
▶ **separate** 分開

🔊 *Track 0447*

If you are far **apart** from your sisters, will you miss them?
如果你跟你的姊妹分離得很遠，你會想念他們嗎？

Without a doubt.
那還用說。

這裡使用的是副詞喔！

approach
n. 方法；態度
v. 接近

Track 0448

The train is **approaching**!
火車來了。

Let's run as fast as we can.
我們快點全力衝刺吧！

這裡使用的是動詞喔！

aquarium
n. 水族館

Track 0449

As far as I know, the **aquarium** here accommodates over 10 thousand species.
據我所知，這裡的水族館包含超過一萬種物種。

That's amazing.
真是太驚人了！

around
adv. 大約；（大概）
prep. 在周圍；（在附近）

同義詞
▶ **approximately**
大約

Track 0450

You have to be especially careful when there is a stranger **around**!
有陌生人在旁邊時，你一定得特別小心。

Yes, mummy! I've heard that from you for the 1000th time!
遵命，媽！我已經聽你說過近千次囉！

這裡使用的是介系詞喔！

arrive
v. 到達；來臨

Track 0451

He had already left when I **arrived**.
我抵達的時候，他已經離開了。

What a pity!
真是可惜！

assemble
v. 聚集；集合

Track 0452

I was busy **assembling** my bike yesterday afternoon.
我昨天下午忙著組裝我的腳踏車

And now? Is it repaired?
那現在呢？修好了嗎？

at
prep. 在

Track 0453

You must stay **at** home this weekend.
你這個週末得待在家。

Why? Will anyone visit us?
為什麼呢？有人要來拜訪我們嗎？

attach
v. 連接;附屬;附加

◀ *Track 0454*

Attach this piece of paper to your passport.
把這張紙黏在你的護照上。

I see. Thanks for the reminder.
我知道了。謝謝你的提醒。

auditorium
n. 禮堂;演講廳

◀ *Track 0455*

Where will the speech be held?
演講會在哪裡舉辦呢?

In the auditorium.
在禮堂。

automobile
n. 汽車

◀ *Track 0456*

The automobile company is the biggest in town.
這間汽車公司是鎮裡最大間的。

Yes. It is where most townsmen work.
是啊,大多的鎮民也都在這裡工作。

avenue
n. 大道;大街

同義詞
▶ thoroughfare
大街

◀ *Track 0457*

The most famous street in New York is called "The Fifth Avenue."
紐約最有名的街道是第五大道。

What is it famous for?
它有名在哪呢?

away
adv. 遠離;離開

◀ *Track 0458*

Go away!
走開!

What's wrong? Are you angry at me?
怎麼了?你在生我的氣嗎?

baggage
n. 行李

◀ *Track 0459*

May I leave my baggage here?
我可以把我的行李留在這嗎?

Sure. Anywhere you want.
可以啊!你想擺哪裡都行!

ban
n. 禁止
v. 禁止

◀ *Track 0460*

My mom **bans** me to play video games after 10 p.m.
我媽媽禁止我十點後玩電玩。

I think she is right. You shouldn't play video games till so late at night.
我覺得那樣是對的，你不該玩電玩玩得這麼晚。

這裡使用的是動詞喔！

bank
n. 銀行；堤；岸

◀ *Track 0461*

Where is Lisa?
麗莎去哪了？

She is at the **bank**.
她在銀行。

basis
n. 根據；基礎

◀ *Track 0462*

The **basis** of his theory is wrong.
他理論的基礎是錯誤的。

No wonder we couldn't figure it out.
難怪我們理不出個頭緒。

besides
prep. 除了……之外；（此外）
adv. 除了……之外

同義詞
▶ **moreover** 此外

◀ *Track 0463*

Besides what I've mentioned, do you have other examples?
除了我剛剛提過的，你還有沒有其他的例子呢？

I haven't come up with any yet.
我還沒想到任何其他的例子。

這裡使用的是介系詞喔！

beyond
adv. 在遠處；超過

◀ *Track 0464*

100 years ago, the invention of the Internet was **beyond** people's imagination.
100 年前，人們無法想像網際網路的誕生。

I agree!
說的沒錯！

bicycle
n. 自行車

同義詞
▶ **bike** 腳踏車

 Track 0465

Do you have a **bicycle** at home?
你家裡有腳踏車嗎？

I used to have, but now it's broken.
我以前有，但是它壞掉了。

---

bill
n. 帳單

 Track 0466

Mom! You forgot to pay my **bill**!
媽，你忘了幫我繳帳單了！

Woops! Is it the end of the month already?
啊！已經月底了嗎？

---

block
n. 街區；木塊；石塊

 Track 0467

How many families are here?
這邊有幾戶人家？

Not sure. I can only say for my own **block**. There are about 10.
不確定，我只知道我們這一區大約有十戶。

---

board
n. 板；佈告欄

 Track 0468

Have you seen the announcement on the **board**?
你看到佈告欄的公告嗎？

Yes! I can't believe that!
有！真不敢相信！

---

boat
n. 船

同義詞
▶ **vessel** 船；艦

 Track 0469

There is a **boat** in our garage.
我們的車庫裡有一艘船。

Is it still in use?
那艘船還有在使用嗎？

booth
n. 棚子；攤子

Track 0470

🧑 I've ordered the ingredients for the bread. What have I missed?
我已經訂了麵包的材料，還有差什麼嗎？

👩 Have you rented the **booth** already?
你租了攤子嗎？

---

bother
v. 打擾

同義詞
▶ **disturb**
妨礙；打擾

Track 0471

🧑 I am sorry to **bother** you, but could I have a second?
很抱歉打擾你，但我可以借個一分鐘嗎？

👩 Certainly.
當然可以！

---

boulevard
n. 林蔭大道

Track 0472

🧑 There is a **boulevard** down the road.
這條路底有一條林蔭大道。

👩 I know. There are a lot of coffee shops there.
我知道，那邊有很多咖啡館。

---

bow
v. 彎腰；鞠躬

同義詞
▶ **bend** 彎腰；行禮

Track 0473

🧑 Even on the phone, Japanese people **bow** unconsciously.
即使在電話中，日本人還是不自覺地鞠躬。

👩 Yeah. Sometimes I nod even when I am on the phone.
是啊。有時我在電話上也會點頭。

---

brake
n. 煞車
v. 煞車

Track 0474

🧑 When you see a cat in the middle of the road, what will you do?
當你看到一隻貓在路中央，你會怎麼做呢？

👩 **Brake**!
剎車！

這裡使用的是動詞喔！

bridge
n. 橋

🔊 *Track 0475*

👦 There is a famous song called "London **Bridge**."
有首有名的歌叫做倫敦鐵橋。

👧 You are talking about the song "London **Bridge** is falling down..."?
你是說倫敦鐵橋垮下來那首歌嗎？

broad
adj. 寬闊的

同義詞
▶ **expansive**
廣闊的

🔊 *Track 0476*

👦 Do you think we can decide our life?
你認為我們可以決定自己的人生嗎？

👧 Yes. Narrow or **broad**, it's up to ourselves.
是的，狹窄或寬闊其實都是由我們自己決定！

brook
n. 川；小河；溪流

🔊 *Track 0477*

👦 There is a **brook** behind my house.
我家後面有一條小溪

👧 Wow. I love it.
哇！我喜歡！

bus
n. 公車

🔊 *Track 0478*

👦 How do you go to school?
你怎麼去學校？

👧 By **bus**.
搭公車。

bypass
n. 旁道
v. 繞過；避開

🔊 *Track 0479*

👦 If it's too crowded, remember to take the **bypass**.
如果太擁擠了，記得繞旁道。

👦 I will. Thank you!
我會的，謝謝你！

這裡使用的是名詞喔！

call

n. 呼叫；打電話
v. （稱呼）；呼叫；打電話

🔊 *Track 0480*

🧑 How many **calls** do you usually receive in a day?
你一天大多都接幾通電話？

👩 About 3.
大約三通。

這裡使用的是名詞喔！

campus

n. 校區；校園

🔊 *Track 0481*

🧑 Look! There is a school over there.
看！那裡有間學校。

👩 Oh! It says that it's the main **campus**.
喔！據説是主校區耶！

canal

n. 運河；人工渠道

🔊 *Track 0482*

🧑 If you go to Italy, what do you want to see?
你去義大利的話，想看些什麼？

👩 **Canals** and churches.
運河和教堂。

canyon

n. 峽谷

🔊 *Track 0483*

🧑 Do you have **canyons** here in Taiwan?
台灣有峽谷嗎？

👩 Not really.
沒有。

car

n. 汽車

🔊 *Track 0484*

🧑 When it's tomb-sweeping day, there are always so many **cars**.
清明節時車總是好多啊！

👩 I can't agree with you more!
你説的真對！

card

n. 卡片；（紙牌）

🔊 *Track 0485*

🧑 Where are you going?
你要去哪裡呢？

👩 To send the **card**.
我要去寄個卡片。

cargo

n. 貨物;船貨

同義詞
▶ **freight** 船運貨物

◀ *Track 0486*

What are those big boxes?
那些大箱子是甚麼?

They are **cargoes**.
是船貨。

---

carriage

n. 車輛;車;馬車

◀ *Track 0487*

In the past, people didn't have cars.
過去,人們沒有汽車。

They had **carriages**.
他們有馬車。

---

carry

v. 攜帶;搬運;拿

反義詞
▶ **drop** 扔下

◀ *Track 0488*

What are you **carrying** with you?
你拿著什麼啊?

A new model!
一個新模型!

---

cart

n. 手拉車;(小推車)

◀ *Track 0489*

Go get a shopping **cart**!
去拉台購物車吧!

Here it is. Let's go.
拉來了!我們走吧!

---

center

n. 中心;中央

同義詞
▶ **core** 中心、核心

◀ *Track 0490*

Where is this place?
這裡是哪裡?

It's the **center** of the city.
這裡是市中心。

central
adj. 中央的；（中心的；重要的）

◀Track 0491

What is the **central** idea of this article?
這篇文章的中心思想是什麼？

No idea!
我也沒頭緒。

channel
n. 通道；頻道；（途徑；航道）

◀Track 0492

Which **Channel** do you usually watch at home?
你在家大多都看哪個頻道？

My favorite, **channel** V!
我都看我最愛的 V 頻道啊！

charge
v. 索價；指控；命令
n. 費用；（價格）；指控

◀Track 0493

I was **charged** 1000 dollars for a ride from my home to here.
從我家搭車到這裡，我被索價 1000 元。

Was the taxi driver crazy?
計程車司機是不是瘋了啊？

這裡使用的是動詞喔！

cheap
adj. 低價的；易取得的

◀Track 0494

Drinks are **cheap** and easy to get in Taiwan.
飲料在台灣很便宜又很好買到。

No wonder all of you carry a bottle of drink with you!
難怪你們身上都帶著一瓶飲料。

church
n. 教堂

◀Track 0495

Where will Nancy's wedding be held?
南希的婚禮會在哪裡舉行？

In the **church**.
在教堂裡。

city
n. 城市

◀Track 0496

Taichung is a friendly **city**.
台中是個很友善的城市。

How can you tell?
怎麼說呢？

cliff
n. 峭壁;斷崖

🔊 *Track 0497*

👦 We saw a woman standing at the edge of a **cliff** yesterday.
昨天我們看到一個女人站在斷崖邊。

👧 That's dangerous!
那很危險呢!

coin
n. 硬幣

🔊 *Track 0498*

👦 Come on! Flip the **coin**.
快!擲出銅板吧!

👧 Stop hurrying!
別急!

come
v. 來;(過來)

🔊 *Track 0499*

👦 **Come** visit me sometime in the week!
這週找個時間來拜訪我吧!

👧 When will you be most convenient?
你哪時最方便呢?

commonplace
adj. 平常的;常見的;(普通的)
n. 平凡的事;(寒暄)

🔊 *Track 0500*

👦 In Scotland, that men wear skirts is a **commonplace**.
在蘇格蘭,男生穿裙子是很平常的事。

👧 Really? I've never heard of that.
真的嗎?我從沒聽過呢!

這裡使用的是名詞喔!

commuter
n. 通勤者

🔊 *Track 0501*

👦 Why do you look so tired?
你看起來怎麼這麼累?

👧 Life as a **commuter** is really tiring!
通勤者的生活真的很累人。

confirm
v. 證實;(確定)

反義詞
▶ **deny** 否認

🔊 *Track 0502*

👦 It is **confirmed** that U.S. beef will be imported.
據證實,美國牛肉會被進口。

👧 I hope the government can make sure of the beef's quality.
我希望政府可以確保牛肉的品質。

115

construct

v. 建造;構築

Track 0503

One emperor **constructed** what is now the National Palace Museum.
有個皇帝建造了現在的故宮博物院。

It is very magnificent indeed.
故宮的確很雄偉。

---

contact

v. 聯絡
n. 聯絡;接觸;關係

Track 0504

Have you **contacted** your relative?
你跟親人聯絡了嗎?

No, I haven't.
不,還沒有。

這裡使用的是動詞喔!

---

convenient

adj. 便利的

Track 0505

There is a grocery shop downstairs.
樓下有間雜貨店。

It is really **convenient** living here.
住在這裡真的很方便。

---

convertible

n. 敞篷車
adj. 可兌換的;可轉變的

Track 0506

Hey, I just bought a car.
嘿!我剛買了部車。

Wow! A **convertible**!
哇!是台敞篷車!

這裡使用的是名詞喔!

---

convey

v. 傳達;運送

Track 0507

The teacher asked me to **convey** a message to you.
老師叫我傳個口訊給你。

What? I'll be flunked?
是什麼?我要被當掉了嗎?

---

corner

n. 角落

Track 0508

I like to stay in a **corner** that belongs only to me.
我喜歡待在一個專屬於我的角落。

Me, too.
我也喜歡這樣。

countryside
n. 鄉間

Track 0509

What is the life like in the **countryside**?
鄉間的生活是怎麼樣的呢？

It's very peaceful.
很平靜。

course
n. 路線；方向；（課程；競賽場；一道菜）

Track 0510

Our **course** is to the west.
我們的路線往西。

Yeah? I thought we are heading east.
是唷？我以為我們往東行。

crash
n. 撞擊；（撞車事故）
v. 撞擊；（墜毀）

Track 0511

The car **crash** was terrible.
這場車禍好可怕。

Yes, but luckily no one was hurt.
是啊！但幸運的是沒人受傷。

這裡使用的是名詞喔！

crawl
v. 爬

Track 0512

A spider **crawled** across my desk in class.
有隻蜘蛛在課堂上爬過我的桌面。

Disgusting!
好噁心啊！

crossing
n. 橫越；橫渡；（路口；渡口）

Track 0513

The **crossing** from east to west was very difficult before.
以前，從東方橫渡到西方很困難。

True, especially when there were no airplanes.
的確，特別是在以前沒有飛機的時候。

cruise
n. 航行；巡航

Track 0514

We'd like to have a **cruise** to Italy.
我們想要航行到義大利去。

Sounds romantic.
聽起來很浪漫。

dam
n. 水壩

The **dam** is famous for its good quality of water resource.

這個水壩因為水質良好而聞名。

So I have heard.

我也這麼聽說。

Track 0515

debt
n. 債；欠款

I paid off my 50-dollar **debt** to you, didn't I?

我把欠你的五十元還你了吧？

Yes, you did.

有，你還給我了。

Track 0516

deck
n. 甲板

People like to go onto the **deck** to watch the view on the boats.

在船上時，人們喜歡到甲板去欣賞風景。

I do, too.

我也喜歡。

Track 0517

delay
n. 延誤
v. 使延誤

When will you be here?

你什麼時候會到這裡？

Because of the **delay**, I will get there at 15:00.

因為有點延誤，我下午三點才會到。

這裡使用的是名詞喔！

Track 0518

deliver
v. 傳送；遞送；（給出；分娩；拯救）

He **delivered** the pizza to us before he got to work.

在他去工作前，他送來了披薩給我們。

It was very kind of him.

他人真好。

Track 0519

depart
v. 離開；走開；（啟程）

He **departed** from America to Japan.

他離開美國，前往日本。

Why is he always so busy?

他怎麼總是這麼忙？

Track 0520

departure
n. 離去；出發

His **departure** to Japan for 1 year makes us sad.
他要離開到日本去一年，我們很難過。

Hey! You should wish him good luck!
嘿！你們應該要祝他好運才對。

Track 0521

desert
n. 沙漠；荒地

There are many landscapes in Taiwan.
台灣有很多種地形。

We have almost landscapes of all kinds, except **deserts** and canyons.
我們幾乎什麼地形都有，大概只沒有沙漠和峽谷吧。

Track 0522

direction
n. 指導；方向

Under the **direction** of my professor, I've learned a lot.
教授的指導讓我學了很多。

How lucky you are!
你真幸運啊！

Track 0523

disappear
n. 消失；不見

He just **disappeared**.
他就這麼不見了。

Why? He didn't say anything to you?
為什麼？他什麼都沒告訴你嗎？

同義字
▶ **vanish** 消失

Track 0524

distance
n. 距離；（疏遠）

The **distance** between school and my house is about 1 km.
學校到我家大約距離一公里。

So you take a bus to school, right?
所以你是搭公車去學校對吧？

Track 0525

distant

adj. 疏遠的；有距離的

同義詞

▶ **remote** 遙遠的

🔊 *Track 0526*

🧑 It is so **distant** to go from where we are to Taipei 101.

從我們所在之處走到台北101好遠哪！

👩 Let's chat along the way so you won't have that feeling.

我們來聊天吧，你就不會這麼覺得了。

---

dock

n. 船塢；碼頭

🔊 *Track 0527*

🧑 The **dock** is so crowded.

碼頭好擁擠啊！

👩 Today is their celebration day.

今天是他們慶祝的日子。

---

doorway

n. 門口；出入口

🔊 *Track 0528*

🧑 Tom! Clean your stuff on the **doorway**.

湯姆！把你放在門口的東西清理掉。

👩 OK! I'm coming!

好，我來了！

---

down

adv. 向下地

prep. 向下；（沿著）

🔊 *Track 0529*

🧑 The elevator is going **down**.

電梯往下。

👩 Ooops! Sorry I am going up!

抱歉！我要往上。

這裡使用的是副詞喔！

---

downstairs

adv. （在）樓下；（往）樓下

🔊 *Track 0530*

🧑 I'll meet you **downstairs**.

我會在樓下與你見面。

👩 See you then!

到時見囉！

---

downtown

adj. 鬧區的

n. 市中心

🔊 *Track 0531*

🧑 Do you prefer living in **downtown**?

你比較喜歡住在市中心嗎？

👩 Yes. It's more convenient!

是的，市中心比較方便。

這裡使用的是名詞喔！

doze
v. 打瞌睡

🔊 *Track 0532*

👦 I **dozed** off in class today.
我今天在課堂上打瞌睡了。

👧 You stayed up too late last night.
你昨晚熬夜太晚了。

---

drift
v. 漂移

🔊 *Track 0533*

👦 He **drifted** on the sea for 3 days.
他在海上漂流了三天。

👧 Fortunately, he survived.
幸運地，他活了下來。

---

drive
v. 駕車
n. 車道

🔊 *Track 0534*

👦 Mom **drives** me to the cram school every day.
媽媽每天都開車載我去補習班。

👧 Your mom is very nice to you.
你媽媽對你很好呢。

> 這裡使用的是動詞喔！

---

driveway
n. 私用車道；車道

🔊 *Track 0535*

👦 Parents must remember not to leave their kids on the **driveway.**
父母親一定要記得不要把小孩留在車道上。

👧 Or they'll easily get hurt.
不然的話，小孩很容易受到傷害。

---

drugstore
n. 藥房

🔊 *Track 0536*

👦 Where are you going?
你要去哪？

👧 The **drugstore**. I want to get some asprine.
藥房，我要去買點阿斯匹靈。

---

earn
n. 賺取；得到

🔗 同義詞
▶ **be paid**
得到報酬

🔊 *Track 0537*

👦 Have you **earned** enough money for a trip?
你賺夠錢去旅遊了嗎？

👧 Almost. I only have to **earn** 2000 more.
快了，我只要再賺2000元就夠了。

earth

n. 地球；陸地；地面

同義字
▶ **hill up** 培土

Track 0538

People on **earth** are searching for new places where they might move to.
地球上的人在尋找他們可能搬去的新地方。

Why would we do that?
我們為何要這麼做呢？

east

adj. 東方

Track 0539

There are four directions: north, south, west, and…?
有四個方位，北方、南方、西方和……？

East.
東方。

eastern

adj. 東方的

Track 0540

Which part of Europe did you visit?
你去了歐洲的哪邊？

Eastern Europe. I loved it.
我去了東歐，我很喜歡。

economical

adj. 節儉的；節省的；（經濟的）

Track 0541

Turning on the fan while having the air conditioning is very **economical**.
開著空調時，打開電風扇，是非常節能的。

I'll try that for sure!
我一定得試試。

elderly

adj. 上了年紀的
n. 長者

Track 0542

What are the priority seats for?
博愛座是設來做什麼的？

They are for children, the **elderly**, and pregnant women.
博愛座是設來給小孩，年長者，和懷孕的女人坐的。

這裡使用的是名詞喔！

elevaor

n. 升降機；電梯

Track 0543

Let's take the **elevator**.
我們搭電梯吧。

No, I'll take the stairs.
不了，我走樓梯。

e-mail
n. 電子郵件

🔊 *Track 0544*

Do you use **e-mail**?
你用電子郵件嗎？

Yes, but I seldom check my mail box.
有，但是我很少收信。

emergency
n. 緊急情況

🔊 *Track 0545*

In any case of **emergencies**, please contact us.
有緊急情況的話，請與我們聯絡。

Thank you!
謝謝你。

enclose
v. 包圍

🔊 *Track 0546*

My house is **enclosed** by high walls.
我家被高牆圍住。

It should be very safe.
應該很安全吧。

engine
n. 引擎

🔊 *Track 0547*

The **engine** is very hot.
引擎很熱。

Let's stop by for a while then.
那我們旁邊暫停一下吧。

entrance
n. 入口

🔊 *Track 0548*

Where is the **entrance** to the building?
請問大樓的入口在哪？

On the left.
在左邊。

entry
n. 入口；（進入）

🔊 *Track 0549*

Where is the **entry** of the movie theater?
電影院的入口在哪？

Right here.
就在這裡。

envelope
n. 信封

🔊 *Track 0550*

Do you have an **envelope** with you?
你身上有信封嗎？

No, what for?
沒有，要做什麼的？

escalator
n. 手扶梯

🔊 *Track 0551*

Please take care of your children while you take the **escalator**.
搭手扶梯時，請照顧好您的孩子。

OK! Thank you!
好的，謝謝！

escape
n. 逃走
v. 逃走

🔊 *Track 0552*

The prisoner has **escaped**!
囚犯逃走了！

Let's go look for him.
我們快去找他。

這裡使用的是動詞喔！

evacuate
v. 撤離

🔊 *Track 0553*

Residents were **evacuated** because of the fire.
居民因火災被撤離了。

Did anyone get hurt?
有人受傷嗎？

exit
n. 出口
v. 離開

🔊 *Track 0554*

When you go to a hotel, remember to check where the emergency **exits** are.
到一間旅館時，記得查看逃生出口在哪。

I will.
我會的。

這裡使用的是名詞喔！

expedition
n. 探險；遠征；（探險隊）

🔊 *Track 0555*

He is going to Africa for an **expedition**.
他要去非洲探險。

Amazing!
好帥啊！

expensive
adj. 昂貴的

🔈 *Track 0556*

The food is so **expensive**! But it tastes weired.
這食物好貴，但嘗起來很詭異。

Yuck! I'll never try it again.
好噁心！我絕不會再嘗試了。

famous
adj. 有名的；出名的

🔈 *Track 0557*

Do you know there is a **famous** TV series recently?
你知道最近有部有名的電視劇嗎？

Are you talking about "Chuck"?
你是說宅男特務嗎？

far
adj. 遙遠的；遠（方）的

🔈 *Track 0558*

My goal is still **far** away from me.
我的目標還離我很遠。

Then you'll have to work harder.
那你得更努力點。

fare
n. 費用；運費

🔈 *Track 0559*

Recently the oil **fare** has been high.
最近油價很高。

Bad news for we drivers!
對我們開車族來說真是個壞消息。

farm
n. 農場；農田

🔈 *Track 0560*

My uncle runs a **farm** in Tainan.
我叔叔在台南開農場。

Sounds interesting. May we visit him sometimes?
聽起來很有趣，我們可能找時間去拜訪他嗎？

farther
adv. 更遠地

🔈 *Track 0561*

He went to America last month, and this month he is going to Canada.
他上個月去了美國，這個月要去加拿大。

Wow, he goes **farther** and **farther** away.
哇！他越跑越遠。

fast
adj. 快速的

🔊 *Track 0562*

😊 He runs as **fast** as thunder.
他跑得跟閃電一樣快。

😊 Yes. He is a **fast** runner.
是啊,他真的跑得很快。

fasten
v. 緊固;繫緊

🔊 *Track 0563*

😊 Sir, please **fasten** your seat belt.
先生,請繫緊你的安全帶。

😊 OK. I see.
好的,我知道了。

fee
n. 費用

🔊 *Track 0564*

😊 It's 336 dollars.
總共是336元。

😊 Does that include the service **fee**?
服務費也包含在內了嗎?

ferry
n. 渡口;渡船

🔊 *Track 0565*

😊 Where can we take **ferries**?
哪裡有渡輪可以搭啊?

😊 A famous place with **ferries** is Seattle.
西雅圖是個有名的渡輪地點。

flight
n. 飛行;(躲避)

🔊 *Track 0566*

😊 hope you enjoyed your **flight**.
我們希望您還滿意您的搭機經驗。

😊 Yes I did. Thank you!
我挺滿意的,謝謝你!

forward
adj. 向前的
adv. 向前的
n. 前鋒

🔊 *Track 0567*

😊 Move **forward** a little.
往前移一點點。

😊 No. I don't want to be too close to the handrail.
不要,我不想太靠近欄杆。

> 這裡使用的是副詞喔!

fountain
n. 噴泉;噴水池

🔊 *Track 0568*

😊 There's a **fountain** in the square.
廣場裡有個噴水池。

😊 There wasn't one last time I came.
上次我來時沒有呢!

freeway
n. 高速公路

Track 0569

How can I go to the town next to us?
隔壁鎮怎麼去呢？

You have to take the **freeway**.
你必須走高速公路。

frequency
n. 時常發生；頻率

Track 0570

The **frequency** of the earthquake is becoming higher and higher.
地震的頻率越來越高了。

That's horrifying!
好嚇人哪！

gallon
n. 加侖

Track 0571

One **gallon** of oil, please.
請給我一加侖的油。

In a minute!
馬上好！

gasoline
n. 汽油

Track 0572

Scientists are discovering substitutes for **gasoline**.
科學家正在找尋汽油的替代品。

Has any result come out?
有什麼結果嗎？

global
adj. 球狀的；全球的

Track 0573

Because of the Internet, the distance between people has narrowed.
因為網路的關係，人與人的距離縮短了！

Right. Now we have a **global** village.
對，現在我們有個地球村！

globe
n. 地球；球

Track 0574

The **globe** now is undergoing a lot of changes.
地球現在正經歷著很多改變。

Like what? Can global warming count?
像是什麼？全球暖化是嗎？

go
v. 去；走
n. 嘗試

Track 0575

Let's **go**! We'll be late.
我們走吧！快遲到了。

One more minute!
再一分鐘！

這裡使用的是動詞喔！

goods
n. 商品；貨物

Track 0576

There are a wide range of **goods** in the market.
市場裡有很多種貨品。

I can't wait to go there!
我等不及要去了！

greet
v. 迎接；問候

Track 0577

He **greeted** us with a loud voice.
他用很宏亮的聲音與我們打招呼。

Sounds like he is a hospitable person.
他聽起來似乎是個很好客的人。

grocery
n. 雜貨店

Track 0578

I'll do **grocery** shopping tomorrow. Do you want me to buy anything for you?
明天我要去採買一些雜貨，你要我幫你買什麼嗎？

Some potato chips will be great.
買一些洋芋片似乎不錯。

handy
adj. 方便的；隨手可得的

Track 0579

In Germany, beer always comes in **handy**.
在德國，啤酒是隨手可得的。

So fascinating!
真吸引人哪！

harbor
n. 碼頭

Track 0580

We were at the **harbor** yesterday.
我們昨天去了港口。

Wow! Did you buy some seafood?
哇！你們有沒有買些海鮮呢？

haste
n. 急忙；急速

Track 0581

In my **haste**, I forgot to bring my cell phone with me.
我在匆忙中忘了帶手機。

That's why I kept calling you and you didn't answer!
難怪我一直打給你都沒接！

128

hasten
v. 趕緊；趕快

Track 0582

- John **hastened** home after he got a call.
  約翰在接到電話後便衝回家了。
- I hope he is alright!
  希望他沒事！

head
v. 出發；船駛往……
n. 頭

Track 0583

- This ship is **heading** for Bali.
  這艘船開往八里。
- How long will it take?
  會花多久時間呢？

> 這裡使用的是動詞喔！

height
n. 高度

Track 0584

- The statue is 300 meters in **height**.
  這座雕像有三百公尺高。
- Is it? I couldn't feel that.
  是嗎？我不覺得它有這麼高。

helicopter
n. 直升機

Track 0585

- What kind of airplane do you want to ride in?
  你想要搭哪種飛機啊？
- A **helicopter**.
  直升機。

here
adv. 這裡

Track 0586

- Here comes the bus.
  巴士來了！
- Let's get on it.
  我們快上車吧！

highly
adv. 大大地、高高地

Track 0587

- She is praised **highly** by the teacher.
  老師極力稱讚她。
- She is a good student.
  她是個好學生。

highway
n. 公路

Track 0588

- This **highway** is built just recently.
  這條公路是最近建的。
- It seems few people know about it.
  似乎還沒什麼人知道。

129

hike
v. 徒步旅行；健行

◀ *Track 0589*

Her hobby is **hiking**.
她的興趣是健行。

So is mine. It makes me healthy.
我也是！健行使我健康。

---

hill
n. 小山

◀ *Track 0590*

Our school is on the **hill**.
我們學校在一座小山上。

The air must be fresh in your school.
你們學校的空氣一定很好。

---

horizon
n. 地平線

◀ *Track 0591*

The sun is rising above the **horizon**.
太陽漸漸自地平線升起。

The view is breathtaking!
這個景緻好美啊。

---

horror
n. 恐怖；畏懼

◀ *Track 0592*

She picked up the phone in **horror**. Who was it?
她恐懼地接起手機，是誰打來的？

I don't know. She wouldn't tell
我不清楚，她不說。

---

hurry
v. 使趕緊
n. 倉促

◀ *Track 0593*

Hurry up! It's going to rain.
快一點！要下雨了。

I am coming!
我來了。

這裡使用的是動詞喔！

---

imposing
adj. 宏偉壯麗的

◀ *Track 0594*

The castle has an **imposing** view.
這個城堡有個宏偉的景致。

It's just like a picture!
簡直就像幅畫。

inspection

n. 檢查;調查

Track 0595

We have to arrive at the airport 2 hours earlier than our flight.
我們必須比班機時間早兩小時到達機場。

I know. We have to go through a lot of **inspections**.
我知道,我們必須經過很多的檢查。

intersection

n. 橫斷;交叉口

Track 0596

Where will we meet?
我們要在哪見面?

At the **intersection** of Wen-Hua Rd. and Ming-Chuan Rd.
在文化路和民權路交叉口。

jam

n. 阻塞;果醬
v. 堵住

Track 0597

There was a traffic **jam** on my way here.
我來這裡時塞車了。

No excuses next time.
下次不許你再有藉口了。

這裡使用的是名詞喔!

jaywalk

v. 不守交通規則;(任意穿越馬路)

Track 0598

People here often **jaywalk**.
這裡的人常常隨意穿越街道。

It is so dangerous since there are so many cars.
這真是危險啊!這裡有很多車。

jeep

n. 吉普車

Track 0599

My dad just bought me a car model.
我爸爸剛剛買了一個汽車模型給我。

Was it a **jeep** or what?
是吉普車還是什麼嗎?

jet

n. 噴射機;噴嘴

Track 0600

There is a flying **jet** in the sky.
有一台噴射機在空中飛。

Where? I can't see it.
在哪?我沒看到啊。

journey
n. 旅程
v. 旅行

Track 0601

Life is like a **journey**.
生命就像一場旅程。

We never know what is in front of us.
我們永遠都不知道會遇到什麼。

這裡使用的是名詞喔！

lake
n. 湖

Track 0602

Do we have a **lake** in Taiwan?
台灣有湖泊嗎？

Yes. The most famous one is Sun-Moon Lake.
有啊，最有名的是日月潭。

land
n. 陸地；土地
v. 降落

Track 0603

The **land** in Taiwan is limited.
台灣的土地有限。

Yes, it is very densely populated here.
是啊，我們這裡人口很密集。

這裡使用的是名詞喔！

landmark
n. 路標；地標

Track 0604

The **landmark** of Paris is the Eiffle Tower.
巴黎的地標是艾菲爾鐵塔。

I really want to visit there.
我很想去那看看。

landscape
n. 風景；山脊

Track 0605

I looked down on the **landscape** and found it so amazing.
我往下看到了一片很美的景色，真的很漂亮。

I've been there. I know it is really beautiful.
我也去過，我知道那裡真的很漂亮。

landslide
n. 山崩

Track 0606

There were several **landslide** accidents last year.
去年有數起山崩的意外。

People should really start making preparations for such accidents.
人們真該開始為這樣的災害做些準備。

lane
n. 小路；巷

Track 0607

> I live in a small **lane**.
> 我住在一條小巷子。

> It must be very quiet there.
> 那裡一定很安靜。

language
n. 語言

Track 0608

> How many languages are there in the world?
> 這個世界上有幾種語言？

> Not sure. Some **languages** are rarely used.
> 不確定，有些語言很少用。

leave
v. 離開
n. 假期

Track 0609

> I will **leave** at 6.
> 我會在六點離開。

> So early? Who will pick you up?
> 這麼早？誰要來接你呢？

這裡使用的是動詞喔！

left
n. 左邊
adv. （向）左邊

Track 0610

> Go straight and then turn **left**.
> 直直走，然後左轉。

> Then there's McDonald's?
> 然後就是麥當勞了嗎？

這裡使用的是副詞喔！

lend
v. 借出

Track 0611

> He **lent** his comic book to me.
> 他借我他的漫畫書。

> He is so nice.
> 他人真好。

lighthouse
n. 燈塔

Track 0612

> Where does the light come from?
> 這燈光從哪來？

> From the **lighthouse**.
> 從燈塔來的。

limo
n. 禮車；大型豪華轎車

Track 0613

> A **limo** came to pick the bride up.
> 一輛豪華轎車來把新娘接走了。

> She must be a very happy bride.
> 她一定是個很幸福的新娘。

location
n. 位置

Track 0614

I don't know about your **location**.
我不知道你位處於哪。

I am currently in central Taichung.
我現在中台中地區。

locker
n. 有鎖的收納櫃；寄物櫃

Track 0615

I don't like to carry a lot of stuff with me.
我不喜歡帶一大堆東西。

You can put them in the **locker.**
你可以把那些東西放到寄物櫃裡。

lounge
n. 交誼廳

Track 0616

Guests are gathering in the **lounge**.
訪客們都聚集在交誼廳裡。

Who is the host?
主人是哪位呢？

luggage
n. 行李

Track 0617

How much is the limit of our **luggage**?
我們的行李限重多少？

30 kg.
三十公斤。

magnificent
adj. 壯觀的；華麗的

Track 0618

I like the **magnifi cent** view of Ali Mountain.
我喜歡阿里山壯麗的景色。

I like that too.
我也很喜歡。

mail
n. 郵件
v. 寄郵件

Track 0619

Have we got any **mails** today?
我們今天有郵件嗎？

Yes, but they are all ads.
有，但都是廣告。

這裡使用的是名詞喔！

maintain
v. 維持

Track 0620

Maintaining our weight is a difficult task.
維持體重真困難。

You can say that again!
你說的真對！

134

a b c d e f g h i j k l m n o p q r s t u v w x y z

market
n. 市場
v. 推銷

Track 0621

Mom just went to the **market**.
媽才剛去市場。

When will she be back?
她什麼時候回來？

這裡使用的是名詞喔！

marvelous
adj. 令人驚訝的

Track 0622

What you did was **marvelous**!
你剛剛做的真棒！

I never thought I could do it.
我從沒想過我可以做到。

massive
adj. 大量的、巨大的

Track 0623

The rock that hit the earth was **massive**.
擊中地球的那塊石頭很巨大。

It led to servere damages.
導致了很大的傷害。

message
n. 訊息
v. （發）訊息

Track 0624

Who left the **message**?
誰留下了這個訊息？

Your dad. He asked you to get home earlier.
是你爸爸，他要你早點回家。

這裡使用的是名詞喔！

middle
n. 中間、在……中間
adj. 中間（的）

Track 0625

There is a dog in the **middle** of the road.
有隻狗在路中央。

I am worried about its safety.
我很擔心牠的安危。

這裡使用的是名詞喔！

milestone
n. 里程碑

Track 0626

World War II was a **milestone** for all humans.
二次大戰對所有人來說，都是一個新的里程碑。

Yes. Many things have changed since then.
是啊，許多事自那時起都改變了。

monument
n. 紀念碑

Track 0627

There is a **monument** of Confucius.
有孔子的紀念碑。

Let's pay our respect.
我們來致敬吧。

motorcycle
n. 摩托車

🔊 *Track 0628*

👦 How will you get there?
你要怎麼去那邊？

👧 By **motorcycle**.
騎摩托車。

mountain
n. 高山

🔊 *Track 0629*

👦 Up in the **mountain** lived a witch.
以前山中住了個女巫。

👧 Really? Unbelievable.
真的嗎？無法置信。

museum
n. 博物館

🔊 *Track 0630*

👦 There's an exhibition in the **museum**.
博物館裡有個展覽。

👧 Is there any extra fee for the exhibition?
去看展覽要額外付費嗎？

navigation
n. 航海、航空

🔊 *Track 0631*

👦 The **navigation** system of the airplane is the most advanced.
這架飛機的導航系統是最先進的。

👧 Then we will never get lost, right?
那我們絕不會迷路了，對吧？

nearby
adv. 短距離地；（附近地）
adj. 短距離的；（附近的）

🔊 *Track 0632*

👦 My parents live **nearby**.
我爸媽住在附近。

👧 So, you can meet them very often.
那你就可以常常見到他們了。

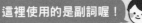 這裡使用的是副詞喔！

north
n. 北、北方
adv. （向）北方
adj. 北方（的）

🔊 *Track 0633*

👦 Canada is in the **north**.
加拿大在北方。

👧 Not the south? I got it wrong before.
不是南方喔？我以前都記錯了。

這裡使用的是名詞喔！

northern
adj. 北方的

🔊 *Track 0634*

👦 Taipei is in **northern** Taiwan.
台北在台灣的北部。

👧 I see.
我知道了。

oasis
n. 綠洲

🧒 When I saw the coke, it was like an **oasis** to me in the desert.
當我看到可樂的時候，那就像在沙漠裡看到綠洲一樣。

👧 Ha-ha, were you that thirsty?
哈哈，你有這麼渴喔？

🔊 *Track 0635*

ocean
n. 海洋

🧒 Do you want to go to the **ocean** park?
你想去海洋公園嗎？

👧 No, I went there last week.
不，我上週才去。

🔊 *Track 0636*

onto
prep. 在……之上

🧒 Remember to put the file **onto** the shelf.
記得把這個文件放到架子上。

👧 Yes, sir. I will do so.
是的先生，我會照辦。

🔊 *Track 0637*

out
adv. 離開；向外
prep. 離開；向外

🧒 Get **out**!
滾出去！

👧 Please let me explain!
請聽我解釋！

這裡使用的是副詞喔！

🔊 *Track 0638*

outdoor
adj. 戶外的

🧒 I like **outdoor** activities a lot!
我很喜歡戶外活動。

👧 I'd rather stay at home.
我寧可待在家。

🔊 *Track 0639*

outside
adj. 在……外面（的）
adv. 在……外面
prep. 在……外面
n. 外部

🧒 Let's have some fresh air **outside**.
我們到外頭呼吸點新鮮空氣吧。

👧 Good idea.
好主意。

這裡使用的是副詞喔！

🔊 *Track 0640*

outward(s)

adv. 向外的；外面的

Bend the metal **outwards** with fire.
用火把這個金屬往外折。

I can't do that! It's too dangerous!
我不會做，太危險了。

overpass

n. 天橋；高架橋

If I became the mayor some day, I'd like to build an **overpass** here.
如果我某天成為市長，我要在這裡蓋座天橋。

I'll vote for you if you become a candidate.
如果你真的變成候選人，我會投你一票。

Pacific

n. 太平洋

Where is the **Pacific** Ocean?
太平洋在哪？

It's on the east coast of Taiwan.
在台灣的東海岸。

package

n. 包裹

Please sign here for your **package**.
領包裹請在此簽名。

I see. Do I only get one?
我知道了。我只有一件包裹嗎？

parachute

n. 降落傘
v. 跳傘

Let's try **parachuting**!
我們去玩降落傘吧！

No! I have height phobia.
不，我有懼高症。

這裡使用的是動詞喔！

park

n. 公園
v. 停放

Who often goes to a **park**?
通常都是誰會去公園呢？

Moms with their kids?
帶著小孩的媽媽吧？

這裡使用的是名詞喔！

passage

n. 通道

A man kept forcing the crowd to make him a **passage** while I was in the market.
我在市場時，有個男人一直推擠人群好讓自己通過。

That was very annoying.
那真的是很惱人。

passenger
n. 旅客

Track 0648

Dear **passengers**, please remain seated.
親愛的乘客，請留在坐位上。

OK! Thank you!
好的，謝謝你。

path
n. 小徑

Track 0649

Go along the **path** in the garden, and you'll see a cave.
沿著花園小徑走，你就會看到一個洞穴。

Is that true? I can't wait to visit it.
真的嗎？我等不及要去那個洞穴看看。

pavement
n. 人行道

Track 0650

The **pavement** is still under construction.
人行道還在建造中。

It brings so much inconvenience.
帶來好多麻煩啊！

peak
n. 山頂；頂點
v. 到達高峰
adj. 高峰的

Track 0651

When you get to the **peak**, you'll forget about all worries.
當你抵達山頂，你會忘了所有煩惱。

Yes, all you will think of is the beauty of life.
是啊！你所能想到的就是生命的美好。

這裡使用的是名詞喔！

peddle
v. 叫賣；兜售

Track 0652

Vendorers **peddle** along the street to have their products sold.
攤販沿街叫賣以賣出商品。

Is it legal to do that?
這麼做是合法的嗎？

pedestrian
n. 行人

Track 0653

This district bans cars to protect the safety of **pedestrians**.
這個區域禁止汽車，以保障行人安全。

It's a paradise for us!
這真是我們行人的天堂啊！

per
prep. 每

🔊 *Track 0654*

👦 There are about 50 customers **per** hour.
每一小時大約有五十位顧客。

👧 That much? Then I'd better work harder.
這麼多？那我可得勤奮點。

pilgrim
n. 朝聖者

🔊 *Track 0655*

👦 What is special about **pilgrims**?
朝聖者有何特別？

👧 The pilgrims are very pious people.
朝聖者是非常虔誠的人。

place
n. 地方；地區；地位
v. 放置

🔊 *Track 0656*

👦 Where is your favorite **place**?
你最喜歡的地方是哪裡？

👧 My grandma's house.
我奶奶家。

這裡使用的是名詞喔！

platform
n. 平臺；月臺

🔊 *Track 0657*

👧 Hey! Don't play on the **platform**.
嘿！別在月台上玩。

👧 Sorry, sir.
抱歉，先生。

polar
adj. 極地的

🔊 *Track 0658*

👧 Have you seen the new-born **polar** bear?
你有看到剛出生的北極熊嗎？

👧 Yes. It is so cute!
有啊！真可愛。

pond
n. 池塘

🔊 *Track 0659*

👧 There is a **pond** near our school.
我們學校附近有個池塘。

👧 Let's go there sometimes.
我們偶爾也去那邊玩吧。

pool
n. 水池

🔊 *Track 0660*

👧 The swimming **pool** is very crowded.
游泳池好擁擠。

👧 Because it is too hot!
因為太熱了嘛！

port
n. 港口

Track 0661

> She visited the **port** yesterday.
> 她昨天去了港口一趟。

> I know, for the best seafood, right?
> 我知道,她要買最新鮮的海鮮嘛。

post
n. 郵件;貼文
v. 張貼

Track 0662

> Where is the **post** office?
> 郵局在哪呢?

> It's next to the only school we have here.
> 在我們僅有的一間學校隔壁。

這裡使用的是名詞喔!

postage
n. 郵資

Track 0663

> Please leave me the **postage** in the envelope.
> 請把郵資留在信封裡。

> I will. Thank you for mailing it for me.
> 我會,謝謝你幫我寄信。

postcard
n. 明信片

Track 0664

> Have you received my **postcard** yet?
> 你收到我的明信片了嗎?

> Yes. I got it. It's beautiful!
> 是,我收到了,很漂亮!

postpone
v. 延緩;延遲

Track 0665

> Don't **postpone** your daily work.
> 不要拖延你每日的例行工作。

> I know, but I can't help it.
> 我知道,但我做不到啊!

quick
adj. 快的
adv. 快地

Track 0666

> CEOs are **quick** at decision making.
> 執行長們通常都能很快做決定。

> True, and they have to be able to!
> 的確,他們也必須有能力這麼做!

這裡使用的是形容詞喔!

raft
n. 木筏

Track 0667

> The **raft** has a hole on it.
> 這木筏上有個洞。

> It's alright. I'll fix it.
> 沒關係。我會把它修好。

railroad
n. 鐵路

Track 0668

This is the old **railroad** built 100 years ago.
這裡是一百年前建的老舊鐵路。

Is it still in use?
現在還有在使用嗎？

rapid
adj. 迅速的

Track 0669

The growth of smart phone users is **rapid**.
智慧型手機的使用人數快速成長。

This is a digital era!
現在是數位時代！

removal
n. 拿開；除去

Track 0670

The **removal** of his tumor is a difficult task.
要把他的腫瘤移除是很困難的工作。

Please try your best to save him!
請盡你最大的力量來救他！

region
n. 區域

Track 0671

Stay in this **region**, or you'll get hurt.
待在這區裡，不然你會很容易受到傷害。

OK. I will stay here.
好的，我會待在這區。

reservoir
n. 水庫；寶庫

Track 0672

Where does the water in the **reservoir** come from?
這水庫的水從哪來？

It's mainly from rainfall.
主要來自雨水。

right
adj. 正確的；右邊的
v. 糾正
n. 權利；（右邊）
adv. 正好

Track 0673

What you did was **right**.
你剛做的是對的。

Thank you, though I know it was not perfect.
謝謝，雖然我知道那樣不是最完美的。

這裡使用的是形容詞喔！

road

n. 路；道路；街道；路線

Track 0674

Do you know where Chungcheng **road** is?
你知道中正路在哪嗎？

It's 2 blocks away.
前面兩個路口就是了。

rock

n. 岩石

Track 0675

Have you ever tried **rock**-climbing?
你試過攀岩嗎？

Yes. That was so exciting!
有啊，那真是太刺激了！

rough

adj. 粗糙的

Track 0676

Your hands are so **rough**!
你的手好粗！

I am starting to use hand cream.
我現在開始用護手霜了。

route

n. 路線

Track 0677

The **route** of the bus is very complicated.
這公車的路線很複雜。

Not for local residents.
對本地人來說是還好啦。

rural

adj. 農村的

Track 0678

The **rural** revolution caused many deaths.
農村運動造成很多死亡。

Oh. That's too bad.
噢！真是太糟了。

rush

v. 倉促行事
n. 匆忙

Track 0679

Don't be in such a **rush**.
別這麼趕。

But we are almost late.
但我們快遲到了。

這裡使用的是名詞喔！

sail

n. 帆
v. 航行

Track 0680

He **sailed** to Penghu last month.
他上個月划船到澎湖。

How brave he was!
他真勇敢！

這裡使用的是動詞喔！

143

send

v. 派遣;寄出

Have you **sent** your resume yet?
你寄出履歷了嗎?

Not yet.
還沒。

shade

n. 蔭涼處;樹蔭;(色調)

Track 0682

Stay in the **shade**, or you'll get a sun stroke.
待在樹蔭裡,不然你會中暑。

It's alright. I can take care of myself.
沒關係,我可以自己照顧自己。

ship

n. 大船;海船
v. 運送

Track 0683

There is a museum for the giant **ships** around the world.
有間博物館專門展示世界上的大船。

I want to visit it someday.
改天我想去參觀。

這裡使用的是名詞喔!

shop

n. 商店;店鋪
v. 購物

Track 0684

The **shop** sells clothes using environmentally friendly material.
這間店賣用環保材質做的衣服。

Is it very expensive?
會很貴嗎?

這裡使用的是名詞喔!

shortcut

n. 捷徑;近路

Track 0685

He took the **shortcut**.
他走捷徑。

But he didn't arrive too much ealier.
但他也沒多早到。

sidewalk

n. 人行道

Track 0686

There are many trees on the **sidewalk**.
人行道上有很多樹。

It's very comfortable walking on it.
走在人行道上很舒服。

signal

n. 信號;號誌
v. (打)信號

Track 0687

The **signal** tells us when to charge our phones.
這個訊號告訴我們什麼時候電話該充電。

Such a wonderful design!
真是個很棒的設計!

> 這裡使用的是名詞喔!

sink

v. 沉沒
n. 水槽

Track 0688

A boat **sank** because of the hurricane.
因為颶風,有艘船沉沒了。

Fingers crossed for them.
我為他們祈禱。

> 這裡使用的是動詞喔!

slippery

adj. 滑溜的

Track 0689

The floor is **slippery**.
地上很滑。

We just waxed it.
我們才剛打蠟。

source

n. 來源;水源地

Track 0690

Do you have a credible **source** for what you said?
你剛剛說的話有甚麼可靠的來源嗎?

It was an official announcement.
那是官方的公告。

south

adj. 南方(的)
n. 南

Track 0691

The climate in the **south** is mild.
南方的天氣很溫和。

So mom says she wouldn't move to the north.
所以媽媽說她不會搬來北方。

> 這裡使用的是名詞喔!

southern

adj. 南方的

Track 0692

Southern Europe is famous for its special buildings.
南歐因為它特別的建築而聞名。

I know they often paint their house white and blue.
我知道他們常把房子漆成白色和藍色。

145

specific

adj. 具體的、特殊的

Track 0693

👦 He didn't talk about any **specific** preference.
他沒有說他明確的偏好。

👧 So anything should be ok?
所以應該什麼東西都可以吧？

speed

v. 急速
n. 速度

Track 0694

👦 The **speed** of the Internet is so slow.
網路的速度好慢。

👧 That's because Jack is downloading.
那是因為傑克在下載東西。

> 這裡使用的是名詞喔！

splash

v. 濺起來

Track 0695

👦 Water **splashed** onto my face when a car passed by.
當一台車經過時，水濺到我臉上。

👧 Poor girl.
可憐的女孩。

squeeze

v. 擠壓

Track 0696

👦 Stop **squeezing** your pimples.
別再擠你的青春痘了。

👧 But they are so ugly.
但是青春痘好醜。

station

n. 車站

Track 0697

👦 I'll drive you to the train **station**.
我會開車載你到火車站。

👧 Thank you very much!
非常謝謝你！

stay

v. 逗留；停留
n. 停留

Track 0698

👦 Don't **stay** out late.
別在外面逗留太晚。

👧 But 7 o'clock isn't really "late."
但七點並不算太晚吧。

> 這裡使用的是動詞喔！

steamer
n. 汽船；輪船

Track 0699

There's a display of how **steamers** were operated.
有個展示示範汽船是如何運作的。

Sounds interesting.
聽起來很有趣。

steep
adj. 險峻的（陡峭的）

Track 0700

The slope is **steep**.
這個斜坡很陡。

Be careful! Grandma!
奶奶，小心點！

step
n. 腳步；步驟

Track 0701

Follow the **steps** on the gound, and you'll find the cabinet.
跟著地上的腳步走，你就會看到小木屋。

I won't be lost, will I?
我不會迷路吧？

strait
n. 海峽

Track 0702

The two countries on the sides of the **strait** work closely with each other.
海峽兩岸的兩個國家緊密的合作。

That's a good thing.
那是好事啊。

stream
n. 小溪

Track 0703

The **stream** is clear.
這條小溪很清澈。

Residents here even drink the water in the stream.
這裡的居民甚至飲用小溪的水呢！

street
n. 街；街道

Track 0704

I saw a weired man on the **street**.
我在街上看到個奇怪的男子。

Don't get too close to him.
別離他太近了。

147

stroll
v. 漫步；閒逛

👦 Let's take a **stroll**.
我們散個步吧。

👧 Wait! I am too full now.
等等！我現在肚子太脹了。

submarine
n. 潛水艇

👦 I've never been in a **submarine**.
我從沒搭過潛水艇。

👧 Me either.
我也沒有。

subway
n. 地下鐵

👦 The **subway** system here offers us a lot of convenience.
這裡的地鐵系統帶給我們很大的方便。

👧 Without it, it'll be very troublesome.
沒有地鐵的話會很麻煩。

supermarket
n. 超級市場

👦 Mom asked me to get some salt in the **supermarket**.
媽媽要我到超市買點鹽。

👧 Get me a can of soda, will you?
幫我帶罐汽水回來好嗎？

surpass
v. 超過；超越

👦 What you've achieved **surpassed** your peers.
你達到的成就比你的同儕高。

👧 I am flattered.
我感到很受賞識。

surround
v. 圍繞

👦 The city is **surrounded** by mountains.
這個城市被山所圍繞。

👧 So it must be very hot during summer.
夏天一定很熱吧。

survivor
n. 生還者

🔊 *Track 0711*

👦 The **survivors** lost everything in the accident.
生還者在這場意外中失去了所有東西。

👩 Can we donate some money to them?
我們可以捐款給他們嗎？

temple
n. 寺院、神殿

🔊 *Track 0712*

👦 I went to the temple for good luck yesterday.
我昨天去寺廟求好運。

👩 Did you draw the lot in the **temple**?
你在寺廟抽籤詩了嗎？

terminate
v. 終止；中斷

🔊 *Track 0713*

👦 Our contract is **terminated**. Can you explain?
我們的合約中止了，你可以解釋原因嗎？

👩 It is just terminated temporarily.
只是暫時中止而已。

through
prep. 經過；通過
adv. 經過；通過

🔊 *Track 0714*

👦 He passed **through** the store he was looking for without noticing it.
他經過了他正在找的店，卻沒發現。

👩 He was being silly!
他那樣很可笑。

這裡使用的是副詞喔！

ticket
n. 車票；入場券

🔊 *Track 0715*

👦 **Tickets** for two.
給我兩個位子的票。

👩 Do you like to sit at the front or back?
你要坐前面還後面呢？

toll
n. 通行費

🔊 *Track 0716*

👦 The **toll** we have to pay is 20 dollars.
我們要付二十元的通行費。

👩 I've had the changes ready.
我已經把零錢準備好了。

tour
n. 旅行；（巡迴）
v. 旅行；（巡迴）

🔊 *Track 0717*

👦 He joined the **tour** to Japan.
他參加了日本的旅行團。

👩 It should be a wonderful experience.
會是個很美好的經驗吧。

這裡使用的是名詞喔！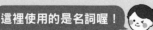

tourist
n. 觀光客

Track 0718

A lot of Chinese **tourists** are coming to Taiwan.
許多中國旅客現在都來台灣。

I met a few yesterday.
我昨天有見到一些。

tower
n. 塔

Track 0719

Get onto the **tower**, and you'll see many stars.
到塔上去，你會看到很多星星。

I feel so much relaxed after seeing the view.
我看到這樣的景致後感到輕鬆了起來。

town
n. 城鎮；鎮

Track 0720

In our **town**, we have several schools.
在我們鎮上有很多間學校。

Why? Is the population big?
為什麼？人口很多嗎？

track
n. 足跡；軌道
v. 追蹤

Track 0721

Look for the **track** of the deers.
找找鹿的足跡。

Come! I've found it!
來啊！我找到了！

這裡使用的是名詞喔！

traffic
n. 交通；走私
v. 走私

Track 0722

The **traffic** is crazy here.
這裡的交通很混亂。

That's true.
千真萬確。

這裡使用的是名詞喔！

trail
n. 痕跡；小徑

Track 0723

I found the **trail** of the black bear.
我發現黑熊的痕跡

Be careful these days!
最近幾天小心點！

train
n. 火車
v. 訓練

Track 0724

Go! Get on the **train**!
快！快上火車！

See you next time!
下次見！

這裡使用的是名詞喔！

trample
v. 踐踏

Track 0725

He **trampled** on the lawn and was fined.
他踐踏草皮，被罰款了。

He deserved it.
他罪有應得。

transportation
n. 輸送；運輸工具

Track 0726

The **transportation** is very convenient here.
這裡的交通很方便。

It is also cheap.
也很便宜呢！

travel
n. 旅行
v. 旅行

Track 0727

I like **traveling** a lot.
我很喜歡旅行。

I like it, too.
我也很喜歡。

這裡使用的是動名詞喔！

traveler
n. 旅行者；旅客

Track 0728

The **traveler** experienced the earthquake and was frightened.
這個旅客經歷了地震，而且嚇壞了。

Poor him.
他真可憐！

trip
n. 旅行

Track 0729

I enjoyed my **trip** to Taiwan.
我很享受到台灣旅行。

It is not only cheap, but also wonderful!
不只便宜，而且很棒！

truck
n. 卡車

Track 0730

He drove the **truck** to see me.
他開卡車來見我。

Sounds funny!
聽起來好好笑。

tunnel
n. 隧道

Track 0731

The **tunnel** links the two countries.
這個隧道連接兩個國家。

That's a breakthrough!
真是一個突破！

underpass
n. 地下道

Track 0732

Many homeless people stay in the **underpass**.
許多遊民會待在地下道裡。

It is warmer there.
那裡比較溫暖。

valley
n. 溪谷；山谷

Track 0733

Don't go to the **valley** over there!
別去那裡的山谷！

I know. There are ghosts there!
我知道，那裡鬧鬼呢！

van
n. 貨車

Track 0734

I want to have a **van** for myself.
我想要有台貨車。

How much will it take?
會花多少錢呢？

vehicle
n. 交通工具；車輛

Track 0735

There are a lot of **vehicles** here.
這裡有很多車。

Strange, isn't it.
很奇怪對吧？

venture
n. 冒險
v. 冒險

Track 0736

He **ventured** to sneak out.
他冒險溜出來。

His brother will be very mad after he finds out about it.
他哥哥發現的話會很生氣。

這裡使用的是動詞喔！

via
prep. 經由

Track 0737

Mail your application **via** post.
將你的申請表以郵寄寄出。

Don't you take emails?
你們不接受電子郵件嗎？

volcano
n. 火山

Track 0738

This is a dormant **volcano**.
這是一座休火山。

I see.
我知道了。

voyage
n. 航海

🧑 This is his first **voyage** as a pilot.
這是他成為領航員以來第一次的航行。

👧 I believe he can do it!
我相信他做得到的！

🔊 *Track 0739*

walk
v. 走；步行

🧑 Keep **walking**!
繼續走啊！

👧 Wait, I've been bitten by a mosquito.
等等，我被蚊子咬了。

🔊 *Track 0740*

warehouse
n. 倉庫；貨棧

🧑 Where is my old bike?
我的舊腳踏車呢？

👧 In the **warehouse**.
在倉庫裡。

🔊 *Track 0741*

waterfall
n. 瀑布

🧑 The view of the **waterfall** is gorgeous.
瀑布的景致真美！

👧 I agree!
我也認為！

🔊 *Track 0742*

way
n. 路；道路

🧑 Where there is a will, there is a **way**.
有志者，事竟成。

👧 It is a famous saying, right?
這是句很有名的諺語，對吧?

🔊 *Track 0743*

west
n. 西；西方

🧑 What are the differences between east and **west**?
東方和西方有何不同呢？

👧 There are many differences. First,...
有許多不同之處。首先……

🔊 *Track 0744*

western
adj. 西方的

Track 0745

Western societies value independence, while eastern societies value filial piety.
西方社會重視獨立，東方社會重視孝道

But I think independence doesn't contradict with filial piety.
但是我覺得獨立和孝順並不衝突啊！

wharf
n. 碼頭；停泊處

Track 0746

Your family will always be your wharf.
你的家永遠會是你的停泊處。

Thank you, mom!
謝謝你，媽！

wheel
n. 輪子；輪

Track 0747

Dad designed wheels for my book bag.
爸爸替我的書包設計了輪子。

That's smart!
真聰明！

wilderness
n. 荒野

Track 0748

In the wilderness, you have to depend on your survival skills.
在野外，你就得靠你的求生技能了。

True. That's why we can't overemphasize the importance of the skills.
真的！這也是為何我們這麼強調這些技能。

In the wilderness.

NOTE

Part

05

要學就學最實用的英文單字，搭配最稀鬆平常的生活對話， 馬上就知道外國人都是這樣用這個單字的喲！＊單字、對話分開錄音，學習目標更明確

absence
n. 缺席

🔈 *Track 0749*

👦 The teacher's angry about your **absence** in her class today.
老師對於你今天課堂上缺席非常生氣。

👧 Oh I'm sorry. I didn't feel well this morning.
噢我很抱歉，我今天早上不太舒服。

academic
n. 學院的；大學的

🔈 *Track 0750*

👦 Why is Jane so busy recently?
為什麼珍最近這麼忙碌？

👧 She is working really hard to pull up her **academic** scores.
她正努力拉高她的大學成績。

academy
n. 學院；專科院校

🔈 *Track 0751*

👦 I heard that your daughter just graduated from high school.
我聽說妳女兒剛從高中畢業。

👧 Yeah, she's going to the National Music **Academy** this fall.
是啊，她今年秋天將進入國立音樂學院就讀。

accounting
n. 會計；會計學

🔈 *Track 0752*

👦 Why are you so upset today?
你今天怎麼那麼沮喪？

👧 I flunked my **accounting** midterm.
我的會計學期中考沒有過。

accurate

adj. 正確的；準確的

Track 0753

How do you get the **accurate** number of birds in this town?
你如何得出這城鎮準確的鳥類數目？

By months of observation.
透過好幾個月的觀察。

achieve

v. 完成；實現

Track 0754

How do you **achieve** your goal of being a lawyer?
你如何達成你當上律師的目標？

I tell myself I should try again every time when I fail.
每一次失敗我都告訴自己我應該再嘗試一遍。

addition

n. 加；加法

Track 0755

Jimmy can do **addition**! He's just three years old.
傑米會加法！他才三歲大。

He's a genius!
他真是個天才！

adjective

n. 形容詞

Track 0756

What's so special about this writer?
這位作家有什麼特別的？

His usage of **adjective** is very accurate.
他形容詞的用法很準確。

admiration

n. 欽佩；讚賞

Track 0757

His courageous behavior has won him **admiration**.
他英勇的行為為他帶來了讚賞。

Yeah, he deserves it.
他應得的。

adverb

n. 副詞

Track 0758

What's an adverb?
副詞是什麼？

An **adverb** is something you use to describe a verb.
副詞是你用來形容動詞的詞。

agriculture
n. 農業（學）；農學

What do you study in college?
你大學主修什麼？

I major in **agriculture**.
我主修農業學。

aim
n. 瞄準；目標
v. 瞄準；（打算）

Why is Lisa practicing tennis so hard lately?
為什麼麗莎最近那麼努力練習網球？

She **aims** at winning the tennis champion.
她將目標放在奪得網球冠軍。

這裡使用的是動詞喔！

alphabet
n. 字母；字母表

How many **alphabets** are there in English?
英文裡有幾個字母？

Twenty-six.
二十六個。

ambition
n. 雄心壯志；志向

What's your **ambition** about the future?
你未來的志向是什麼？

Being a teacher.
當上老師。

ancient
adj. 古老的；古代的

This **ancient** scroll is said to be at least ninety years old!
這個古代卷軸據説至少有九十年歷史！

It's even older than my grandfather!
它甚至比我的爺爺還老。

angle
n. 角度；立場

I'm so angry about my mom's punishing me for coming home late.
我非常生氣我媽媽因為我晚歸處罰我。

Think from a different **angle**, your mother was worried about you.
換個角度想，你媽媽也是擔心你。

answer
v. 回答
n. 答案

🔊 Track 0765

👦 I called Sandy yesterday, but no one **answered** the phone.
我昨天打電話給珊蒂，可是沒有人接。

👧 They went to the restaurant last night.
他們昨晚去餐廳。

> 這裡使用的是動詞喔！

apply
v. 申請；應用

🔊 Track 0766

👦 She **applied** for scholarship, but got rejected.
她申請獎學金，但被拒絕了。

👧 That's too bad!
真糟糕。

argue
v. 爭辯；辯論

🔊 Track 0767

👦 Do your parents **argue** often?
你的父母經常爭執嗎？

👧 No, they get along very well.
不，他們相處得很好。

argument
n. 爭論；議論

🔊 Track 0768

👦 They support different political parties, so they often have **arguments** during the election.
他們支持不同的政黨，所以在選舉期間經常有爭執。

👧 Maybe you should calm them down.
也許你應該讓他們冷靜下來。

arithmetic
n. 算術

🔊 Track 0769

👦 Does your son go to cram school?
你兒子有去補習嗎？

👧 Yes, his **arithmetic** is poor.
對啊，他算術很差。

$x = \sqrt{3}$

article
n. 文章；論文

🔊 *Track 0770*

😊 How's your **article** on environmental protection?
你那篇環境保護的論文怎麼樣了？

😊 My teacher gave me an A!
我的老師給了我A。

ask
v. 問；要求

🔊 *Track 0771*

😊 Did you **ask** Jay about his midterm?
你有問過傑的期中考考得如何嗎？

😊 No, but I can guess from his sad look.
沒有，但我從他傷心的表情可以猜出一二。

assignment
n. 功課；作業

🔊 *Track 0772*

😊 Our teacher gave us an **assignment** today.
老師今天出作業給我們。

😊 Then you'd better turn off the TV and work on it.
那你最好關掉電視，然後去寫功課。

attention
n. 注意；專心

🔊 *Track 0773*

😊 She didn't pay **attention** to the class, so the teacher sent her to detention.
她上課不專心，所以她老師罰她留校察看。

😊 I hope she will learn a lesson!
希望她學到教訓。

attitude
n. 態度；心態；看法

🔊 *Track 0774*

😊 What's your **attitude** toward this issue?
你對這件事的看法是什麼？

😊 No comments.
我不予置評。

autobiography
n. 自傳

🔊 *Track 0775*

😊 His **autobiography** published this year got really good comments.
他今年出版的自傳得到很多好評。

😊 That's for sure, after his success in romance novels.
在他寫愛情小說大成功之後，這無庸置疑。

bachelor
n. 單身漢;學士

Track 0776

I got my **bachelor**'s degree in computer science studies.
我得到電腦科學研究的學士學位。

Then you must be good at programming.
那你一定很會寫程式!

backward
adj. 向後方的;面對後方的
adv. 向後

Track 0777

What did she do when she met the strange guy?
她遇見奇怪的男子時的反應是什麼?

She moved **backward** slowly.
她緩緩地向後退。

這裡使用的是副詞喔!

basic
adj. 基本的

Track 0778

Learning addition is considered **basic** in Mathematics.
學習加法在數學裡非常基本。

But my child seems to have difficulties.
但我的小孩似乎有障礙。

beginner
n. 初學者

Track 0779

This book is designed for **beginners**.
這本書是為初學者設計的。

Then I'll buy it for my son.
那我要買給我的兒子。

behave
v. 行動;舉止

Track 0780

He **behaves** strangely in front of Judy.
他在茱蒂面前表現得很奇怪。

That's because he has a crush on Judy.
那是因為他暗戀茱蒂。

believe
v. 認為;相信

Track 0781

I saw a cow flying last night.
我昨晚看見母牛在飛。

I don't **believe** you.
我不相信。

biological
adj. 生物學的

The DNA test shows he is the little boy's **biological** father.
DNA檢驗顯示他是那小男孩的親生父親。

But he's just eighteen, he's too young to be a father.
但他才十八歲，就當爸爸而言他太年輕了。

◀ Track 0782

Bible
n. 聖經

You took a class about **Bible** last year, how was it?
你去年修了聖經的課，結果如何？

It was interesting.
很有趣。

◀ Track 0783

biography
n. 傳記

Do you enjoy reading the **biography** of the politician?
你享受閱讀那位政治人物的傳記嗎？

Not at all.
一點也不。

◀ Track 0784

biology
n. 生物學

What's your favorite subject in high school?
你高中最喜歡的科目是什麼？

Biology of course!
當然是生物學！

◀ Track 0785

blackboard
n. 黑板

I can't see the sentence on the **blackboard**.
我看不見黑板上的句子。

Maybe you should get a pair of glasses.
也許你該配副眼鏡。

◀ Track 0786

blank

adj. 空白的
n. 空格

What were you thinking when you jump off the cliff?
你從懸崖跳下去時腦袋裡想什麼？

Nothing, but my mind went **blank**.
什麼都沒想，我的腦袋一片空白。

這裡使用的是形容詞喔！

Track 0787

brainstorming

n. 腦力激盪；集思廣益

Our teacher separates us into small groups and tells us to do **brainstorming**.
我們老師把我們分成小組並讓我們腦力激盪。

It's a good way to come up with good ideas.
這是個能激出好點子的方法。

Track 0788

brilliant

adj. 有才氣的；出色的

Your son draws really well, he has **brilliant** talents!
你兒子畫得真的很好，他有出色的才華。

Really? Thanks.
真的嗎？謝謝。

Track 0789

capable

adj. 有能力的

I failed again.
我又失敗了。

I think you're **capable** of doing it, you just need to try harder.
我認為你絕對有能力做到，你只需要更努力地去試。

Track 0790

celebrate

v. 慶祝；慶賀

Mom, what's that cake for?
媽，那個蛋糕是要幹嘛的？

We're **celebrating** your father's promotion!
我們要慶祝你爸的升遷！

Track 0791

chalk
n. 粉筆

I don't like writing with **chalk**, it makes my hand dirty.
我不喜歡用粉筆寫字，會把我手弄髒。

Maybe someday you can invent something to replace it.
有許有天你可以發明東西來取代它。

chapter
n. 章；章節；（分會）

Which chapter in this book is your favorite?
這本書裡你最喜歡哪一章？

Chapter five.
第五章。

chart
n. 圖表

I can't understand the financial management of this company.
我不懂這家公司的財務管理。

It's OK, I'll make you a **chart**.
沒關係，我作張圖表給你。

cheat
v. 欺騙；（作弊；出軌）

John told me that he saw a flying pig yesterday.
約翰說他昨天看到飛天豬。

He **cheats** all the time.
他總是在欺騙人。

chemistry
n. 化學

Why is **chemistry** your favorite subject?
為什麼化學是你最喜歡的科目？

I like doing experiments.
我喜歡做實驗。

choice

n. 選擇；（選項）
adj. 精選的

Track 0797

I hate multiple **choice** questions, I always get the wrong answer.

我討厭多重選擇題，我總是選到錯的答案。

Maybe next time you should try to cross out those that are wrong.

也許下次你應該先刪去錯的答案。

> 這裡使用的是名詞喔！

choose

v. 選擇

Track 0798

Mom, our teacher **chooses** me as the class leader!

媽，我們導師選我當班長！

That's great.

太棒了。

claim

v. 主張；要求

Track 0799

He **claims** that we shouldn't go to school for education.

他主張我們不應該去學校接受教育。

That's ridiculous.

真荒謬。

class

n. 班級；階級；種類

Track 0800

Our flight to Tokyo was full, so we got promoted to first **class**.

我們的班機座位滿了，所以我們被升到頭等艙。

You are so lucky!

你們真幸運。

clever

adj. 聰明的；伶俐的

Track 0801

Cliff is a **clever** kid.

克里夫是個聰明的孩子。

But he likes to play tricks on other kids.

但是他喜歡捉弄其他孩子。

collect
v. 收集

🔊 *Track 0802*

👦 What's your hobby?
你的嗜好是什麼？

👧 I like to **collect** stamps.
我喜歡集郵。

---

college
n. 學院；大學

🔊 *Track 0803*

👦 Which college do you go to?
你讀哪間大學？

👧 I go to King's **College** in London.
我就讀倫敦的國王學院。

---

commentary
n. 注釋；說明

🔊 *Track 0804*

👦 I don't know the meaning of this word.
我不懂這個字的意思。

👧 Check the **commentary** below.
看下面的說明。

---

competent
adj. 有能力的

🔊 *Track 0805*

👦 Why is father smiling?
爸爸為什麼在笑？

👧 He is smiling because he has a **competent** daughter like you.
他在笑是因為有個像你一樣能幹的女兒。

---

comprehension
n. 理解力

🔊 *Track 0806*

👦 The exam's purpose is to check students' **comprehension** of the lesson.
這考試的目的是要確認學生對該課的了解。

👧 But I think it's a bit too hard for them.
但我覺得對學生來說有點太難。

Confucius
n. 孔子

🔊 *Track 0807*

👦 **Confucius** once said education without discrimination.
孔子曾說：有教無類。

👧 That's my favorite sentence as a teacher.
那是我做為老師最喜歡的一句話。

congratulations
n. 祝賀；恭喜

Track 0808

😀 Mom, I won the swimming contest!
媽，我贏了游泳比賽！

😊 **Congratulations**.
恭喜你。

conjunction
n. 連接；關聯

Track 0809

😀 What's the **conjunction** between these two events?
這兩件事情的關聯是什麼？

😊 They both happened in Taipei.
同樣都發生於台北。

conservative
n. 保守主義者
adj. 保守的；傳統的

Track 0810

😀 My mother is a **conservative**, she doesn't allow us to stay out for the night.
我媽媽是保守主義者，她不准我們在外過夜。

😊 You can't be too careful.
小心點總沒錯。

這裡使用的是名詞喔！

consider
v. 仔細考慮

Track 0811

😀 Have you decided to work for our company?
你決定要為我們公司效力了嗎？

😊 I'm still **considering**.
我仍在考慮。

contest
n. 比賽

Track 0812

😀 When is the speech **contest**?
演講比賽是什麼時候？

😊 Next week.
下星期。

contradiction
n. 矛盾；對立

Track 0813

😀 I see **contradictions** in his argument.
我在他的論點裡看見矛盾。

😊 Maybe he didn't think carefully.
也許他沒有仔細想清楚。

controversial
adj. 有爭議的

🔊 *Track 0814*

👦 Why do you take debate class?
你為什麼上辯論課？

👧 I want to discuss **controversial** issues.
我想要討論爭議性的話題。

correct
adj. 正確的
v. 更正

🔊 *Track 0815*

👦 Do you know the **correct** answer to this question?
你知道這一題的正確答案嗎？

👧 No, but I'll ask my teacher.
不知道，但我會問我的老師。

> 這裡使用的是形容詞喔！

course
n. 課程；講座；路線

🔊 *Track 0816*

👦 Why do you want to take this **course**?
為什麼你想修這堂課程？

👧 I heard it's quite interesting.
我聽說蠻有趣的。

crayon
n. 蠟筆

🔊 *Track 0817*

👦 Can you lend me your **crayon**?
你能借我你的蠟筆嗎？

👧 Sure.
當然

create
v. 創造

🔊 *Track 0818*

👦 He **created** a story about her childhood.
他創造了一個關於她童年的故事。

👧 I can't wait to read it!
我等不及要讀了！

creation
n. 創造；創世

🔊 *Track 0819*

👦 No one really knows when exactly the **creation** of Earth happened.
沒有人確切地知道地球是什麼時候誕生的。

👧 It must be a long time ago.
一定是很久以前。

creativity
n. 創造力

James is a kid with amazing **creativity**.
詹姆士是個擁有驚人創造力的小孩。

I've heard that, too.
我也有聽說。

Track 0820

criticism
n. 評論；批評

His teacher's **criticism** on his writing made him cry.
他的老師對他文章的批評使他哭了。

Poor him.
真可憐。

Track 0821

criticize
v. 批評；批判

Dick likes to **criticize** others.
迪克喜歡批評他人。

That's definitely not something good.
這絕非好事。

Track 0822

curriculum
n. 課程

So far, what do you know about your school's **curriculum** plan?
到目前為止你對學校的課程安排知道多少？

Nothing.
什麼都不知道。

Track 0823

data
n. 資料；事實；材料

Where did you get this **data**?
你從哪裡得到這數據的？

From the Internet.
從網路。

Track 0824

descend
v. 下降；突襲

As my scores **descend**, my mom gets angrier.
我的成績一下降媽媽就更生氣了。

Well, good luck!
祝你好運囉！

Track 0825

debate

v. 討論；辯論
n. 討論；辯論

What are they doing here?
他們在這裡幹嘛？

They're **debating** over whether we should import American beef.
他們正在辯論是否該進口美國牛肉。

這裡使用的是動詞喔！

decision

n. 決定

Track 0827

It's time to make your final **decision**.
是時候做最後決定了！

Can I have five more minutes?
可以再給我五分鐘嗎？

define

v. 下定義

Track 0828

How do you **define** a good friend?
你如何給好朋友下定義？

Someone who is always on your side to back you up.
一個總是站在你這邊挺你的人。

definition

n. 定義

Track 0829

What's the **definition** of this word?
這個字的定義是什麼？

I'll look up in the dictionary.
我查查字典。

degree

n. 學位；程度

Track 0830

It's so hot today!
今天真熱！

Of course, it's thirty **degrees** Celcius out here!
當然囉！這裡現在攝氏三十度呢！

description

n. 敘述；說明

Track 0831

His detailed **description** helps the police to arrest the thief.
他對小偷詳細的描述幫助警察逮到他。

He must have a good memory.
他記性一定很好。

design
v. 設計
n. 設計

Track 0832

Did you **design** this dress?
這件衣服是你設計的嗎？

No, my mother did.
不，是我媽設計的。

> 這裡使用的是動詞喔！

dictate
v. 口授；聽寫；（命令）

Track 0833

Students, listen carefully and **dictate** what I say.
學生們，仔細聽然後寫下來。

Alright Mr. Lin.
是的林老師。

differentiate
v. 辨別；區分

Track 0834

He doesn't know how to **differentiate** right and wrong.
他無法分辨是非。

You should teach him.
你應該教導他。

difference
n. 差異；差別

Track 0835

What's the **difference** between a lime and a lemon?
萊姆和檸檬有什麼不同？

They are of different colors.
它們的顏色不同。

dig
v. 挖掘；探究

Track 0836

He is good at **digging** secrets.
他善於挖掘秘密。

I should be careful.
那我應該小心點。

diploma
n. 文憑；畢業證書

Track 0837

I lost my **diploma**!
我的文憑不見了！

Apply for another at school tomorrow.
明天去學校再申請一張。

disagreement
n. 意見不合;（不同意見）

Track 0838

He thinks men are better than women.
他認為男人比女人好。

I have **disagreement** on that.
我不同意。

discipline
n. 紀律;訓練

Track 0839

His mother helps him learn about **discipline** and responsibility.
他媽媽教導他紀律與責任。

What a good mother!
真是個好媽媽!

discover
v. 發現

Track 0840

His great grandfather **discovered** the moon.
他的曾祖父發現月亮。

I don't believe it.
我不相信。

discuss
v. 討論;商議

Track 0841

We'll **discuss** it at night, OK?
我們晚上討論,好嗎?

Sure.
當然。

discussion
n. 討論;商議

Track 0842

After an hour's **discussion**, they finally have an agreement.
經過一小時的討論他們終於達成共識。

Finally!
終於!

dishonest
adj. 不誠實的

Track 0843

James is **dishonest**, he lies all the time.
詹姆士不誠實,他總是説謊。

Maybe it's not true.
也許這不是真的。

division
n. 分割；除去

Track 0844

👦 The **division** of opinions has led to the failure of the company.
意見相左導致該公司的失敗。

👧 That's too bad.
真不幸。

doubt
n. 懷疑；疑問
v. 懷疑

Track 0845

👦 I **doubt** whether the government will realize all its promises.
我懷疑政府是否會實現所有承諾。

👧 Oh don't be stupid!
別傻了！

這裡使用的是動詞喔！

draft
n. 草稿
v. （打）草稿

Track 0846

👦 Our teacher asks us to hand in our first **draft** tomorrow.
我們老師要我們明天先交第一份草稿。

👧 You'd better hurry up!
你最好趕快！

這裡使用的是名詞喔！

ecology
n. 生態學

Track 0847

👦 Our teacher is always educating us about **ecology**.
我們老師總是教育我們生態學。

👧 You must learn a lot.
你們一定學了很多。

economics
n. 經濟學

Track 0848

👦 Why did you study **economics** in college?
你為什麼大學讀經濟？

👧 I thought that would make me rich.
我以為這會使我富有。

education
n. 教育

Track 0849

👦 **Education** paves way for your future.
教育為你的未來鋪路。

👧 Did your teacher said that?
你的老師說的？

effort
n. 努力

Despite all his **efforts**, he still couldn't succeed.
儘管努力，他仍然不成功。

He doesn't have the right attitude.
他態度不正確。

electronics
n. 電機工程學；電子

For beginners, **electronics** could be really hard to learn.
對初學者而言，電子工程學可能很難學會。

True.
沒錯。

elementary
adj. 基本的

My brother is studying in an **elementary** school now.
我弟弟正在念小學

So is my sister.
我妹妹也是。

eliminate
v. 消除

I can't **eliminate** the mark on my desk.
我擦不掉桌上的記號。

Maybe you should use some water.
也許你該用點水。

eloquent
adj. 辯才無礙的

James won the debate contest again.
詹姆士又贏了辯論賽。

That's for sure, he's so **eloquent**!
當然，他是如此的辯才無礙！

encyclopedia
n. 百科全書

The making of an **encyclopedia** sometimes takes dozens of years.
編一本百科全書有時耗費數十年。

True.
沒錯。

engineering
n. 工程學

Engineering includes many fields of studies.
工程學涵蓋許多領域的研究。

Really?
真的嗎？

Track 0856

enlighten
v. 啟發

He was **enlightened** by his mother to become a doctor to help people.
他母親啟發他成為一位助人的醫生。

His mother must be so proud.
他母親一定很驕傲。

Track 0857

equation
n. 相等

The **equation** of their age makes them good play mates.
他們年齡相仿促使他們成為要好的玩伴。

They might still be good friends in the future.
他們未來也可能還是好朋友。

Track 0858

equivalent
adj. 相等的

Criticizing someone harshly is **equivalent** to hurting them mentally.
嚴厲批評某人與傷害他們心靈是一樣的。

So it's better not to criticize.
所以最好不要隨意批評。

Track 0859

eraser
n. 橡皮擦

Did you see my **eraser**?
你有看到我的橡皮擦嗎？

It's on the floor.
在地上。

Track 0860

error
n. 錯誤

I made an **error** on my exam.
我考試時犯了個錯誤。

Don't worry, you'll pass.
別擔心，你會過的。

Track 0861

essay
n. 短文;隨筆;論說文

Track 0862

My teacher returned my **essay** without even reading it.
我的老師讀也不讀便退回了我的短文。

Maybe it's because you handed in after the deadline.
也許是因為你截稿後才交。

ethical
adj. 道德的

Track 0863

Human cloning issue involves **ethical** discussions.
複製人的議題包含道德方面的討論

I agree.
我也同意。

examination
n. 考試

Track 0864

When is your final **exam**?
你什麼時候期末考?

Tomorrow.
明天。

examine
v. 檢查

Track 0865

The security guard is **examining** people who are entering the building.
警衛正在檢查進入大樓的人。

What for?
為什麼?

example
n. 榜樣;例子

Track 0866

As a father, you need to set good example for your children.
身為一位父親,你需要為孩子建立好榜樣。

I know.
我知道。

exhibition
n. 展覽

Track 0867

Do you want to go to the **exhibition** with me?
你想跟我一起去看展覽嗎?

Sure.
好啊。

expertise
n. 專門知識；（專長）

Track 0868

What's your **expertise** in this field?
你在這個領域的專門知識是什麼？

Physics.
物理學。

explain
v. 解釋

Track 0869

Can you **explain** what happened in here?
你能解釋這裡發生了什麼事嗎？

No, I just got here.
不，我也是剛剛才來的。

express
v. 表達；說明
adj. 特快的
n. 快遞

Track 0870

You're really good at **expressing** your feelings through words.
你真的很會運用文字表達自己情感。

Thanks.
謝謝。

> 這裡使用的是動名詞喔！

extensive
adj. 廣泛的；廣大的

Track 0871

Biology is an **extensive** knowledge.
生物學是門廣泛的知識。

So is linguistics.
語言學也是。

extract
v. 摘錄
n. 摘錄

Track 0872

After reading this **extract** from his book, I want to buy one.
看了他這本書的摘錄，我也想買一本。

So do I.
我也是。

> 這裡使用的是名詞喔！

extracurricular
adj. 課外的

Track 0873

Do you have any **extracurricular** activity experience?
你有任何課外活動經驗嗎？

I used to volunteer as a social worker when I was in high school.
我高中時曾任社工志工。

fable
n. 寓言

🔊 *Track 0874*

👦 What's your favorite fable?
你最喜歡的寓言故事是什麼？

👩 Actually, I don't like any **fable**.
其實我不喜歡寓言。

faculty
n. 全體教員；系所

🔊 *Track 0875*

👦 All of the **faculty** should have a break tomorrow after being busy all day.
忙了一整天的全體教職員明天應該放假一天。

👩 Yeah, I agree.
我同意。

fact
n. 事實

🔊 *Track 0876*

👦 Are you telling me the **fact**?
你說的是實話嗎？

👩 Of course, just trust me.
當然了，相信我。

fail
v. 失敗；不及格
n. 不及格

🔊 *Track 0877*

👦 It is said that he never **fails**.
據説他從未失敗。

👩 Sometimes it may not be a good thing.
這不全然是好事。

> 這裡使用的是動詞喔！

false
adj. 錯誤的；假的；虛偽的

🔊 *Track 0878*

👦 I only got five points from my true-or-**false** questions.
我的是非題只得了五分。

👩 So did I.
我也是。

fancy
n. 想像力；愛好
adj. 花俏的

🔊 *Track 0879*

👦 Your daughter is really good at drawing.
你女兒真的很會畫畫。

👩 Yeah, she has a lively **fancy**.
是啊，她想像力豐富。

> 這裡使用的是名詞喔！

fiction
n. 小說；虛構

🔊 *Track 0880*

😀 Do you like science **fiction** novels?
你喜歡科幻小說嗎？

🙂 It depends.
不一定。

fill
v. 填空；填滿

🔊 *Track 0881*

😀 Can you help me **fill** this bottle with water?
你能幫我把這瓶子裝滿水嗎？

🙂 Sure.
當然

finance
n. 財政學；財務

🔊 *Track 0882*

😀 What's your major in college?
你大學主修什麼？

🙂 **Finance**.
財政學。

find
v. 找到；發現

🔊 *Track 0883*

😀 What did you **find** in the sand?
你在沙裡發現什麼？

🙂 A piece of glass.
一塊玻璃。

fluency
n. 流暢的說話（或寫作）

🔊 *Track 0884*

😀 You have good **fluency** of English speaking.
你英文說得很流利。

🙂 Thanks.
謝謝。

flunk
v. 打不及格分數；考試不及格

🔊 *Track 0885*

😀 I **flunked** my Chinese.
我國文被當。

🙂 That's because you didn't work hard.
那是因為你不努力。

folklore
n. 民間傳說；民俗

🎧 *Track 0886*

😀 Is there any **folklore** near this town.
這城鎮附近有什麼民間傳說嗎？

😊 Ask Gina, she knows the most.
問吉娜吧，她知道得最多。

foolish
adj. 愚笨的；愚蠢的

🎧 *Track 0887*

😀 Calling someone **foolish** is rude.
罵某人愚笨是非常不禮貌的。

😊 I agree.
我同意。

form
n. 形式；表格
v. 型塑

🎧 *Track 0888*

😀 I want to apply for scholarship.
我想要申請獎學金。

😊 Please fill the **form** here.
請先填好表格。

這裡使用的是名詞喔！

formula
n. 公式；法則

🎧 *Track 0889*

😀 Which **formula** should we apply to this math question?
這一題數學該套用什麼公式？

😊 Maybe you should ask your math teacher.
你應該問你的數學老師。

freshman
n. 新生；大一生

🎧 *Track 0890*

😀 Hi, I'm a **freshman** here, can you introduce me to the campus?
嗨你好，我是大一新生，你能為我介紹校園嗎？

😊 No problem.
沒問題。

gain
v. 得到；獲得
n. 收穫

🎧 *Track 0891*

😀 What did you **gain** from this class.
你從這堂課獲得什麼？

😊 A good attitude.
好的態度。

這裡使用的是動詞喔！

genetics
n. 遺傳學

🔊 *Track 0892*

👦 By studying **genetics**, we know humans are connected with other animals.
藉由解讀遺傳學，我們知道人和其他動物有關連。

👧 Even insects?
甚至是昆蟲？

genius
n. 天才；英才

🔊 *Track 0893*

👦 He goes to college when he's just fifteen.
他十五歲就上大學了。

👧 He's really a **genius**.
他真是天才。

geography
n. 地理（學）

🔊 *Track 0894*

👦 You can also learn about **geography** by playing this game.
藉由玩這遊戲你也能學習地理。

👧 I can't wait.
我等不及了。

giant
n. 巨人
adj. 巨大的

🔊 *Track 0895*

👦 Due to his height, his classmates call him a **giant**.
因為他的身高，他同學都喊他巨人。

👧 That's so rude.
真不禮貌。

> 這裡使用的是名詞喔！

gifted
adj. 有天賦的；有才能的

🔊 *Track 0896*

👦 His teacher thinks he's **gifted** in writing.
他的老師認為他寫作很有天賦。

👧 I bet his teacher's right.
我想他的老師是對的。

goal
n. 目標；終點

🔊 *Track 0897*

👦 He almost reached his **goal** of being a doctor.
他幾乎達到他當醫生的目標。

👧 He will, only if he tries again.
他會的，只要再試一次。

grade

n. 年級；等級；分數
v. 分級；打分數

🔊 *Track 0898*

👦 Which **grade** are you in?
你幾年級？

👧 I'm in second grade.
我二年級。

> 這裡使用的是名詞喔！

graduate

n. 畢業生
v. 畢業

🔊 *Track 0899*

👦 Are you a **graduate** from this college?
你是這個大學的畢業生嗎？

👧 No, I'm only a freshman.
不，我只是大一新生。

> 這裡使用的是名詞喔！

graduation

n. 畢業

🔊 *Track 0900*

👦 His parents took him to a party celebrating his **graduation**.
他父母帶他去派對以慶祝畢業。

👧 How I envy him.
我真羨慕他。

grammar

n. 文法

🔊 *Track 0901*

👦 His **grammar** is poor, but his speaking is fantastic.
他文法很差但口説很強。

👧 I'm just like him.
我跟他一樣。

grammatical

adj. 文法上的

🔊 *Track 0902*

👦 Students, do you have any more **grammatical** questions?
學生們，還有其他文法問題嗎？

👧 No.
沒有。

graph

n. 曲線圖；圖表

🔊 *Track 0903*

👦 What does this **graph** suggest?
這圖表在表達什麼？

👧 I have no idea.
我也不知道。

graphic
adj. 圖解的;生動的

Track 0904

The **graphic** explanation helps me understand the book.
這圖解幫助我了解這本書。

I agree.
我也同意。

grasp
v. 掌握;領悟;抓牢

Track 0905

Grasp this and don't let go.
抓緊了不要放開。

OK.
好的。

growth
n. 成長;發育

Track 0906

I can see his **growth** day by day.
我每天都能看見他的成長。

Of course, you're his mother!
當然了!你是他母親!

guide
n. 引導者;指南
v. 引導 .

Track 0907

We really need a tour **guide**.
我們真的需要一個導遊。

I'll go ask.
我去問問。

這裡使用的是名詞喔!

headline
n. 標題

Track 0908

What's the **headline** of today's news?
今天的新聞頭條是什麼?

The earthquake in Japan.
日本地震。

helpful
adj. 有用的

Track 0909

He is **helpful** when we're doing a project together.
一起做報告時他很有用。

That's not what I heard.
我聽到的不是這樣耶!

hero
n. 英雄；勇士

◀ *Track 0910*

He saved the residents from the fire.
他從火災中救了當地居民。

He is a **hero**.
他真是英雄。

---

hint
v. 暗示
n. 提示

◀ *Track 0911*

I really don't know the answer.
我真的不知道答案。

I'll give you a **hint**.
我給你個提示。

這裡使用的是名詞喔！

---

history
n. 歷史

◀ *Track 0912*

Do people learn anything from **history**?
人類有從歷史學習嗎？

Sometimes.
有時候。

---

hobby
n. 興趣；嗜好

◀ *Track 0913*

What's your **hobby**?
你的嗜好是什麼？

Collecting stamps.
集郵。

---

homework
n. 家庭作業

◀ *Track 0914*

Did you do your **homework** today?
你今天做功課了嗎？

Not yet.
還沒。

---

honest
adj. 誠實的；耿直的

◀ *Track 0915*

Is he an **honest** man to you?
對你而言他是誠實的人嗎？

I'm not sure.
我不確定耶。

humble
adj. 身份卑微的；謙虚的

Track 0916

I passed the exam by luck.
我通過這個考試真的只是運氣好。

You're so **humble**.
你真謙虚。

hypothesis
n. 假說；前提

Track 0917

The **hypothesis** of this experiment isn't clear.
這個實驗的假說不太明確。

I'll fix it again.
我會再修改。

idea
n. 主意；想法；觀念

Track 0918

Does anyone have any good **idea** in mind?
有沒有人心中有好點子呢？

Yes, I do.
我有。

ignorant
adj. 無知的

Track 0919

The gangsters are usually **ignorant**.
流氓們通常都沒受什麼教育。

It's only your prejudice.
那只是你的偏見而已。

illustrate
v. 舉例說明；畫插圖

Track 0920

So far, do you understand this question?
到目前為止，大家都了解這問題嗎？

Can you **illustrate** more?
你可以再舉例說明嗎？

illustration
n. 說明；插圖

Track 0921

Why do you like the book?
你為什麼喜歡這本書？

Because it has clear **illustration** for every specific term.
因為它有對每個專有名詞的清楚說明。

importance
n. 重要性

The **importance** of friendship is known to everyone.
友誼的重要大家都知道。

That's why I treat friends well.
所以我善待朋友。

individual
adj. 個別的
n. 個人

In this big project, all the **individual** company will work with another.
在這個大計畫案裡，每個個別公司都要互相合作。

It must be difficult for them.
對它們而言一定很難。

 這裡使用的是形容詞喔！

inference
n. 推理

His **inference** of this case is believable.
他對此案的推理很可信。

He is clever and has a keen observation of the case.
他很聰明且對此案有銳利的觀察。

influence
n. 影響

The **influence** of global warming is getting bigger.
地球暖化的影響越來越大。

We really need to care for the environment more.
我們應該更加關心環境。

information
n. 知識；見聞；（資訊）

You can visit the counter there for more **information**.
你可以到那裡的櫃台以得到更多資訊。

Thank you.
謝謝你。

ingenious
adj. 有獨創性的

Track 0927

His idea of this project is **ingenious**!
他對此案的想法非常具有獨創性。

He's been working on it for three months.
他投入此案已有三個月。

inherent
adj. 天生的；固有的

Track 0928

His intelligence is **inherent**, but he also studies hard.
他的聰明是天生的，但他也十分努力。

No wonder he can be a lawyer.
難怪他能成為律師。

insist
v. 堅持；強調

Track 0929

The host **insists** that the guest should wear ties.
主人堅持賓客要打領帶。

I guess I'll have to buy one.
那我可能需要去買一條。

instance
n. 實例

Track 0930

There are many kinds of fruits, for **instance**, apples, oranges etc.
水果有很多種，舉例來說有蘋果和柳橙等。

I love to eat fruits.
我愛吃水果。

instruct
v. 教導；指令

Track 0931

You are really my best student ever!
你真是我有史以來最棒的學生！

That's because you **instruct** me well.
那是因為您教導得好。

instruction
n. 指令；教導

Track 0932

Follow the **instructions** on the book and you can make an apple pie.
照著書上指示你就能做出蘋果派。

But the **instructions** are in French.
但是指示是法文耶！

integrity
n. 正直；誠實；完整

Track 0933

He was promoted as manager due to his **integrity**.
他被升為經理，因為他為人正直。

Good for him.
恭喜他。

intellect
n. 理解力

Track 0934

He can understand everything in the textbook without instruction.
他不經指導便能讀懂課文。

He must have superior **intellect**.
他一定有超群的理解力。

interpret
v. 解讀；翻譯

Track 0935

My teacher ask me to help **interpret** for her foreign friend.
我的老師要求我幫忙當她外國朋友的翻譯。

You should go, it's a good opportunity!
你應該去，這是很好的機會！

IQ
n. 智商

Track 0936

In Linda's opinion, high **IQ** doesn't mean anything.
琳達認為高智商不代表什麼。

I sort of agree with her.
我有點同意。

journal
n. 期刊

Track 0937

What does Jack do for a living?
傑克目前靠做什麼過活？

He is an editor for a **journal**.
他是一本期刊的編輯。

journalism
n. 新聞學；新聞業

Track 0938

This college is famous for its department of **journalism**.
這所大學以新聞系聞名。

A lot of noted reporters graduated from here.
許多知名記者都從這裡畢業。

judgment

n. 判斷；判斷力；（審判）

🔊 *Track 0939*

👦 Do you believe in instinct?
你相信直覺嗎？

👩 I don't, but I believe in my judgment.
我不相信，但我相信我的判斷。

kindergarten

n. 幼稚園

🔊 *Track 0940*

👦 How old is your little brother?
你小弟幾歲？

👩 He's just five, he goes to kindergarten now.
他才五歲，正在念幼稚園。

know-how

n. 本事；竅門

🔊 *Track 0941*

👦 I'm stuck on this question.
我被這個問題困擾。

👩 That's because you lack the know-how to solve it.
那是因為你缺乏竅門。

knowledge

n. 知識

🔊 *Track 0942*

👦 Do you believe that **knowledge** is power?
你相信知識就是力量嗎？

👩 That's my favorite sentence!
這是我最喜歡的一句話。

knowledgeable

adj. 博學的

🔊 *Track 0943*

👦 Professor Chen is **knowledgeable**.
陳教授博學多聞。

👩 That's why she's favored by students.
所以她深受學生喜愛。

laboratory

n. 實驗室

🔊 *Track 0944*

👦 Did you see Tom this morning?
你今早有看到湯姆嗎？

👩 I remember he was in the **laboratory**.
我記得他那時在實驗室。

lazy
adj. 懶惰的

Track 0945

Tim is **lazy**, he never does homework.
提姆很懶散，從不寫功課。

You should be more strict on him.
你應該對他嚴厲點！

learn
v. 學習；知悉；瞭解

Track 0946

What did you **learn** from Tom's behavior?
你從湯姆的行為學到什麼？

Courage.
勇氣。

lecture
n. 講座；教訓
v. 講授；教訓

Track 0947

Whenever his mom **lectures** him, he falls asleep.
他媽媽一對他說教他就睡著。

It's his nature.
這是他的天性。

這裡使用的是動詞喔！

legend
n. 傳奇

Track 0948

Did you know the **legend** of King Arthur?
你知道亞瑟王的傳奇嗎？

Of course, everyone knows that.
當然了，每個人都知道。

lesson
n. 課

Track 0949

Lesson two is hard, so he spends more time on it.
第二課很難，所以他多花了很多時間讀。

He's so hard working.
他真努力。

letter
n. 字母；信

Track 0950

Do you know any word that starts with **letter** A?
你知道任何A開頭的字嗎？

Apple!
蘋果！

level
n. 水準；標準；（等級）

🔊 *Track 0951*

👦 This school separates its students into three **levels.**
此校將其學生分為三級。

👧 Which **level** are you in?
你在哪一級？

liberal
adj. 自由主義的；開明的；慷慨的

🔊 *Track 0952*

👦 He comes from a **liberal** family.
他來自非常開明的家庭。

👧 I can see that.
我看得出來。

library
n. 圖書館

🔊 *Track 0953*

👦 Where is Tim now?
提姆現在在哪裡？

👧 He's in the **library**.
他在圖書館。

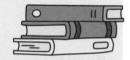

link
n. 關聯
v. 相連結

🔊 *Track 0954*

👦 I don't see any **link** between these two events.
我看不出這兩件事的關聯。

👧 Me either.
我也是。

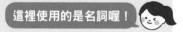
這裡使用的是名詞喔！

literacy
n. 讀寫能力

🔊 *Track 0955*

👦 This test is designed to test the **literacy** of students.
此測驗的目的在測驗學生的讀寫能力。

👧 I think it's hard.
我覺得測驗很難。

literal
adj. 文字的；照字面的；原義的

🔊 *Track 0956*

👦 When you read, you can't just know the literal meaning.
你讀書時不能只知道字面意思。

👧 That's what my teacher says.
跟我的老師說的一樣。

literature
n. 文學

Track 0957

- Tony likes **literature**.
  東尼喜歡文學。
- Maybe he'll become a writer in the future.
  也許他未來會成為作家。

logic
n. 邏輯；道理

Track 0958

- There's no **logic** in your writing.
  你的文章裡沒有邏輯。
- I'll fix it.
  我會修改。

logical
adj. 邏輯上的；合理的

Track 0959

- He never studies, so failure is a **logical** result.
  他從不讀書，因此失敗是合邏輯的結果。
- I can't agree with you more.
  我十分同意。

main
adj. 主要的

Track 0960

- What's the **main** idea of your essay?
  你文章的主要論點是什麼？
- People should care for animals more.
  人類應該更關懷動物。

major
v. 主修
adj. 主要的；重大的
n. 少校

Track 0961

- I **major** in English when I was in college.
  我大學主修英文。
- No wonder your English is so good.
  難怪你英文這麼好。

  這裡使用的是動詞喔！

manner
n. 方法；（方式）；（舉止）

Track 0962

- She really has good **manners**, look at the way she talks!
  她真的很有禮貌，看看她講話的方式！
- She goes to **manner** classes!
  她有上禮儀班。

a b c d e f g h i j k **l** m n o p q r s t u v w x y z

manners
n. 禮貌；風俗

👦 I'm not familiar with the local **manners**.
我對本地風俗不熟悉。

👧 It's OK, I'll teach you.
沒關係，我會教你。

🔊 *Track 0963*

manuscript
n. 手稿；原稿

👦 Where did you find that **manuscript**?
你從哪裡找到那張手稿？

👧 My father gave it to me.
我爸爸給我的。

🔊 *Track 0964*

mark
n. 標記
v. 標記

👦 He **marks** the paper with a blue pen.
他用藍筆標記在那張紙上。

👧 That's very smart!
真聰明！

這裡使用的是動詞喔！

🔊 *Track 0965*

master
n. 碩士；大師；主人
v. 精通
adj. 技藝精湛的

👦 I got my **master's** degree from King's college.
我從國王學院取得碩士學位。

👧 It must be hard.
一定很難。

這裡使用的是名詞喔！

🔊 *Track 0966*

material(ism)
n. 材質；材料；唯物論

👦 The **materials** of a window include glass.
這窗戶的材料包括玻璃。

👧 But my teacher says it is made of plastic.
但我的老師說這是塑膠做的。

🔊 *Track 0967*

mathematics
n. 數學

👦 Jim is good at **math**, but not so good at English.
吉姆數學好，但英文不好。

👧 A lot of boys are like that.
很多男生都這樣。

🔊 *Track 0968*

matter

n. 事情；（物質）
v. 有關係

🔊 *Track 0969*

👦 What's the **matter** with you?
你出了什麼事？

👧 I don't feel well.
我身體不舒服。

這裡使用的是名詞喔！

meaning

n. 意義

🔊 *Track 0970*

👦 How do I know the **meaning** of this word?
我如何知道這個字的意思？

👧 Check the dictionary.
查字典。

mechanics

n. 機械學；力學

🔊 *Track 0971*

👦 Tony learned some **mechanics** from his father.
東尼從他爸那裡學到了一點機械學。

👧 What does his father do?
他爸爸是做什麼的？

meditate

v. 沉思；（冥想）

🔊 *Track 0972*

👦 I'm so stressed!
我壓力好大！

👧 Try to **meditate**, it helps you calm.
試試冥想，可以幫助你冷靜。

memorize

v. 記憶

🔊 *Track 0973*

👦 He can **memorize** all his classmates' name!
他能記住所有同學的名字！

👧 Amazing!
真厲害！

mentality

n. 心態

🔊 *Track 0974*

👦 Being under stress for a long time can lead to the sickness of **mentality**.
長期處於壓力下可能導致心理疾病。

👧 Really?
真的嗎？

mind
n. 頭腦；思想
v. 介意；當心

🔊 *Track 0975*

👦 What's in your **mind**?
你心裡想什麼？

👧 Nothing.
沒什麼。

這裡使用的是名詞喔！

---

minor
v. 副修
n. 未成年人
adj. 次要的

🔊 *Track 0976*

👦 Did you **minor** in English last year?
你去年有輔修英語嗎？

👧 No, I was too busy.
沒有，我太忙了。

這裡使用的是動詞喔！

---

mistake
n. 錯誤；過失
v. 誤會

🔊 *Track 0977*

👦 It's not your **mistake**.
這不是你的錯。

👧 I know, but I feel guilty.
我知道，但我感到罪惡。

這裡使用的是名詞喔！

---

monthly
n. 月刊
adj. 每月的
adv. 每月的

🔊 *Track 0978*

👦 I buy this kind of **monthly** regularly.
我定期買這種月刊。

👧 What is it about?
這月刊是關於什麼的？

這裡使用的是名詞喔！

---

morality
n. 道德；德行

🔊 *Track 0979*

👦 Our teacher talks about the importance of **morality** all the time
我們老師總強調道德的重要。

👧 That's really an important lesson in life.
那的確是人生重要課程。

---

motto
n. 座右銘

🔊 *Track 0980*

👦 Do you have a **motto**?
你有座右銘嗎？

👧 Never give up!
永不放棄！

multiply
v. 相乘

Track 0981

👦 Four **multiplied** by two is…?
四乘以二是？

👧 Eight.
八。

myth
n. 神話；傳說

Track 0982

👦 I like reading Greek **myth**.
我喜歡讀希臘神話。

👧 I prefer Chinese myth.
我比較喜歡中國神話。

narrator
n. 敘述者；講述者；（旁白）

Track 0983

👦 Who is the **narrator** in this drama?
這齣戲的旁白是誰？

👧 Amy.
艾咪。

narrate
v. 敘述；講故事

Track 0984

👦 John **narrates** really well.
約翰很會講故事。

👧 No wonder kids love him.
難怪小孩喜歡他。

note
n. 筆記；便條
v. 注意

Track 0985

👦 You should hand in your homework tomorrow.
你明天應該要交作業。

👧 I'll put it in on my **note**.
我會把它記在筆記上。

這裡使用的是名詞喔！

noun
n. 名詞

Track 0986

👦 Is apple a **noun**?
蘋果是名詞嗎？

👧 Yes.
是的。

nursery
n. 托兒所

Track 0987

I grew up in a **nursery**.
我在托兒所長大。

Did you like it?
你喜歡那裡嗎？

observation
n. 觀察力

Track 0988

Tom has keen **observation**.
湯姆有銳利的觀察力。

So does Lily.
莉莉也有。

opinion
n. 觀點；意見

Track 0989

What's your **opinion** on this issue?
你對此事的看法是什麼？

I strongly agree with Tim.
我非常同意提姆的看法。

optimism
n. 樂觀主義

Track 0990

He never feels sad, even when he fails his test!
他從不悲傷，即使他考試不及格！

He must be a believer of **optimism**.
他一定是樂觀主義者。

oral
n. 口試
adj. 口語的；（口頭）

Track 0991

When is your **oral** test for graduate school?
你研究所口試是什麼時候？

Tomorrow.
明天。

這裡使用的是形容詞喔！

outlook
n. 觀點；（前景）

Track 0992

Take a different **outlook**, and things will be different.
採取不同觀點，事物也會變得不一樣。

I'll try.
我會試試。

page
n. （書上的）頁

Track 0993

Turn to **page** six and you will see the picture.
翻到第六頁就能看到這張圖。

I see.
我了解了。

pass
n. 及格；通行證
v. 傳遞；通過

Track 0994

Did you **pass** the math final exam?
你數學期末考有過嗎？

No, I'll have to take the make-up test.
沒有，我必須要補考了。

這裡使用的是動詞喔！

pen
n. 鋼筆；原子筆

Track 0995

There's a **pen** on the floor.
地上有枝筆。

Where?
哪裡？

pencil
n. 鉛筆

Track 0996

Our teacher requires us to draw first with a **pencil**.
我們的老師要求我們先用鉛筆畫底稿。

But I don't have a pencil!
但是我沒有鉛筆！

perceive
v. 感知；察覺

Track 0997

How do you **perceive** the world?
你如何感知這世界？

I perceive with my eyes, ears and mouth.
我用眼睛、耳朵和嘴巴感知。

personality
n. 個性；人格

Track 0998

Everyone agrees that he has a good **personality**.
大家都同意他個性很好。

And he's easy to get along with.
他也十分好相處。

pessimism
n. 悲觀；悲觀主義

Amy is a believer of **pessimism**, she always thinks on the negative side.
艾咪是悲觀主義者，她總是往負面想。

You should talk to her about the importance of being positive.
你應該向她訴説正面想法的重要。

Track 0999

philosophy
n. 哲學

Some people think **philosophy** is essential to life.
有人覺得哲學對人生是必要的。

I've heard that.
我也聽説過。

Track 1000

phrase
n. 片語

There are so many **phrases** in English.
英文裡有好多片語。

Learn them step by step!
一步一步學吧！

Track 1001

physics
n. 物理學

He studies **physics** whenever he has time.
他一有時間就讀物理。

I don't know he's so crazy about physics!
我不知道他對物理如此狂熱！

Track 1002

plagiarize
v. 剽竊；抄襲

Plagiarizing other people's work is illegal.
剽竊他人作品是違法的。

Does that include information on the Internet?
包括網上的資料嗎？

Track 1003

plus
prep. 加
n. 加號；優勢

He learned how to **plus** when he was three.
他三歲就學會加法。

What a prodigy!
真是個神童！

此為口語化用法

Track 1004

poem
n. 詩

🔊 *Track 1005*

> I write **poems** when I feel sad.
> 我難過時就會寫詩。

> Can I read them?
> 我可以讀嗎？

politics
n. 政治學

🔊 *Track 1006*

> Some people say **politics** is very complicated.
> 有人説政治學非常複雜。

> I agree.
> 我也同意。

positive
adj. 確信的；積極的；正的

🔊 *Track 1007*

> Are you **positive** that John got married?
> 你確定約翰結婚了嗎？

> I'm positive
> 我確定。

possibility
n. 可能性

🔊 *Track 1008*

> Is John really the son of the president?
> 約翰真的是總統的兒子嗎？

> The **possibilities** are high.
> 可能性很高。

practice
n. 實踐；練習；熟練
v. 實踐；練習

🔊 *Track 1009*

> You should **practice** English everyday.
> 你應該天天練習英文。

> It's easier said than done.
> 説的比做容易

這裡使用的是動詞喔！

preparation
n. 準備

🔊 *Track 1010*

> How much time did you spend on **preparation**?
> 你準備了多久時間？

> A month.
> 一個月。

presence
n. 出席

🔊 *Track 1011*

> Your **presence** pleases me!
> 你的出席使我高興！

> I'm flattered.
> 你太誇獎了。

preview
n. 預習

Track 1012

Tony **previews** each lessen before the class.
東尼在課前都會預習。

He's so hard-working.
他真努力。

problem
n. 問題

Track 1013

Is there any **problem**?
有問題嗎？

No.
沒有。

pronounce
v. 發音

Track 1014

He can **pronounce** long words easily.
他能夠輕易唸出長單字的發音。

He must have learned English for a long time.
他一定學了很久英文。

prose
n. 散文

Track 1015

Our homework today is to preview the **prose**.
我們的今日作業是預習散文。

It must be easy for you.
對你而言一定很簡單！

psychology
n. 心理學

Track 1016

His passion for **psychology** is inspired by Freud.
他對心理學的熱情是被佛洛伊德啟發的。

And now he's going to study that in college.
而且他大學也將要讀心理學。

pupil
n. 小學生；（瞳孔）

Track 1017

Teaching **pupils** can be harder than teaching college students!
有時候教小學生比教大學生還難！

I agree.
我同意。

puzzle
n. 難題；謎
v. 使困惑

Track 1018

I still can't solve this **puzzle**.
我仍解不出這難題。

You should ask your teacher for help.
你應該向老師求救。

這裡使用的是名詞喔！

qualify
v. 使合格

Track 1019

Her language proficiency **qualifies** her as an English guide.
她流利的語言使她能夠成為一名英語導覽。

That's for sure!
當然了！

query
n. 問題；疑問
v. 詢問

Track 1020

If you still have any **query** in mind, consult me after class.
如果你心裡還有疑問，下課再來問我。

OK.
好的。

這裡使用的是名詞喔！

question
n. 疑問；（問題）
v. 詢問

Track 1021

The president was **questioned** by a group of reporters.
總統被一群記者詢問。

I think it's because of his recent act on protecting the environment.
我想應該是因為他最近保護環境的措施。

這裡使用的是動詞喔！

quiz
n. 測驗
v. 測驗

Track 1022

Our teacher likes to give pop **quizzes**.
我們老師喜歡出隨堂測驗。

Then you have to review after class.
那你課後都該複習。

這裡使用的是名詞喔！

quote
v. 引用；引證

Track 1023

The famous poet was **quoted** frequently.
那位名詩人經常被引用。

I just quoted him in my last report.
我才在上一份報告中引用他。

range
n. 範圍

🔊 *Track 1024*

👦 The **range** of the midterm exam isn't clear.
期中考的範圍並不清楚。

👩 You should ask your teacher as soon as possible.
你應該盡早問老師的。

read
v. 讀、看（書、報等）；朗讀

🔊 *Track 1025*

👦 Jane, can you **read** the first paragraph?
珍，妳能唸一下第一段嗎？

👩 Of course.
當然。

realize
v. 實現；瞭解

🔊 *Track 1026*

👦 Why is he so happy?
他為何如此高興？

👩 His dream is **realized**.
他實現了他的夢想。

recite
v. 背誦

🔊 *Track 1027*

👦 He read the article several times that he can almost **recite** the whole article!
他看了那文章數遍，甚至都會背了！

👩 That's amazing!
真厲害！

remember
v. 記得

🔊 *Track 1028*

👦 Do you still **remember** his name?
你還記得他的名字嗎？

👩 No, but I remember him.
不記得，但我記得他的人。

report
v. 報告；報導
n. 報告；報導

🔊 *Track 1029*

👦 Did you watch the **report** about our school yesterday?
妳昨天有看關於我們學校的報導嗎？

👩 No, what is it?
沒有耶，是什麼？

這裡使用的是名詞喔！

respect

v. 尊重
n. 尊重；（方面）

🔈 *Track 1030*

👦 Students should show **respect** to their teacher.
學生應對老師表達尊重。

👧 I think it's important!
我認為這很重要！

這裡使用的是名詞喔！

result

n. 結果
v. 導致

🔈 *Track 1031*

👦 What's the **result** of your speech contest?
妳演講比賽結果如何？

👧 I won!
我贏了！

這裡使用的是名詞喔！

review

v. 複習；評論；審查
n. 評論；審查

🔈 *Track 1032*

👦 Students nowadays seldom **review** lessons after class.
現在的學生很少課後複習。

👧 Yeah, they spend more time on the Internet.
是啊，他們花更多時間上網。

這裡使用的是動詞喔！

sanitation

n. 公共衛生

🔈 *Track 1033*

👦 The school should pay more attention to the **sanitation** of restrooms.
學校應該更注意廁所衛生。

👧 My father has suggested our principle.
我父親已經建議校長了。

scholarship

n. 獎學金

🔈 *Track 1034*

👦 Have you applied for **scholarship** this semester?
妳這學期申請獎學金了嗎？

👧 Not yet.
還沒。

school

n. 學校

🔈 *Track 1035*

👦 Where were you this afternoon?
妳今天下午在哪？

👧 I stayed at **school** with my classmates.
我和同學一起留在學校。

scope
n. 範圍；領域

◀ Track 1036

The thing you talk about is beyond the **scope** of my field of study.
妳所談論之事不在我的研究範圍內。

I guess I'll have to ask another teacher.
那我想我應該去問其他老師了。

---

score
n. 分數
v. 得分

◀ Track 1037

What's your **score** on English writing?
妳的英語寫作分數幾分？

I don't want to talk about it.
我不想說。

這裡使用的是名詞喔！

---

search
v. 搜索；搜尋
n. 搜索

◀ Track 1038

The police **searched** his house and found illegal drugs.
警察搜索他家並發現違法毒品。

He's in a big trouble.
他有大麻煩了。

這裡使用的是動詞喔！

---

section
n. 部分；區域

◀ Track 1039

How many **sections** are there in the city?
這個城市有幾個區域？

Fifteen.
十五個。

---

seminar
n. 研討會

◀ Track 1040

Will you go to the economic **seminar**?
你會去經濟研討會嗎？

I'll go if you go.
你去，我就去。

---

sentence
n. 句子；判決
v. 判處

◀ Track 1041

Our teacher asked us to make ten **sentences** today.
我們老師要我們今天造十個句子。

Then do it now.
那現在就做吧。

這裡使用的是名詞喔！

simple
adj. 簡單的

🔊 *Track 1042*

😀 The Math midterm is really **simple**!
數學期中考很簡單。

😊 Maybe no one will fail!
也許不會有人被當。

simplify
v. 使……單純

🔊 *Track 1043*

😀 My father thinks that I over **simplify** the problem.
我爸爸認為我把問題過於簡化。

😊 I think your father is right.
我想妳爸是對的。

skill
n. 技能

🔊 *Track 1044*

😀 You should work on your writing **skills**.
你應該加強你的寫作技巧。

😊 I know, I'm taking a writing class this semester.
我知道,我這學期有上寫作課。

slang
n. 俚語

🔊 *Track 1045*

😀 **Slangs** are not proper in formal occasions.
俚語在正式場合不適當。

😊 They should be avoided in formal occasions.
應該避免在正式場合使用俚語。

smart
adj. 聰明的

🔊 *Track 1046*

😀 David is a **smart** boy.
大衛是個聰明的男孩。

😊 He is humble, too.
他也很謙虛。

sociology
n. 社會學

🔊 *Track 1047*

😀 **Sociology** explores into the formation of society.
社會學探討社會的形成。

😊 Sounds hard to me.
聽起來很難。

sophomore

n. （大學、高中）二年級學生

Track 1048

What grade are you in now?
你今年幾年級？

I'm a **sophomore**.
我今年高二。

species

n. 物種

Track 1049

Have you heard of Darvin's book *The Origin of Species*?
你聽過達爾文的《物種起源》嗎？

Of course! It's a must-know.
當然，這是一定要知道的。

specify

v. 詳述；詳載

Track 1050

Can you **specify** reasons why you were absent this morning?
你可以詳述你今早缺席的原因嗎？

I was sick and stayed in the hospital.
我生病，然後住院了。

speculate

v. 沉思；推測

Track 1051

Stop **speculating**! Gary and I are not in a relationship.
別妄自猜測！我跟蓋瑞沒有在一起。

I don't believe that.
我不相信。

speech

n. 演講；（說話）

Track 1052

When is the **speech** contest?
演講比賽是什麼時候？

Next Monday.
下禮拜一。

spelling

n. 拼讀；拼法

Track 1053

My **spelling** is weak.
我拼字很差。

You should work on it!
你應該加強！

spoil
v. 寵壞；損壞

🔊 Track 1054

👦 Mary is **spoiled** by her parents.
瑪莉被她的父母寵壞了。

👧 She gets angry so easily.
她很容易生氣。

squad
n. 小隊；班

🔊 Track 1055

👦 Are we in the same **squad**?
我們在同一隊嗎？

👧 I guess so.
我想應該是吧。

stationery
n. 文具

🔊 Track 1056

👦 Let's go to that shop, I need to buy some **stationery**.
我們去那家店一下，我需要買一些文具。

👧 Me, too.
我也要。

structure
n. 構造；結構
v. 建構

🔊 Track 1057

👦 The **structure** of this building is designed by Tony.
這棟建築物的構造是東尼設計的。

👧 He is so talented.
他真有才華。

> 這裡使用的是名詞喔！

student
n. 學生

🔊 Track 1058

👦 As a **student**, you should study hard.
身為一名學生，你應該認真讀書。

👧 That's what my mother says.
我媽媽也這麼説。

study
v. 學習
n. 學習；（研究）

🔊 Track 1059

👦 Tony **studies** for five hours each day.
東尼一天讀五小時書。

👧 Isn't that too much for a junior high school student?
對國中生來説是不是太多了？

> 這裡使用的是動詞喔！

stupid
adj. 愚蠢的；笨的

Track 1060

It's rude to call someone **stupid**.
罵別人笨很失禮。

I never use that word.
我從不這麼説。

subject
n. 主題；科目
adj. 服從的；取決於

Track 1061

What's the **subject** of your essay?
你文章的主題是什麼？

The importance of education.
教育的重要。

> 這裡使用的是名詞喔！

subjective
adj. 主觀的

Track 1062

I think your essay is too **subjective**.
我覺得你的文章太主觀了。

I'll fix it.
我會再修改。

subtract
v. 扣除；移走

Track 1063

Why did they **subtract** her from the list?
他們為什把她從名單上扣除？

She's not coming!
她不來了！

summarize
v. 總結；概述

Track 1064

Can you **summarize** this article for me?
你可以為我概述一下這一段嗎？

Sure.
當然。

supplement
n. 副刊；補充

Track 1065

Why do you like that newspaper?
你為什麼喜歡那份報紙？

Its **supplement** is interesting.
它的副刊很有趣。

talent
n. 天份；天賦

Track 1066

I really think you have **talent** in drawing.
我真的覺得你畫圖有天份。

Thank you so much.
很謝謝你。

talented
adj. 有才能的

Track 1067

He can write interesting stories.
他能寫出有趣故事。

He is very **talented**.
他很有才華。

teach
v. 教；教書；教導

Track 1068

He **teaches** junior high school.
他在國中任教。

Students must love him so much!
學生一定很喜歡他。

technology
n. 技術學；工藝學；（科技）

Track 1069

Do you know anything about **technology**?
你知道關於技術學的東西嗎？

I have no idea.
我不知道耶。

tell
v. 告訴；說明；分辨

Track 1070

Can you **tell** me what's going on?
你能告訴我發生了什麼事嗎？

Sure.
當然了。

test
n. 考試
v. 測驗

Track 1071

Is the **test** hard.
考試難嗎？

No, it's easy.
不，很簡單。

這裡使用的是名詞喔！

text
n. 課文;本文;簡訊
v. 傳簡訊

Track 1072

Do you understand the whole **text**?
你了解課文全文嗎?

No, I have few questions.
不,我還有些問題。

這裡使用的是名詞喔!

textbook
n. 教科書

Track 1073

I forgot my **textbook** today!
我忘了帶課本!

Well, we can share.
我們可以一起看。

theme
n. 主題;題目

Track 1074

The **theme** of today's lesson is education in Taiwan.
今日課程的主題是台灣的教育。

Sounds interesting!
聽起來很有趣!

theory
n. 理論

Track 1075

I don't believe this **theory**.
我不相信這個理論。

Well, you can try to prove it wrong.
那麼你可以試著證明它是錯的。

think
v. 想;思考
n. 思考

Track 1076

Do you want to enter this school?
你想要就讀這間學校嗎?

I'll **think** about it.
我會想想看。

這裡使用的是動詞喔!

thought
n. 沉思;推測;(想法)

Track 1077

What's your **thought** on this case?
你對此案的推測是什麼?

I'm still thinking.
我仍在思考。

title
n. 稱號；標題

🔊 *Track 1078*

👦 What's the **title** of your essay?
你的文章標題是什麼？

👧 The Story of Me.
我的故事。

topic
n. 主題

🔊 *Track 1079*

👦 The **topic** of today's lesson is hobby.
今天課程的主題是嗜好。

👧 It must be interesting.
一定很有趣。

trait
n. 特色；特性

🔊 *Track 1080*

👦 You need to discover your personal **traits**.
你需要挖掘你的個人特質。

👧 But how?
應該如何做？

translate
v. 翻譯

🔊 *Track 1081*

👦 **Translate** this sentence into Chinese.
把這句話翻成中文。

👧 Give me one minute.
給我一分鐘。

translation
n. 譯文；翻譯

🔊 *Track 1082*

👦 The **translation** of this book will be out tomorrow!
這本書的翻譯明天會出來！

👧 I can't wait!
我等不及了！

truant
n. 蹺課的學生
v. 蹺課

🔊 *Track 1083*

👦 All **truants** will be punished by school.
所有蹺課者都會被學校處罰。

👧 I know.
我知道。

這裡使用的是名詞喔！

truth
n. 真相；真理

Are you telling the **truth**?
你說的是實話嗎？

Yes.
是的。

Track 1084

tuition
n. 教學；講授；學費

The tuition of my school is almost unaffordable.
我學校的學費幾乎令人無法負擔。

My school's **tuition** is even more expensive.
我學校的學費比你更貴。

Track 1085

undergraduate
n. 大學生

Are you an **undergraduate** of this college?
你是這所大學的大學生嗎？

No, I'm a high school student.
不是，我只是高中生。

Track 1086

understand
v. 瞭解；明白

Can you **understand** what he says?
你聽得懂他說的嗎？

No, it's too hard.
不，太難了。

Track 1087

university
n. 大學

Can you drive me to my **university**?
你可以載我去我的大學嗎？

Sure.
當然。

Track 1088

upbringing
n. 養育；教養

He thanks his mother for all the years of **upbringing**.
他感謝他母親多年的養育。

His mother must be so happy.
他的母親一定很高興。

Track 1089

useful

adj. 有用的；有益的；有幫助的

Track 1090

A second language can be a **useful** tool.
第二外語可以是很好的工具。

Especially when you go abroad.
尤其當你出國時。

---

versatile

adj. 多才多藝的；多用途的

Track 1091

He can sing, dance, and play a piano!
他能唱、能舞、更能彈琴！

He's so **versatile**.
他真多才多藝。

---

version

n. 說法；版本

Track 1092

Did you get the new **version** of this book?
你拿到這本書的新版了嗎？

Not yet.
還沒。

---

verb

n. 動詞

Track 1093

Can you give me an example of **verb**?
你可以給我一個動詞的例子嗎？

Run is a verb.
跑就是動詞。

---

verse

n. 詩；詩句

Track 1094

Do you like Shakespeare's **verses**?
你喜歡莎士比亞的詩句嗎？

I love them!
我很喜歡。

---

view

n. 景觀；見解
v. 看見

Track 1095

You can **view** the beautiful beach from here.
從這裡你可以望見美麗的沙灘。

Wow, it is breathtaking.
哇，真令人嘆為觀止。

這裡使用的是動詞喔！

a
b
c
d
e
f
g
h
i
j
k
l
m
n
o
p
q
r
s
t
u
v
w
x
y
z

vocabulary
n. 單字；字彙

🔊 *Track 1096*

👦 The **vocabulary** of the lesson is a bit hard.
這一課單字有些難。

👧 I agree.
我也同意。

vulgar
adj. 粗糙的；粗魯的

🔊 *Track 1097*

👦 You shouldn't call him **vulgar** just because you dislike him.
你不應該只因為你討厭他而罵他粗鄙。

👧 I'm sorry.
我很抱歉。

wisdom
n. 智慧

🔊 *Track 1098*

👦 He is considered a man with true **wisdom**.
他被認為是有真實智慧的人。

👧 I also admire his knowledge.
我也敬佩於他的學問。

wise
adj. 有智慧的；聰明的

🔊 *Track 1099*

👦 A **wise** man should never stop pursuing knowledge.
一位聰明的人不應停止追求知識。

👧 I can't agree with you more.
我再同意不過。

write
v. 書寫；寫下；寫字

🔊 *Track 1100*

👦 Can you **write** down your phone number on this sheet?
你可以把你的電話寫在這張紙上嗎？

👧 Sure.
當然。

write down your phone number.

Part
06

要學就學最實用的英文單字，搭配最稀鬆平常的生活對話，馬上就知道外國人都是這樣用這個單字的喲！＊單字、對話分開錄音，學習目標更明確

album	😊 Is this guy your favorite singer?
n. 相簿；專輯	這個人是你最喜歡的歌手嗎？
	😊 Sure! I've already purchased his latest **album** in advance!
🔊 *Track 1101*	當然啊，我已經預購了他最新的專輯呢！

amuse	😊 Why is everybody laughing?
v. 娛樂；消遣	為什麼大家都在笑？
	😊 Because what you say truly **amuses** us.
🔊 *Track 1102*	因為你講的話真的很逗我們笑。

amusement	😊 What's your **amusement** in leisure time?
n. 娛樂；有趣	你休閒時的娛樂是什麼？
	😊 Well, shopping, shopping, and shopping.
🔊 *Track 1103*	嗯，就是逛街、逛街、還有逛街嘍。

animation	😊 Did you see the latest Disney **animation** movie?
n. 動畫	你看了迪士尼最新的動畫電影嗎？
	😊 No, what's the title of the movie?
🔊 *Track 1104*	還沒耶，電影的名字叫什麼？

antique	😊 It's said that the sword is an invaluable **antique**.
n. 古董	聽說這把劍是價值連城的古董。
adj. 古董的	😊 Fine. We'd better leave it alone.
	很好，那我們還是別動它了吧。
🔊 *Track 1105*	這裡使用的是名詞喔！

applaud

v. 鼓掌；喝采；誇讚

Track 1106

> The show was so fantastic!!!
> 那場表演真的太精彩了！

> I remember the audience **applauded** for more than ten minutes.
> 我還記得觀眾鼓掌超過十分鐘呢。

applause

n. 喝采

Track 1107

> Did you hear the **applause**?
> 你聽到掌聲了嗎？

> Yeah! I can't believe they liked our performance!
> 嗯！我沒想到他們會喜歡我們的表演！

appreciate

v. 欣賞；鑑賞

Track 1108

> Why don't they **appreciate** my talent?
> 為什麼他們不賞識我的才華？

> Maybe they're lack of judgement.
> 他們大概不懂得欣賞吧。

art

n. 藝術

Track 1109

> Those who major in **art** look very elegant.
> 學藝術的人感覺都很有氣質。

> Like those who major in music.
> 學音樂的人也是啊。

artistic

adj. 藝術的；美術的

Track 1110

> Be good. Don't waste your **artistic** skill.
> 好好加油。別浪費你的藝術天份。

> I will, Professor Ryan.
> 我會的，萊恩教授。

ascend

v. 上升；登

Track 1111

> I wonder when Prince Charles will **ascend** the throne.
> 我在想到底查爾斯王子什麼時候會登上王位。

> I'm sure it won't be soon.
> 絕對不會是最近。

auction
n. 拍賣

Track 1112

Is this Lamborghini? The price is astronomical!
這是藍寶堅尼嗎？它是天價耶！

Actually, I bought it from a car **auction**.
其實呢，我是在汽車拍賣會買的。

---

audience
n. 聽眾；（聽眾）

Track 1113

The gym is crowded with **audiences**!
整個體育館都是聽眾！

You see! They all come to hear you sing!
看吧！大家都來聽你唱歌了！

---

ball
n. 舞會；球

Track 1114

There's a **ball** on the grass.
草地上有顆球。

Let's kick it and play a game.
那我們用它來場比賽吧。

---

balloon
n. 氣球

Track 1115

We should decorate the classroom with red **balloon**.
我們應該要用紅色氣球裝飾教室。

No. I think yellow is better.
不，我覺得黃色的比較好。

---

band
n. 帶子；隊；樂隊

Track 1116

Which rock **band** do you like the best?
你最喜歡哪個搖滾團體？

Of course it's Oasis. Their music is gorgeous.
當然是綠洲。他們的音樂實在太棒了。

---

beach
n. 海灘

Track 1117

How are you gonna spend your summer break?
你要怎麼過暑假？

I'm going to sunbath on the **beach**.
我要去海灘做日光浴。

beat
v. 敲打；打敗
n. 節拍

🔊 *Track 1118*

😮 Do you hear the **beat** of the drum?
你聽到鼓點的聲音了嗎？

😊 Sure! I'm getting excited now!
有！我越來越興奮了！

這裡使用的是名詞喔！

beauty
n. 美；美人；美的東西

🔊 *Track 1119*

😮 How do you define **beauty** of a girl?
你所定義的美女是什麼樣子？

😊 She must be confident to herself.
一定要對自己有自信。

bell
n. 鐘；鈴；門鈴

🔊 *Track 1120*

😮 The **bell** is ringing.
門鈴響了。

😊 I have Sam answer it.
我叫山姆去應門了。

bingo
n. 賓果遊戲

🔊 *Track 1121*

😮 Which gambling games do you want to play?
你想玩哪種賭博遊戲？

😊 How about **Bingo**?
賓果怎麼樣？

blow
v. 吹；打擊

🔊 *Track 1122*

😮 The wind is **blowing** your skirts up.
風把妳的裙子吹起來了。

😊 Nonsense! I am aware of it!
胡說！我有在注意啦！

blues
n. 憂鬱；藍調

🔊 *Track 1123*

😮 Do you know any **blues** bar in Taipei?
你知道台北哪裡有藍調酒吧嗎？

😊 I am not clear about it.
這我不是很清楚。

broadcast

n. 廣播
v. 播出
adj. 廣播的

🔊 *Track 1124*

👦 What if our electricity shut off and we can't watch newscast?
如果停電了看不到新聞怎麼辦？

👧 Take it easy. We can hear **broadcast**.
放心，我們可以聽廣播。

這裡使用的是名詞喔！

bungee-jumping

n. 高空彈跳

🔊 *Track 1125*

👦 Dear, why don't we have a **bungee-jumping** wedding?
親愛的，為什麼我們不辦一場高空彈跳婚禮呢？

👧 No way! I have acrophobia!
不行！我有懼高症！

cartoon

n. 卡通

🔊 *Track 1126*

👦 I've not seen **cartoon** for a long while.
我已經很久沒有看卡通了。

👧 Why? Do you think it's childish?
為什麼？你覺得卡通很幼稚嗎？

CD

n. 光碟

🔊 *Track 1127*

👦 Did you bring the **CD** I borrowed you yesterday?
你有帶我昨天借你的CD嗎？

👧 Oh! I left it in my computer!
噢！它還在我的電腦裡面！

chess

n. 西洋棋

🔊 *Track 1128*

👦 You can't beat me in **chess**.
你沒辦法在下棋方面贏過我的。

👧 It's impossible! Let me try again!
不可能！讓我再試一次！

chord

n. 琴弦；（和弦）

🔊 *Track 1129*

👦 Try to strike a **chord** on the guitar.
試著用吉他刷個和弦。

👧 Like this? Oh no, it's awful.
像這樣嗎？噢不，聽起來超慘的。

cinema
n. 電影院；電影

🎵 *Track 1130*

👦 There is a good **cinema** on screen tomorrow.
明天有部好電影要上映了。

👧 Really? It seems I need to spare some time.
是哦？看來我要空點時間出來了。

circus
n. 馬戲團

🎵 *Track 1131*

👦 Have you ever seen a **circus**?
你有看過馬戲團表演嗎？

👧 Yeah, my grandfather took me to it once when I was a kid.
有啊，我小時候爺爺帶我去看過一次。

clap
v. 鼓掌；拍擊
n. 鼓掌

🎵 *Track 1132*

👦 Why do we have to **clap** hands after the lecture?
為什麼我們要在演講完後鼓掌？

👧 Because that's how we show our respect.
這樣才能顯示我們的尊重。

這裡使用的是動詞喔！

classic
adj. 古典的；經典的
n. 經典

🎵 *Track 1133*

👦 It's said that **classic** music can make you graceful.
聽說聽古典樂會讓人變得優雅。

👧 A little bird told you, right?
道聽塗説的，對吧？

這裡使用的是形容詞喔！

clay
n. 黏土

🎵 *Track 1134*

👧 Do you know playing **clay** can increase creativity?
你知道玩黏土可以增加創造力嗎？

👦 Yeah. I've played it, man and boy.
知道啊，我從小玩到大。

clown
n. 小丑；丑角

🎵 *Track 1135*

👦 I don't like the mask on the **clown**.
我不喜歡那個小丑的面具。

👧 Me, neither. It looks a little horrible.
我也是。它看起來有點可怕。

club
n. 俱樂部;社團

🔊 *Track 1136*

😃 Which **club** are you going to join?
你要去哪個社團?

😊 Football club seems interesting.
足球社看起來滿有趣的。

comedy
n. 喜劇

🔊 *Track 1137*

😃 *The Big Bang Theory* is my favorite **comedy**.
我最喜歡的喜劇是《宅男行不行》。

😊 Tell you something, I've collected all seasons!
跟你說,我買了全套!

comic
adj. 好笑的;喜劇的
n. 漫畫

🔊 *Track 1138*

😃 See this **comic** book! It's really funny!
看這本漫畫書!真的很好笑!

😊 Not interested.
沒興趣。

> 這裡使用的是名詞喔!

compare
v. 比較

🔊 *Track 1139*

😃 **Compared** to our car, theirs is shabby.
跟我們的車一比,他們的車就顯得很寒酸了。

😊 Don't be that mean.
別這麼苛薄啦。

concert
n. 音樂會;演奏會;(演唱會)

🔊 *Track 1140*

😃 I'm sorry. The **concert** is temporarily canceled.
很抱歉,音樂會臨時取消了。

😊 What? I spent 10 hours traveling here!
什麼?我花了十個小時到這裡耶!

dance
v. 舞蹈
n. 舞蹈

🔊 *Track 1141*

😃 Let's **dance** the whole night!
我們去跳整晚的舞!

😊 Awesome! Call some more friends to come with us!
好耶!那就再多找些朋友一起去吧!

> 這裡使用的是動詞喔!

disco
n. 迪斯可；小舞廳

Track 1142

If you want to relax, go to **disco** tonight.
如果你想放鬆一下，晚上就去迪斯可吧。

But I have some paper to read...
但是我還有論文要讀……

display
v. 展示
n. 展示；（櫥窗）

Track 1143

I'm very touched by the old photos **displayed** in the hall.
大廳展示的舊照片讓我很感動。

They remind us of the good old days.
它們讓我們想起了以前的美好時光。

這裡使用的是動詞喔！

dive
v. 潛水
n. 潛水

Track 1144

I'm a **diving** club member.
我是潛水社團的社員。

Cool! Where do you think is the best diving destination?
好酷！那你覺得哪裡是最棒的潛水點？

這裡使用的是動名詞喔！

documentary
n. 紀錄片
adj. 文件的；紀實的

Track 1145

These **documentaries** are all worth collecting.
這些紀錄片都很有收藏的價值。

Yeah, some of them truly present the social nature.
恩，有些片子的確反應了社會現況。

這裡使用的是名詞喔！

doll
n. 玩具娃娃

Track 1146

What did you buy for your daughter's birthday?
妳買什麼給妳女兒做生日禮物？

A **doll**, which looks p retty much like her.
一個長的很像她的娃娃。

download
v. 下載
n. 下載

Track 1147

Where do you **download** these films?
你去哪裡下載這些電影的？

I can't tell you. The source is illegal.
我不能跟你說。來源是非法的。

這裡使用的是動詞喔！

drama
n. 戲劇

🔊 *Track 1148*

I don't like to watch **drama**. It's a waste of time.
我不喜歡看戲劇。那很浪費時間。

You're so freaky.
你真是個怪人。

---

disk
n. 唱片；碟片；圓盤狀的東西

🔊 *Track 1149*

What do you want to be when you grow up?
你長大後想當什麼？

I want to be a **disk** jockey.
我想當一個 DJ。

---

dramatic
adj. 戲劇性的

🔊 *Track 1150*

I've been arrested once, divorced twice, and bankrupted four times.
我被逮捕過一次，離婚兩次，還有破產四次。

Your live is extremely **dramatic**.
你的人生超級戲劇化的耶！

---

draw
v. 拉；拖；提取；畫；繪製

🔊 *Track 1151*

Are you **drawing** your grandmother?
你在畫你的奶奶嗎？

You're rude! This is my girlfriend!
你真失禮！我是在畫我女朋友！

---

drum
v. 敲打
n. 鼓

🔊 *Track 1152*

What's your position in the band?
你在樂團玩什麼樂器？

I play the **drums**.
我是鼓手。

這裡使用的是名詞喔！

DVD
n. 影音光碟

🔊 *Track 1153*

Nowadays everyone watches **DVD** and HD.
現在大家都在看 DVD 跟 HD 了。

My family still watch VHS occasionally.
我家偶爾還是會看錄影帶。

earphone
n. 耳機

Track 1154

🧑 Oh! I can't concentrate because of the noise.
噢！都是那噪音害我不能專心。

👧 Here is an **earphone**. Wear it.
這裡有耳機，戴上它吧。

enjoyable
adj. 快樂的；放鬆的

Track 1155

🧑 Making snacks is really **enjoyable**.
做點心真的很好玩。

👧 Right. Especially when the snacks are tasty.
對啊，尤其是當你做出好吃的點心時。

enjoyment
n. 享受；愉快

Track 1156

🧑 Why do you guys dress so cute today?
你們今天怎麼打扮得這麼可愛？

👧 Just for **enjoyment**.
就感覺開心囉。

entertain
v. 招待；娛樂；接受

Track 1157

🧑 What did you prepare to **entertain** your friends?
你準備了什麼招待朋友？

👧 There's Wii and some snacks.
一台 Wii 跟一些點心。

entertainment
n. 款待；娛樂

Track 1158

🧑 Sorry, there are few **entertainments** in this village.
抱歉，這個村子沒什麼娛樂。

👧 It's alright. Let's take a walk.
沒關係，我們就散步吧。

enthusiasm
n. 熱情

Track 1159

🧑 Only with great **enthusiasm** can you be qualified for this work.
你必須有強大的熱情才能勝任這個工作。

👧 I will bear that in mind.
我會謹記在心的。

expressive
adj. 意味深長的

🔊 *Track 1160*

👦 Did the man you like give you any response?
你喜歡的那個男生有給你任何回應嗎？

👧 No, he just gave me an **expressive** eyesight.
不，他只給了我一個意味深長的眼神。

fabulous
adj. 傳說中的；極好的

🔊 *Track 1161*

👦 Is that the **fabulous** actor?
那是那位超棒的演員嗎？

👧 Probably. Maybe he's here for the charity activity.
大概吧。他應該是為了這個慈善活動來的。

fad
n. 一時的流行

🔊 *Track 1162*

👦 I haven't seen you wear snow boots for a while.
我有一陣子沒看妳穿雪靴了。

👧 Come on. That's not a **fad** anymore.
拜託，那已經不流行了好嗎？

fake
v. 仿造
adj. 假的
n. 冒牌者

🔊 *Track 1163*

👦 The diamond you received is **fake**.
你收到的那顆鑽石是假的。

👧 You kidding! How do you know that?
開玩笑的吧！你怎麼知道？

> 這裡使用的是形容詞喔！

fan
n. 粉絲；風扇
v. 扇動

🔊 *Track 1164*

👦 I used to be a super big **fan** of Michael Jackson.
我以前是麥可傑克森的超級粉絲。

👧 So you must feel sad when he passed away.
那他去世的時候你一定很難過。

> 這裡使用的是名詞喔！

film
n. 電影；膠捲
v. 拍攝

🔊 *Track 1165*

👦 I saw more than five hundred **films** when I was in college.
我在大學時看了超過五百部電影。

👧 You're really a movie buff!
你還真是個電影狂！

> 這裡使用的是名詞喔！

firework
n. 煙火

Track 1166

🧑 **Firework** Festival will be held in Taipei this year.
今年的煙火節會在台北舉行。

👩 Well, then we can just stay at home to see **firework** this year.
那我們今年在家就可以看到煙火了。

flute
n. 橫笛

Track 1167

🧑 Which instrument will you play in music class?
你音樂課要演奏什麼樂器？

👩 **Flute**. It seems the easiest.
長笛。那個感覺是最簡單的。

full
adj. 滿的；充滿的；（飽的）

Track 1168

🧑 The room we're gonna live is **full** of odds and ends.
我們要住的房間堆滿了雜物。

👩 Shall we empty some space first?
我們要不要先清出一些空間？

fun
n. 樂趣；玩笑
adj. 有趣的

Track 1169

👩 My husband and I will take a trip to Hawaii.
我和我老公要去夏威夷旅行。

🧑 How nice! Enjoy your trip and have **fun**.
好棒哦！祝你們玩的開心。

這裡使用的是名詞喔！

funny
adj. 滑稽的、有趣的

Track 1170

🧑 Did you see Alan today? He looked so **funny** today.
你今天有看到愛倫嗎？他今天看起來超好笑的。

👩 Ha! I know, He lost half of his eyebrows!
哈我知道！他眉毛有一半不見了！

gallery
n. 畫廊；美術館

Track 1171

Please describe your present career.
請描述一下你現在的工作。

I'm a painter and I own a **gallery**.
我是個畫家，而且有一間畫廊。

gamble
v. 賭博

Track 1172

Stop **gambling**, or I will leave you one day.
不要再賭博了，不然我總有一天會離開你。

Just one more, OK? I will win this time.
再一次就好了，可以嗎？我這次會贏的。

game
n. 遊戲、比賽

Track 1173

Are you interested in NBA?
你對 NBA 有興趣嗎？

Absolutely. That's the most exciting basketball **game** on earth.
有啊，那是世界上最令人興奮的籃球比賽了。

garden
n. 花園

Track 1174

I want a **garden** behind our new house.
我希望我們的新家後面有個花園。

No problem, what do you want to plant?
沒問題，你想在裡面種什麼？

grab
v. 急抓；搶奪

Track 1175

I am afraid of falling down.
我很怕掉下去。

You just need to **grab** my hand tightly.
你只要緊緊抓著我的手就好了。

group
n. 團體；組；群
v. 聚集

Track 1176

Mom, I will go riding with a **group** of my friends.
媽，我要跟一群朋友去騎腳踏車。

Take care. Be punctual for dinner.
小心點，準時回來吃晚飯啊。

這裡使用的是名詞喔！

guitar
n. 吉他

Track 1177

I think Jimmy Hendrix is the greatest **guitar** player.
我覺得吉米漢醉克斯是最厲害的吉他手。

You bet, he is the king of rock **guitar**.
沒錯,他是搖滾吉他之神。

haircut
n. 理髮

Track 1178

I wanna have a **haircut**, any suggestion?
我想去理髮,有什麼好意見嗎?

You can choose a sweet short hairstyle.
你可以剪個甜美的短髮。

hangover
n. 宿醉

Track 1179

Why did you leave the office?
你怎麼離開辦公室了?

I had a terrible **hangover**, could you help to ask for leave?
我嚴重宿醉了,你可以幫我請個假嗎?

harmonica
n. 口琴

Track 1180

Whenever I hear the sound of **harmonica**, all the pain vanishes.
每次我聽到口琴的聲音,所有痛苦就不見了。

The sound is really healing.
口琴的聲音真的很療癒人心。

horn
n. 喇叭

Track 1181

Can you stop sounding the **horn**?
你可以不要再按喇叭了嗎?

But if I stop, all the pedestrians keep jaywalking.
我不按的話,所有行人就會繼續一直違規過馬路了。

humor
n. 詼諧;幽默

Track 1182

What do you think about our teacher?
你覺得我們老師怎麼樣?

She is a person with sense of **humor**.
她很有幽默感。

233

humorous
adj. 幽默的；滑稽的

Track 1183

How do you catch your audience's attention during a lecture?
你在演講時怎麼抓注觀眾的注意力？

I always weave some **humorous** stories from time to time.
我都會不時穿插一些幽默的故事。

idol
n. 偶像

Track 1184

You know what happened yesterday?
你知道昨天發生什麼事嗎？

I've heard, you had a meal with your **idol**, right?
我知道，你昨天跟你的偶像吃飯，對吧？

illusion
n. 錯覺；幻覺

Track 1185

Do you see a girl wearing a red dress standing over there?
你有看到一個穿紅色洋裝的女生站在那裡嗎？

No, that's your **illusion**.
沒有啊，那是你的幻覺吧。

image
n. 影像；形象

Track 1186

The **image** of this video is not clear.
這影片的影像不是很清楚。

Ok, I'll show you the other one.
好，我換另外一段影片給你看好了。

imagination
n. 想像力；創作力

Track 1187

My girl is full of **imagination**. She talks nonsense all day.
我女兒很有想像力，整天都在胡說八道。

It doesn't matter. All kids behave like this.
沒關係，每個小孩都一樣。

imagine
v. 想像；設想

Track 1188

Can you **imagine** a world without laughter?
你可以想像一個沒有笑聲的世界嗎？

Thanks to endless tests, I'm living in such a world now.
多虧了永無止境的考試，我現在已經活在這種世界了。

impress
v. 深刻印象；使感動

Track 1189

Her beauty and politeness really **impress** me.
她的美貌和禮儀真的很讓我印象深刻。

If you like her, go get her.
如果你喜歡她，就去追她啊。

impressive
adj. 印象深刻的

Track 1190

Very **impressive** performance.
很讓人印象深刻的表演。

Thank you very much. I'm honored.
謝謝，我很榮幸。

introduce
v. 介紹；引進

Track 1191

Thanks for **introducing** your sister to me.
謝謝你介紹你妹妹給我。

Piece of cake. How have you been recently?
沒什麼。你們最近如何？

invitation
n. 請帖；邀請

Track 1192

I sent an **invitation** to Ring but she didn't reply.
我寄請帖給玲了，但她沒有答覆我。

Maybe she didn't receive it.
或許她還沒收到。

invite
v. 邀請；招待

Track 1193

I won't **invite** Patrick to my birthday party.
我不會邀請派翠克來我的生日派對。

What happened between you two?
你們之間發生什麼事了？

instrument
n. 樂器；器具

Track 1194

The sound of this **instrument** is weird.
這樂器的聲音好奇怪。

It's a traditional Japanese musical instrument, called Shamisen.
這是一種日本傳統樂器，叫三味線。

interest

n. 興趣；嗜好；利益；利息

v. 使感興趣

🔊 *Track 1195*

Actually, I don't have any special **interests**.
其實，我並沒有什麼特別的興趣。

To most of people, martial art is a very very special interest.
對大部份的人來説，練武術是個非常非常特別的興趣。

這裡使用的是名詞喔！

jazz

n. 爵士樂

🔊 *Track 1196*

My father is an excellent **jazz** player.
我爸是個很優秀的爵士樂手。

I love **jazz**! Can you introduce your father to me?
我愛爵士樂！你可以介紹你爸給我嗎？

joke

n. 笑話；玩笑

v. 玩笑

🔊 *Track 1197*

The **joke** Josh told made us laugh very hard.
賈許講的笑話害我們笑的肚子好痛。

Really? Then I'll ask him to tell me again.
真的嗎？那我要叫他再講一次給我聽。

這裡使用的是名詞喔！

lantern

n. 燈籠

🔊 *Track 1198*

While I was a child, I always hold a lantern hanging around on **Lantern** Festival.
我小時候都會在元宵節提著燈籠亂晃。

Ha, you must have scared many passers-by.
哈，你一定嚇到很多路人了。

laugh

n. 笑；笑聲

v. 笑；（嘲笑）

🔊 *Track 1199*

Don't **laugh** so loud, you'll wake your mother.
別笑這麼大聲，會把你媽吵醒。

Sorry, dad, I just can't stop!
抱歉，老爸，我就是忍不住！

這裡使用的是動詞喔！

laughter

n. 笑聲

🔊 *Track 1200*

I heard **laughter** from the empty room.
我聽到那間空房間傳出笑聲。

Don't scare me, I'm timid!
別嚇我，我很膽小！

listen
v. 聽

🔊 *Track 1201*

👦 I am always a good listener.
我一直都是個好聽眾。

👧 Liar! You never **listen** to what I say!
騙人！你從來都沒聽我講話啊！

lottery
n. 樂透彩

🔊 *Track 1202*

👦 I heard that you won a **lottery** last week.
我聽說你上禮拜贏了一張樂透彩。

👧 That was not true. Who told you that?
那不是真的，是誰跟你說的？

loud
adj. 大聲的；響亮的
adv. 大聲的；響亮的

🔊 *Track 1203*

👦 Janet's voice is really **loud**.
珍娜的聲音真的很大聲。

👧 Yeah, sometime it's intolerant.
對，有時候真的很難以忍受。

> 這裡使用的是形容詞喔！

low
adj. 低聲的；低的
adv. 低的

🔊 *Track 1204*

👦 Tell you a secret about Jane.
跟你說個跟珍有關的祕密。

👧 Then your voice should be **low**, cause she's right behind us.
那你聲音要小一點，她就在我們的後面。

> 這裡使用的是形容詞喔！

magazine
n. 雜誌

🔊 *Track 1205*

👧 I've subscribed to Voce for a year.
我訂了一年份的 Voce 了。

👧 You mean the beauty **magazine**? Then, can I borrow yours every month?
你說那本美容雜誌嗎？那我可以每個月都跟你借嗎？

magic
n. 魔術
adj. 有魔力的

🔊 *Track 1206*

👦 I practice **magic** tricks everyday.
我每天都在練習魔術。

👧 Oh, I know, you want to attract girls, don't you?
噢，我知道，你要去把妹對不對？

> 這裡使用的是名詞喔！

magical
adj. 魔術的;神奇的

Track 1207

Do you know what just happened?
你知道剛剛發生什麼事了嗎?

A bird flew from her mouth! That's **magical**!
一隻鳥從她嘴巴飛了出來!太神奇了!

mall
n. 購物中心

Track 1208

We need to buy some daily necessities.
我們必須買生活用品了。

Let's go to a shopping **mall** this afternoon.
我們下午去購物中心吧。

medium
n. 媒體
adj. 中等的

Track 1209

The **medium** said you were bribed by the gangland.
有媒體說你被黑社會收買了。

Believe me, that was not true.
相信我,那不是真的。

這裡使用的是名詞喔!

melody
n. 旋律

Track 1210

The **melody** is beautiful.
這旋律真美。

You like it? This is my own song.
你喜歡嗎?這是我自己寫的歌。

membership
n. 會員

Track 1211

How much does a **membership** cost?
會員費要多少?

50,000 dollars a year, Sir.
一年五萬元,先生。

memory
n. 記憶;回憶

Track 1212

What's the best **memory** of your life?
你一生中最美好的回憶是什麼?

The time when I broke up with my ex-boyfriend.
跟我前男友手的時候。

microphone
n. 麥克風

Track 1213

Please set up the **microphone**. I'm going to give the lecture.
請架一下麥克風，我要開始上課了。

I can't find the **microphone**, professor.
教授，我找不到麥克風耶。

model
n. 模型；模特兒

Track 1214

I think Vivian is the top **model** in Taiwan.
我覺得薇薇安是台灣最頂尖的模特兒。

She isn't, it's Elle!
不是她，是艾兒！

music
n. 音樂

Track 1215

Do you listen to **music** while reading books?
你會邊聽音樂邊看書嗎？

Sure, I always do.
對啊，我都這樣。

musical
adj. 音樂的
n. 音樂劇

Track 1216

How was your **musical** competition?
你的音樂比賽怎麼樣了？

Very terrible, cause I forgot to bring my violin bow.
超糟的，我忘了帶我的小提琴弓。

> 這裡使用的是形容詞喔！

MV/music video
n. 音樂錄影帶

Track 1217

I want to see the **music video** you showed me yesterday.
我想看你昨天秀給我看的 MV。

Sorry, I've deleted it.
抱歉，我已經把它刪掉了。

news
n. 新聞；消息

Track 1218

Justin Bieber is going to hold a concert in Taiwan!
小賈斯汀要來台灣開演唱會耶！

How did you know the **news**?
你怎麼知道這個消息？

noise
n. 喧鬧聲；噪音；聲音

🔊 *Track 1219*

The **noise** is everywhere.
這裡到處是噪音。

Let's hurry up and get out of here.
我們動作快一點然後離開這裡吧。

noisy
adj. 吵鬧的

🔊 *Track 1220*

Darling, I can't bear this **noisy** street anymore.
親愛的，我再也受不了這條吵鬧的街道了。

Let's move to somewhere quiet.
我們搬去安靜的地方住吧。

novel
n. 小說
adj. 新穎的

🔊 *Track 1221*

I can't stop crying while reading the novel.
我在讀那本小說的時候哭到停不下來。

You are too sentimental. And by the way, that's a funny **novel**!
你太多愁善感了吧。而且，那是一本爆笑小說！

> 這裡使用的是名詞喔！

opera
n. 歌劇

🔊 *Track 1222*

I don't know how to appreciate an **opera**.
我不知道該怎麼欣賞歌劇。

I can teach you some tips. Next time we can go see an opera together.
我可以教你一些方法，下次我們一起去看歌劇吧。

orchestra
n. 樂隊；樂團

🔊 *Track 1223*

I've seen the performance of London Philharmonic **Orchestra** before.
我以前看過倫敦愛樂交響樂團的表演。

You have? How did you like it?
你看過？那你覺得怎麼樣？

outfit
n. 裝備
v. 裝備

🔊 *Track 1224*

I bought a sport **outfit** yesterday.
我昨天買了運動裝。

What did you buy that for? You never exercise.
你買那幹麻？你又不運動。

> 這裡使用的是名詞喔！

outlet
n. 暢貨中心

◀ *Track 1225*

Have you ever bought items from **outlet**?
你有在暢貨中心買過東西嗎？

No, the quality of those items is lower.
沒，那些東西的品質都比較不好。

painting
n. 繪畫

◀ *Track 1226*

Excuse me, I don't really know what it is.
不好意思，我真的不知道這是什麼。

It is an abstract **painting**.
這是一幅抽象畫啊。

palace
n. 宮殿

◀ *Track 1227*

I can't believe there are so many servants in this **palace**.
我不敢相信這座宮殿居然會有這麼多僕人！

Neither can I! The king has countless servants!
我也不能！這個國王有數不完的僕人！

paper
n. 紙；報紙；（論文）

◀ *Track 1228*

He is doing a job of morning **paper** delivery.
他現在的工作是送早報。

What's his former job? Did he quit?
他之前的工作呢？辭掉了嗎？

parachute
v. 跳傘
n. 降落傘

◀ *Track 1229*

Can you believe Verna dare go **parachuting** alone?
你相信芙兒娜敢一個人去跳傘嗎？

Well, I bet she dare.
這個嘛，我猜她敢。

這裡使用的是動名詞喔！

parade
n. 遊行
v. 遊行

◀ *Track 1230*

The **parade** will last till 11 o'clock.
這個遊行會持續到11點。

Then we can't see the whole **parade**. We have to go home early.
那我們就無法看完整個遊行了，我們得早點到家。

這裡使用的是名詞喔！

241

party
n. 派對
v. 狂歡

Track 1231

What will you dress to the Halloween **party** tonight?
你今天晚上要穿什麼去萬聖節派對？

I'll be a vampire, how about you?
我會扮成吸血鬼，你呢？

這裡使用的是名詞喔！

pastime
n. 消遣

Track 1232

Fishing is my favorite **pastime**.
釣魚是我最喜歡的消遣。

Come on, you're like an old man!
拜託，你好像老人哦！

perform
v. 表演

Track 1233

The show was **performed** terrifically well!
這個表演真的超極棒的！

Of course it's the best circus in the world!
當然啦，這是全世界最棒的馬戲團！

performance
n. 演出；（表現）

Track 1234

Where is the next stop of the **performance**?
下次在哪裡會有這場表演？

I don't know very well. You'd better ask the staff.
我不太清楚，你最好問一下工作人員。

photograph
n. 照片
v. 攝影

Track 1235

Tell me the truth, who is the woman in the **photograph**?
跟我說實話，這照片上面的女人是誰？

I've told you one hundred times, that's my sister.
我跟你說過一百次了，那是我姐姐。

這裡使用的是名詞喔！

piano
n. 鋼琴

Track 1236

Lisa is good at playing **piano** and guitar.
麗莎很會彈鋼琴跟吉他。

Sounds like she's very talented in music.
感覺她很有音樂才華。

picture
n. 圖片；相片
v. 想象

◀️ *Track 1237*

Why is there a spot on the **picture**?
為什麼這圖片上有污點？

I accidentally dropped ink on it.
我不小心把墨汁滴了上去。

 這裡使用的是名詞喔！

---

picturesque
adj. 如畫的

◀️ *Track 1238*

Do you remember the **picturesque** mountain?
你記得那座像畫一樣漂亮的山嗎？

You mean the one located in Northern Italy?
你說在義大利北邊的那個嗎？

---

pirate
v. 盜版；剽竊
n. 海盜

◀️ *Track 1239*

My best friend **pirated** my composition. What shall I do?
我最好的朋友剽竊了我的作品，我該怎麼辦？

Forgive him, or get a lawyer and sue him.
原諒他，或者你要找個律師然後控告他。

 這裡使用的是動詞喔！

---

play
n. 玩耍；（戲劇）
v. 遊戲；玩耍；（吹奏）

◀️ *Track 1240*

Jill, let's **play** Super Mario!
吉兒，我們來玩超級瑪利歐！

Alright, but after I finish my homework.
是可以，不過要等我寫完功課。

 這裡使用的是動詞喔！

---

playground
n. 運動場；遊戲場

◀️ *Track 1241*

A girl got serious injured on the **playground**!
有個女生在運動場受了重傷！

Did anybody call an ambulance?
有沒有人叫救護車了？

---

plot
n. 陰謀；情節
v. 陰謀

◀️ *Track 1242*

The movie's **plot** is too complicated to figure out.
這部電影的情結太複雜了，我完全無法理解。

That's only because you didn't pay attention to the movie.
那是因為你沒有認真看電影。

 這裡使用的是名詞喔！

243

poetry
n. 詩；詩集

Track 1243

I can recite all the **poetry** of Wordsworth.
我可以背出所有華茲華斯的詩。

You have a pretty good memory.
你的記憶力很好。

pop
adj. 流行的

Track 1244

You know Lady Gaga?
妳知道女神卡卡嗎？

Absolutely! She is the most crazy **pop** star on earth!
當然啊！她是世界上最瘋狂的流行歌手！

portrait
n. 肖像

Track 1245

The **portrait** of my grandfather was stolen!
我爺爺的肖像被偷走了！

That's ridiculous! I can't imagine who would steal that!!
太好笑了吧！我想不到誰會偷那種東西啊！

poster
n. 海報

Track 1246

Wow, you post so many *Rocky*'s **posters** on your wall.
哇，你在牆上貼了好多《洛基》的海報。

I've collected them since childhood.
我從小時候就開始就開始收集了。

print
n. 印跡；印刷字體；版
v. 印刷

Track 1247

The words **printed** here are too small.
印在這裡的字太小了。

I think it's acceptable.
我覺得可以接受啊。

這裡使用的是動詞喔！

program
n. 節目；程式

Track 1248

Did you see the **program** last night?
你昨天有看那節目嗎？

No, but I can see the record on the Internet.
沒有，不過我可以在網路上看錄影。

puppet
n. 木偶；傀儡

🔈 *Track 1249*

👦 Allan Davis is a brilliant enterpriser.
艾倫戴維斯是個傑出的企業家。

👧 No he's not. He's just a **puppet** of his father.
他才不是，他只是他爸爸的傀儡。

radio
n. 收音機

🔈 *Track 1250*

👦 Would you please turn on the **radio**?
你可以打開收音機嗎？

👧 No way, you're driving now and I need you to concentrate!
不行，你現在在開車，我要你專心！

rehearsal
n. 排演

🔈 *Track 1251*

👦 It's almost time for **rehearsal**.
排演的時間快到了。

👧 But Amy is not here, can anybody call her?
但是艾咪不在這裡，有誰可以打電話給她嗎？

record
n. 紀錄；唱片
v. 紀錄

🔈 *Track 1252*

👦 Tell you something, the baseball player breaks the world **records**!
跟你說，那個棒球選手破世界紀錄了！

👧 I'm not surprised. He's always an outstanding player.
我不驚訝，他一直是一個很優秀的選手。

> 這裡使用的是名詞喔！

recreation
n. 娛樂

🔈 *Track 1253*

👦 Do you think doing exercise is a **recreation**?
你認為運動是一種娛樂嗎？

👧 Not at all. I hate exercise.
才不呢，我討厭運動。

relax
v. 放鬆

🔈 *Track 1254*

👦 I'm exhausted!
我快要累死了！

👧 You can **relax** a while, just five minutes.
你可以休息一下，但只有五分鐘。

resort
n. 休閒勝地

🔊 *Track 1255*

This wasteland will become a **resort** one day.
這塊荒地以後會變成休閒勝地。

How do you know that?
你怎麼知道？

restrict
v. 限制

🔊 *Track 1256*

Don't **restrict** me, I'm not your puppet.
別再限制我了，我不是你的玩偶。

Oh dear, it's all for your own good.
噢親愛的，這完全是為了你好啊。

rhythm
n. 節奏；韻律

🔊 *Track 1257*

The little girl is so cute!
那個小女生好可愛！

Yeah, especially when she dances with the **rhythm**.
對啊，尤其是她跟著節奏跳舞的時候。

riddle
n. 謎語

🔊 *Track 1258*

Guess the **riddle**: what can't be used unless broken?
猜個謎語：什麼東西要破了以後才能使用？

Let me think…is it egg?
讓我想想……是蛋嗎？

rock
v. 搖動
n. 搖滾樂；（岩石）

🔊 *Track 1259*

If you like **rock** music, then you should know Guns and Roses.
如果你喜歡搖滾樂，你應該就知道槍與玫瑰吧。

I know them very well!
我可知道的清楚咧！

這裡使用的是名詞喔！

role
n. 角色

🔊 *Track 1260*

What's your **role** in the play?
你在這齣劇的角色是什麼？

A gay man who lives with a group of women.
跟一群女人同居的同性戀男子。

saloon
n. 酒店;酒吧

Track 1261

How about go to the **saloon** and have a drink?
要不要去酒吧喝個酒?

No thanks, I'm a little bit tired.
不謝了,我有一點累。

sanctuary
n. 聖所;聖堂;庇護所

Track 1262

I need somewhere to commit my spirit, a **sanctuary**.
我需要某個地方寄託我的心靈,一個聖堂那樣的地方。

Maybe what you really need is just a box of chocolate.
也許你要的只是一盒巧克力而已。

scene
n. 戲劇的一場;風景

Track 1263

The **scene** is too impressive to forget!
那一幕戲真是太另人難忘了!

You mean when the killer tried to say I love you to the girl?
你說的是那個殺手要向女孩告白的那一幕嗎?

scenery
n. 風景;景色

Track 1264

I will never forget the **scenery** of this place.
我永遠不會忘記這個地方的景色。

I hope you won't, because this is the first place we met.
我希望你記得,因為這是我們第一次相識的地方。

script
n. 原稿;劇本

Track 1265

Are you crazy? Why are you throwing away the **script**?
你瘋了嗎?為什麼要把劇本丟掉啊?

It's not good enough. I'll write a new one.
寫得不夠好,我要寫個新的。

sculpture

n. 雕刻；雕塑；雕像
v. 雕塑

Track 1266

My goodness, are you the one who broke the **sculpture**?
天啊，就是你打破雕像的嗎？

I'm sorry…I didn't mean it.
我很抱歉……我不是故意的。

這裡使用的是名詞喔！

seesaw

n. 翹翹板

Track 1267

How many **seesaws** are there in the No.4 park?
四號公園裡有幾個翹翹板？

I have no idea, you can ask those children.
不知道，你可以去問那些小孩。

shore

n. 岸；濱

Track 1268

My house is located by a **shore**.
我家就住在海岸邊。

Sounds wonderful. The view must be very beautiful.
聽起來很棒，視野一定很好。

show

n. 秀；表演
v. 秀；（展示）

Track 1269

What if the **show** is terrible?
如果表演很難看怎麼辦？

Just relax and enjoy the show!
你就放輕鬆然後好好享受這場表演吧！

這裡使用的是名詞喔！

shrine

n. 廟；祠

Track 1270

My grandmother used to pray at the **shrine** every morning.
我奶奶以前每天早上都會去廟裡拜拜。

Then why doesn't she do that anymore?
那她為什麼現在不這麼做了？

sightseeing

n. 觀光；遊覽

Track 1271

I'm planning to do **sightseeing** in Egypt.
我正計劃要去埃及觀光。

Will you go alone or with your friends?
你要自己去還是跟朋友去？

sign
n. 記號；標誌
v. 簽署

🔊 *Track 1272*

👦 If anybody finds anything, make a **sign** on the wall.
如果任何人發現了任何東西，就在牆上做記號。

👧 Roger!
收到！

這裡使用的是名詞喔！

---

sociable
adj. 愛交際的；社交的

🔊 *Track 1273*

👦 I have a **sociable** personality.
我的個性很愛社交。

👧 I can tell, we will be good friends then.
看得出來，那我們可以當好朋友。

---

song
n. 歌曲

🔊 *Track 1274*

👦 Hello, this is ICRT, which **song** do you want to request?
哈嚕，這裡是 ICRT 電台，你想要點播什麼歌？

👧 "Crazy in Love" by Beyonce.
碧昂絲的「瘋狂的愛」。

---

sound
n. 聲音
v. 聽起來
adj. 完好的

🔊 *Track 1275*

👦 Stop making the disgusting **sound**, please.
請你不要再製造那個噁心的聲音了。

👧 Sorry, just one more minute.
抱歉，再一分鐘就好。

這裡使用的是名詞喔！

---

souvenir
n. 紀念品；特產

🔊 *Track 1276*

👦 I bought some **souvenirs** from Thailand for you.
我從泰國買了些紀念品給你。

👧 Thank you! They are beautiful!
謝謝！它們好漂亮哦！

---

spectacle
n. 奇觀

🔊 *Track 1277*

👦 The building is designed by the legendary architect.
這棟建築物是由那個傳奇建築師設計的。

👧 No wonder it is a **spectacle**.
難怪它會是個奇觀。

spectacular
n. 大場面
adj. 壯觀的

Sorry, my son never sees such a **spectacular**. He's frightened.
抱歉，我兒子從來沒看過這種大場面，他嚇壞了。

That's OK. Take him somewhere for a rest.
沒關係，帶他去旁邊休息吧。

這裡使用的是名詞喔！

spot
n. 汙點；地點
v. 識別

There's a **spot** on the floor.
地板上有個污點。

Ask the servant to clean it.
叫僕人去弄乾淨。

這裡使用的是名詞喔！

statue
n. 鑄像；雕像

We intend to build a marble **statue** on the center of the city.
我們打算在市中心蓋一座大理石雕像。

What's the shape of the **statue** going to be?
那雕像的外形會是什麼？

story
n. 故事

Tell me more **stories** about you and your boyfriend.
多跟我説一點妳跟妳男朋友的事。

Nothing special.
沒有什麼特別的啊。

subscribe
v. 捐助；訂閱；預訂

Hey, miss, would you like to **subscribe** *Times* for a year?
嗨小姐，妳想不想訂閱一年份的《時代雜誌》？

Not interested, thanks.
沒興趣，謝謝。

surf
n. 衝浪

What did you do this summer? You are so dark!
你夏天做了什麼事？你看起來很黑！

I went **surfing** every weekend.
我每個週末都去衝浪。

symphony

n. 交響樂；交響曲

Track 1284

I have two tickets for a **symphony** concert.
我有兩張交響樂音樂會的票。

You don't look like the guy who likes classic music.
你看起來不像會喜歡古典音樂的人。

theater

n. 戲院；劇場

Track 1285

Do you want to go to the **theater** tomorrow?
你明天想要去看電影嗎？

I'll think about it.
讓我考慮一下。

thriller

n. 恐怖小說；恐怖電影

Track 1286

I really dare not to watch a **thriller**.
我真的不敢看恐怖片。

What are you afraid of? They are all fake.
你在怕什麼？他們都是假的啊。

vogue

n. 時尚；流行物

Track 1287

I bet the hairstyle will become a **vogue** sooner or later.
我覺得這個髮型遲早會流行起來。

You sure? It looks weird!
你確定嗎？它看起來很怪耶！

I bet the hairstyle will become a vogue sooner or later.

Part

07

"家庭與社會"

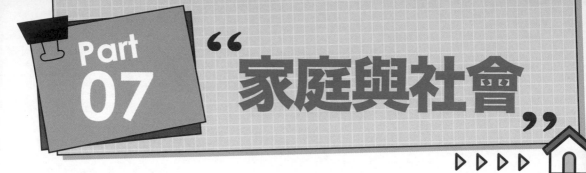

要學就學最實用的英文單字，搭配最稀鬆平常的生活對話，馬上就知道外國人都是這樣用這個單字的囉！＊單字、對話分開錄音，學習目標更明確

abandon
v. 放棄；拋棄

◀ *Track 1288*

The orphan was **abandoned** by his parents.
那個孤兒從小就被他的父母所拋棄

That's such a terrible thing to do!
那是多麼糟糕的一件事呀！

---

abide
v. 容忍；忍耐

◀ *Track 1289*

I can't **abide** her bad attitude anymore.
我再也不能忍受她糟糕的態度了。

Neither can I.
我也不能。

---

accessible
adj. 容易接近的

◀ *Track 1290*

The drugs should not be **accessible** to kids.
藥品不應該很容易被孩童取得。

I always put them high enough that they can't reach.
我總是把它們放在夠高的地方，讓他們拿不到。

---

acquaintance
n. 認識的人；熟人

◀ *Track 1291*

Do you know Jennifer?
你認識珍妮佛嗎？

Of course, she's an **acquaintance** of mine.
當然，她是我的熟人。

---

adopt
v. 收養

◀ *Track 1292*

My sister **adopted** an orphan yesterday.
我姊姊昨天收養了一個孤兒。

Wow, what a kind-hearted person.
哇！多麼有愛心的人。

adore
v. 崇拜；喜愛

Track 1293

I **adore** playing basketball.
我喜歡打籃球。

Me too.
我也是。

adulthood
n. 成年期

Track 1294

Happy Birthday Jason! Congratulation you reached **adulthood**.
生日快樂傑森！恭喜你成年了。

Thanks a lot.
多謝。

advise
v. 勸告

Track 1295

I **advise** you to go to sleep immediately.
我建議你馬上去睡覺。

Yeah, I have to get up early tomorrow.
對呀，我明天還要早起。

affection
n. 親情；情愛；愛慕

Track 1296

Linda can't hide her **affection** to Terry.
琳達藏不住對泰瑞的愛慕。

Even I can see that too.
就連我也看得出來。

affectionate
adj. 摯愛的

Track 1297

My mother is very **affectionate** to me.
我媽媽非常的愛我。

So be good to her.
所以對她好一點。

affirm
v. 斷言；證實

Track 1298

It's **affirmed** that the school is out for next week.
確定學校下個禮拜不上課了。

Wow! I can't wait to take a break and have fun.
哇！我等不及要休息一下然後好好玩了。

afford
v. 給予；供給；能負擔

Track 1299

I can't **afford** that much to buy a car.
我沒辦法負擔那麼多去買一輛車。

Maybe I can lend you some.
也許我可以借你一些。

---

against
prep. 反對；不同意

Track 1300

I'm **against** having sex before marriage.
我反對婚前性行為。

Interesting, tell me about your opinion.
有趣，說說你的看法。

---

agree
v. 同意；贊成

Track 1301

I totally **agree** Steven to study abroad.
我完全贊成史蒂芬出國念書。

Yeah! We should support him.
對呀，我們應該要支持他。

---

agreement
n. 同意；一致；協議

Track 1302

I Hope we can reach an **agreement** after today's conference.
希望我們能在今天的會議上達成一個協議。

Me too.
我也是。

---

alike
adj. 相似的；相同的
adv. 相似地；相同地

Track 1303

Wilson and Jim are so **alike**!
威爾森和吉姆真是太像了。

No wonder they are brothers.
難怪他們是兄弟。

這裡使用的是形容詞喔！

---

allow
v. 允許；准許

Track 1304

I'm **allowed** to take some days off from work.
我被允許放幾天假不用工作。

Wow, How nice.
哇！多麼好呀。

---

annoy
v. 煩擾；使惱怒

Track 1305

The fly is so **annoying** around here.
那些在附近的蒼蠅好煩。

I hate bugs.
我討厭蟲子。

apologize
v. 道歉；認錯

Track 1306

I **apologize** for yelling at you yesterday.
我為昨天對你大吼而道歉。

Never mind, it's alright.
別在意，沒關係。

application
n. 應用；申請

Track 1307

Photoshop is such an useful **application** software to use.
Photoshop 真是個有用的應用軟體。

Maybe you should teach me how to use it someday.
也許你應該找一天教教我。

appreciation
n. 賞識；鑑識

Track 1308

I really **appreciated** your hard work on this team report.
我很欣賞你在這個團隊報告上面的用心。

You're welcome.
不客氣。

approval
n. 承認；同意

Track 1309

I got the **approval** from my parents to take a trip to Japan by myself.
我爸媽同意我可以自己去日本旅行。

How badly I wish I could go along with you.
我多麼希望我可以跟你一起去。

arouse
v. 喚醒

Track 1310

The fierce dog was **aroused** by the sound.
那隻凶狠的狗被聲音所喚醒。

Let's stay away from it.
我們離牠遠一點。

assist
v. 援助

Track 1311

Tom, Can you give me some **assists** on this work?
湯姆，你可以在這個工作上幫我一下嗎？

Sure, I'll do my best.
當然好，我會盡我所能。

auntie
n. 伯母;姑;嬸;姨

Track 1312

Auntie Susan is going to visit us next Sunday.
蘇珊阿姨下個禮拜天要來拜訪我們。

I can't wait to see her.
我等不及要見她了。

---

awaken
v. 使……覺悟

Track 1313

Thanks for awaken me to pay more attention studying.
謝謝你使我覺悟,讓我更認真在課業上。

Don't mention about it.
別客氣。

---

award
n. 獎品;獎賞
v. 獎賞

Track 1314

Ken should get an award for all the contributions he did for the company.
阿肯應該要因為他多年來為公司的付出而得到獎賞。

Let's give him a gift on his retirement party.
我們在他的退休派對上送他禮物吧。

這裡使用的是名詞喔!

---

baby-sit
v. (臨時)照顧嬰孩

Track 1315

I baby-sit for my sister's child yesterday afternoon.
我昨天下午幫我姊姊照顧小孩。

It sounds like a big work to do.
聽起來像是個大工程。

---

bankrupt
adj. 破產的

Track 1316

The millionaire was bankrupted after the global economy crisis.
那位百萬富翁在全球金融危機後破產了。

I was shock when I heard the news.
我聽到消息時很震驚。

---

belong
v. 屬於

Track 1317

Who's the owner of this pen?
這支筆的主人是誰?

It belongs to Mike.
它為麥克所有。

belongings
adj. 所有物；財產

Track 1318

My house is one of my **belongings**.
房子是我的財產之一。

And it cost you a lot of money too.
它也花了你很多錢。

benefit
n. 益處；利益
v. 造福

Track 1319

Mary won't do a thing that she can't get **benefits** from.
瑪莉不做任何不能獲取利益的事。

What a selfish person she is.
她是個多自私的人呀。

這裡使用的是名詞喔！

blame
v. 責備
n. 責備

Track 1320

What's wrong with Alan?
艾倫發生什麼事了？

He was **blamed** by his Dad for skipping classes.
他因為翹課而被他父親責備。

這裡使用的是動詞喔！

bless
v. 祝福

Track 1321

I had an car accident this morning.
我早上出車禍了。

God **bless** you! What happened?
上帝保佑你！發生什麼事了？

bosom
adj. 知心的；親密的

Track 1322

Jenna and Olivia have been **bosom** friends for many years.
珍娜和奧莉薇亞當了多年的好友。

What a great friendship.
多麼好的一段友誼。

boy
n. 男孩

Track 1323

Who's Leon?
誰是李昂？

He's the **boy** right beside the door.
他是那個在門口旁的男孩。

boyhood

n. （男生的）少年期；童年

🔊 *Track 1324*

👦 How long have we been friends?
我們當朋友多久啦？

👦 I remember we met since **boyhood**.
我記得我們自從兒時就相識了。

break up

v. 分散；分手；瓦解

🔊 *Track 1325*

👦 The glass **broke up** into many tiny pieces on the floor.
那片玻璃在地板上碎裂成許多小碎片。

👧 Watch out not to step on it.
小心不要踩到它。

bribery

n. 行賄

🔊 *Track 1326*

👦 The candidate was accused for **bribery**.
那位候選人因為行賄而被起訴。

👧 I can't believe it.
我不敢相信。

bride

n. 新娘

🔊 *Track 1327*

👧 I'm going to be a **bride** tomorrow!
我明天就要當新娘了！

👦 Congratulations that you're finally going to be married.
恭喜妳終於要結婚啦。

bring

v. 帶來

🔊 *Track 1328*

👦 Why are you always praying?
你為什麼總是在祈禱？

👧 Because I believe it'll **bring** me good fortune.
因為我相信它將帶給我好運。

burden

n. 負荷；負擔
v. 負擔

🔊 *Track 1329*

👦 Will this **burden** you a lot?
這會造成你很大的負擔嗎？

👧 No, not at all.
不，完全不會。

這裡使用的是動詞喔！

case

n. 情形；情況；箱；案例

🔊 *Track 1330*

👦 We should carefully notice every **case** that may occur.
我們應該小心的注意每個可能會發生的情況。

👧 Sure, it's always better to be cautious.
當然，小心點總是比較好的。

a b c d e f g h i j k l m n o p q r s t u v w x y z

ceremony
n. 慶典；儀式

🔊 *Track 1331*

👦 Will you attend tonight's wedding **ceremony**?
你會出席今晚的婚禮嗎？

👧 Of course I will!
我當然會。

---

certificate
n. 證書；憑證
v. 證明

🔊 *Track 1332*

👦 You'll get a **certificate** after you have fully participated in this camp.
你會在全程參與這個營隊後得到一個證書。

👧 Thanks for mentioning about it.
謝謝你特別提到這點。

這裡使用的是名詞喔！

---

consideration
n. 考慮；（體貼）

🔊 *Track 1333*

👦 Haven't you decided yet?
你還沒決定好嗎？

👧 I'm still under some **consideration**.
我還在考慮當中。

---

conversation
n. 交談；談話

🔊 *Track 1334*

👦 Mrs. Jim wants to have a **conversation** with you.
吉姆太太想跟你談談。

👧 Got it.
知道了。

---

cost
n. 代價；費用
v. 價值

🔊 *Track 1335*

👦 How much is this?
這個多少？

👧 It **costs** ten thousand NT dollars.
一萬塊台幣。

這裡使用的是動詞喔！

---

couple
n. 配偶；一對

🔊 *Track 1336*

👦 They are such a great **couple**.
他們真的是很配的一對。

👧 I'm so jealous of them.
我好嫉妒他們。

---

cousin
n. 堂（表）兄弟姊妹

🔊 *Track 1337*

👦 Where did you go yesterday?
你昨晚去哪了？

👧 I went out for dinner with my **cousin**.
我和我表哥出去吃晚餐了。

criminal

adj. 犯罪的；刑事的
n. 罪犯

🔊 *Track 1338*

👦 The **criminal** was sentenced to a 5 years imprisonment.
那個罪犯被判處五年有期徒刑。

👧 He deserves it.
他罪有應得。

這裡使用的是名詞喔！

curiosity

n. 好奇心

🔊 *Track 1339*

👦 Kids are always full with **curiosity**.
小孩子總是充滿著好奇心。

👧 It seems like they are interested in everything!
他們彷彿對每件事情都有興趣。

curse

v. 詛咒；罵

🔊 *Track 1340*

👦 It's wrong to **curse** anybody.
罵任何人都是不對的。

👧 I know, but sometimes I still can't hold my temper.
我知道，但有時候我還是不能控制我的脾氣。

cute

adj. 可愛的；聰明伶俐的

🔊 *Track 1341*

👦 Jessie is popular among her class.
潔西在她的班上很受歡迎

👧 She's such a **cute** girl to make friends with.
她是個多麼可愛的女孩，大家都想跟她當朋友。

damn

v. 指責
adj. 討厭的
adv. 非常

🔊 *Track 1342*

👦 The captain **damned** his team members for not paying attention.
隊長指責他的隊員不專心。

👧 It's always important to stay focus when you are in a team.
在團隊合作中永遠要保持專注認真。

這裡使用的是動詞喔！

danger

n. 危險

🔊 *Track 1343*

👦 Don't drive too fast, you'll be in **danger**.
別開太快，很危險。

👧 Okay, I know.
好的，我知道。

darling
n. 親愛的人

Track 1344

Darling, would you pick me up at 4 o'clock in the afternoon?
親愛的，你能夠在下午四點接我嗎？

No problem.
沒問題。

daughter
n. 女兒

Track 1345

My grandmother has 8 **daughters**.
我的祖母有八個女兒。

That's a large number!
那真是個龐大的數目。

dear
adj. 昂貴的；親愛的
n. 親愛的人

Track 1346

I didn't mean to be late, my **dear**.
親愛的，我不是故意要遲到的。

I don't want to hear any excuses.
我不想要聽到任何藉口。

這裡使用的是名詞喔！

decide
v. 決定

Track 1347

I **decided** to buy this furniture.
我決定要買這個家具。

Do you have enough money?
你有足夠的錢嗎？

delinquency
n. 犯罪

Track 1348

Juvenile **delinquency** becomes a serious problem of our society.
青少年犯罪變成社會上很嚴重的問題。

Maybe we should keep an eye on our children's education.
也許我們應該注意我們孩童的教育。

depend
v. 依賴；依靠

Track 1349

You **depend** on Kevin too much.
你太依賴凱文了。

I know, he's such an important friend of mine.
我知道，他是我非常重要的一個朋友。

detail
n. 細節
v. 詳細描述

🔊 *Track 1350*

You should be careful when you shop online.
你在網路購物的時候應該要小心謹慎。

Okay, I'll pay attention to the **details**.
好的,我會注意細節的。

這裡使用的是名詞喔!

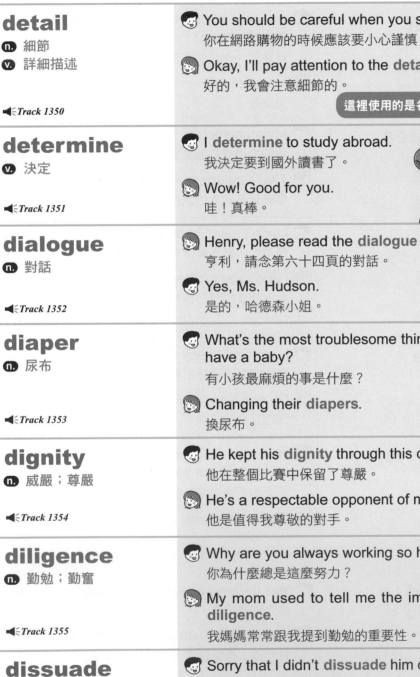

determine
v. 決定

🔊 *Track 1351*

I **determine** to study abroad.
我決定要到國外讀書了。

Wow! Good for you.
哇!真棒。

dialogue
n. 對話

🔊 *Track 1352*

Henry, please read the **dialogue** on page 64.
亨利,請念第六十四頁的對話。

Yes, Ms. Hudson.
是的,哈德森小姐。

diaper
n. 尿布

🔊 *Track 1353*

What's the most troublesome thing when you have a baby?
有小孩最麻煩的事是什麼?

Changing their **diapers**.
換尿布。

dignity
n. 威嚴;尊嚴

🔊 *Track 1354*

He kept his **dignity** through this competition.
他在整個比賽中保留了尊嚴。

He's a respectable opponent of mine.
他是值得我尊敬的對手。

diligence
n. 勤勉;勤奮

🔊 *Track 1355*

Why are you always working so hard?
你為什麼總是這麼努力?

My mom used to tell me the importance of **diligence**.
我媽媽常常跟我提到勤勉的重要性。

dissuade
v. 勸阻;勸止

🔊 *Track 1356*

Sorry that I didn't **dissuade** him on time.
抱歉我沒能及時勸阻他。

He's such a stubborn person.
他真是個頑固的人。

distinctive
adj. 個別的；獨特的

Track 1357

This place is **distinctive**.
這個地方好特別。

I wonder why we never noticed here.
我很好奇為什麼我們以前沒有注意到這裡。

distinguish
v. 辨別；分辨；區分

Track 1358

Do you know how to **distinguish** the species in this garden?
你知道怎麼分辨這花園內的物種嗎？

I don't think so, I'm not professional in this field.
我不知道，我不是這方面的專家。

divorce
v. 離婚；解除婚約
n. 離婚

Track 1359

Do you know Lillian and Edward **divorced** last week?
你知道莉莉安和艾德華上個禮拜離婚了嗎？

What a shocking news!
真是令人震驚的消息！

這裡使用的是動詞喔！

donate
v. 贈與；捐贈

Track 1360

Mr. Duncan **donated** a lot of money to the orphanage.
鄧肯先生捐了很多錢給孤兒院。

He's such a charitable person.
他是個多麼有慈善心的人呀。

donor
n. 寄贈者；捐贈人

Track 1361

Mr. Kim is the **donor** of the blood which you received.
金先生是你血液的捐贈者。

Words can't describe how appreciated I am.
言語無法表達我有多感激。

doom
n. 命運
v. 注定

Track 1362

I think he's going to fail.
我覺得他會失敗。

Yeah, He's about to meet his **doom**.
對呀，我覺得他要完蛋了。

這裡使用的是名詞喔！

eager
adj. 渴望的

Track 1363

What do you want for your birthday present?
你想要什麼當作生日禮物？

I've **eagered** to have a car of my own for a long time.
我渴望擁有自己的車子很久了。

earnings
n. 收入

Track 1364

I always save half of my **earnings** to the bank.
我總是把收入的一半存入銀行。

It's important to have good manage on your own finance.
擁有良好的財務管理是很重要的。

effect
n. 影響；效果
v. 招致

Track 1365

The **effect** of global warming is more and more apparent.
全球暖化的影響已經越來越明顯了。

We should really face this issue seriously.
我們應該認真地面對這個問題。

這裡使用的是名詞喔！

elder
adj. 年長的
n. 長輩

Track 1366

Who's that girl over there?
那邊那位女孩是誰？

Oh, she's my **elder** sister.
喔，她是我的姐姐。

這裡使用的是形容詞喔！

embrace
v. 包圍；擁抱

Track 1367

I want to have an adventure in the forest and **embrace** the nature.
我想要去森林冒險並且擁抱大自然。

Please count me in.
我也要參加。

engage
v. 僱用；訂婚；從事

Track 1368

Polly and Hank was **engaged** last week.
波麗和漢克上個禮拜訂婚了。

I'm so happy for them.
我為他們感到高興。

engagement
n. 預約；訂婚

🔊 *Track 1369*

👦 Wow, your ring is so beautiful.
哇！你的戒指好漂亮。

👧 Thanks! It's an **engagement** ring given from my boyfriend.
謝謝！這是我男朋友給我的訂婚戒指。

estate
n. 財產

🔊 *Track 1370*

👦 I need a real **estate** agent.
我需要一個房地產經理人。

👧 What for?
為了什麼？

esteem
n. 尊重

🔊 *Track 1371*

👦 Please show your **esteem** to all status of people.
請尊重各個階層的人。

👧 I'll remember that.
我會記得的。

excellent
adj. 傑出的

🔊 *Track 1372*

👦 The performance was **excellent**.
那個表演很棒。

👧 Wow, that's a great praise to me.
哇！那對我來說是很大的讚美。

exchange
v. 交換
n. 交換

🔊 *Track 1373*

👦 Do you want to **exchange** Christmas gift?
你想要交換聖誕節禮物嗎？

👧 Sounds great!
聽起來很棒！

> 這裡使用的是動詞喔！

exciting
adj. 令人興奮的；刺激的

🔊 *Track 1374*

👦 The game is so **exciting**.
這場比賽太刺激了。

👧 I can hardly hear my heart beat.
我幾乎可以聽到我的心跳聲。

expect
v. 期望

🔊 *Track 1375*

👦 I **expect** you to be a leader of us.
我期待你能成為我們的領導者。

👧 I'll try my best.
我會盡我所能。

expectation
n. 期望

Track 1376

Don't have too much **expectation** on me.
別對我有太高的期望。

Oh, you'll be just fine.
喔，你會做得很好的。

expense
n. 費用

Track 1377

The **expense** on maintaining the engine is so high.
花在維修引擎上的費用太高了。

But we still have to get it fixed.
但我們還是得把它修好。

faithful
adj. 忠實的；耿直的

Track 1378

The dog is a **faithful** friend to humans.
狗是人們忠實的朋友。

I agree.
我同意。

familiar
adj. 熟悉的；親密的

Track 1379

This restaurant is so **familiar**.
這間餐廳好熟悉。

You forgot we've been here last month.
你忘了我們上個月曾來過。

family
n. 家庭；（家人）

Track 1380

I have five brothers and two sisters.
我有五個兄弟和兩個姊妹。

Wow! You got a big **family**!
哇！你有一個很大的家庭！

fate
n. 命運；宿命

Track 1381

I don't believe in **fate**.
我不相信命運。

Neither do I.
我也不信。

fiance
n. 未婚夫

Track 1382

Mary, please meet my **fiancé**.
瑪麗，來見見我的未婚夫。

Nice to meet you, Tom.
很高興認識你，湯姆。

finance
n. 財務

🔊 *Track 1383*

👦 Her **finance** condition is bad.
她的財務狀況很糟。

👩 Maybe she needs someone to give her a hand.
也許她需要別人幫她一點忙。

---

forgive
v. 原諒；寬恕

🔊 *Track 1384*

👦 He's gone way too far this time.
他這次真的是太過分了。

👩 I won't **forgive** him anymore.
我不會再原諒他了。

---

found
v. 建立；打基礎

🔊 *Track 1385*

👦 This school was **founded** in the early 1950's.
這所學校在六零年代前期時就創建了。

👩 It sounds like it has a long history.
聽起來它有一段很長的歷史。

---

friend
n. 朋友

🔊 *Track 1386*

👦 Do you have a Facebook account number?
你有臉書的帳號嗎？

👩 Yeah, I have 800 **friends** online.
嗯，我有八百個線上好友。

---

friendship
n. 友誼；友情

🔊 *Track 1387*

👦 May our **friendship** last forever.
希望我們的友誼能到永遠。

👩 Cheers!
乾杯！

---

frustrated
adj. 氣餒的；受挫的

🔊 *Track 1388*

👦 I felt so **frustrated**.
我感到好挫折。

👩 What's wrong with you?
你怎麼了？

---

gang
n. 一幫；一群

🔊 *Track 1389*

👦 A **gang** of workers are working on the new building.
一群工人在為建立新大樓工作著。

👩 They worked so hard.
他們工作地很辛苦。

gathering
n. 集會；聚集

Track 1390

Why is people **gathering** around there?
為什麼那邊有人群聚集？

Let's check out what's happening.
讓我們看看發生了什麼事。

gender
n. 性別

Track 1391

I don't think the performance on this job will differ by **gender**.
我不認為這個工作的表現會跟性別有關。

I agree with you.
我同意你的說法。

generosity
n. 慷慨；寬宏大量

Track 1392

Thanks for your **generosity**.
感謝你的寬宏大量。

You're welcome.
不客氣。

give
v. 給；提供；捐助

Track 1393

Can you **give** me a hand?
你可以幫我一點忙嗎？

Sure, what for?
當然，要做什麼？

glory
n. 榮耀；光榮

Track 1394

We fight for **glory**.
我們為光榮而戰。

I'm proud to be a NAVY.
我以身為海軍的一員為傲。

grandchild
n. 孫子

Track 1395

Who's that cute boy in the picture?
照片裡面那個可愛的小男孩是誰？

He's my **grandchild**.
他是我的孫子。

granddaughter
n. 孫女；外孫女

Track 1396

My **granddaughter** visited me yesterday.
我的孫女昨天來拜訪我。

It's been a long time since her last visit.
距離她上次拜訪已經過了好久了。

grandfather
n. 祖父；外祖父

🔊 *Track 1397*

My son is going to have a baby!
我兒子即將要有孩子了！

You are about to be a **grandfather**!
你快要成為爺爺了！

grandmother
n. 祖母；外祖母

🔊 *Track 1398*

My **grandmother** used to told me bed time stories when I was little.
我祖母在我小時候都會跟我講床邊故事。

Mine too.
我的祖母也是。

grandson
n. 孫子；外孫

🔊 *Track 1399*

Your **grandson** is excellent.
你的孫子很傑出。

I'm so proud of him.
我為他感到驕傲。

guarantee
v. 擔保；作保
n. 擔保；（保證）

🔊 *Track 1400*

No one can **guarantee** to always win.
沒有人能夠保證永遠的獲勝。

I know that.
我知道。

這裡使用的是動詞喔！

guest
n. 客人

🔊 *Track 1401*

Jim, you have a **guest** waiting for you.
吉姆，你有位訪客在等你。

Okay, I'll be there just a minute.
好的，我馬上就過去。

heir
n. 繼承人

🔊 *Track 1402*

He is the **heir** of his family.
他是他們家的繼承人。

So he takes on a lot of responsibility.
所以他負起了很大的責任。

heritage
n. 遺產

🔊 *Track 1403*

The millionaire left a huge **heritage** for his son.
那個百萬富翁留下了一大筆遺產給他的兒子。

That's a lot of money!
那真是很大一筆錢！

hometown
n. 家鄉

Track 1404

Pennsylvania is my **hometown**.
賓州是我的家鄉。

How often do you go back?
你多久回去一次？

---

honeymoon
n. 蜜月

Track 1405

We went on a **honeymoon** to Hawaii.
我們去夏威夷度蜜月。

Was it fun?
好玩嗎？

---

hope
v. 希望；期望
n. 希望

Track 1406

I **hope** I can get high scores this semester.
我希望可以在這學期拿到好的成績。

Me too.
我也是。

這裡使用的是動詞喔！

---

host
n. 主人
v. 主辦

Track 1407

The **host** of this hotel treats us well.
這間旅館的主人對我們真好。

Yeah, he is such a kind person.
對呀，他真是個好人。

這裡使用的是名詞喔！

---

housewife
n. 家庭主婦

Track 1408

What's your mother's occupation?
妳母親的職業是什麼？

Oh, she's just a **housewife**.
喔，她只是一個家庭主婦。

---

housework
n. 家事

Track 1409

There is so much **housework** to do.
有好多的家事要做。

Maybe I can help you.
也許我可以幫你。

---

humanity
n. 人類；人道

Track 1410

Technology comes from **humanity**.
科技始終來自於人性。

I can't agree you more.
我很贊同你。

husband
n. 丈夫
Track 1411

My husband is a dentist.
我的先生是個牙醫。

Does he have a clinic?
他有自己的診所嗎？

identical
adj. 相同的
Track 1412

This two pictures are so identical.
這兩張照片好相像。

Because the background is the same.
因為背景是一樣的。

identification
n. 身分證
Track 1413

Please show your personal Identification.
請出示妳的個人身分證件。

Yes, officer.
是的長官。

identity
n. 身分
Track 1414

What's the most important thing of being a secret agent?
對於一個特務來講什麼是最重要的呢？

Not to disclose their identity.
不要洩漏他們的身分。

important
adj. 重要的
Track 1415

Today is an important day of mine.
今天對我來說是個重要的日子。

Why?
為什麼？

indulge
v. 沉溺；放縱；遷就
Track 1416

I was once indulge in alcohol.
我曾經沉溺在酒精當中。

Glad that you keep away from it now.
很高興你現在已經遠離它了。

income
n. 收入
Track 1417

There is no income today.
今天沒有任何的收入。

We have to find out what's the problem.
我們必須要找出問題在哪。

inherit

v. 繼承；接受

🔊 *Track 1418*

😀 What will Mike do after he graduates?
麥可在畢業後會做什麼？

😊 He'll **inherit** his father's company.
他會繼承他父親的公司。

inheritance

n. 繼承；繼承權

🔊 *Track 1419*

😀 Who has the **inheritance** of this shop?
誰有這間店的繼承權？

😊 Mr. Kunes.
肯納斯先生。

inspiration

n. 鼓舞；激勵

🔊 *Track 1420*

😀 The speech gave me a lot of **inspiration**.
這個演講給了我好多激勵。

😊 Yeah, it was great.
對呀，這場演講棒極了。

inspire

v. 啟發；鼓舞；激起

🔊 *Track 1421*

😀 Thank you for **inspiring** me to complete this job.
謝謝你鼓勵我完成這項工作。

😊 You are welcome.
不客氣。

instead

adv. 替代

🔊 *Track 1422*

😀 Do you want to have some steak for lunch?
你要吃點牛排當午餐嗎？

😊 No, I would rather eat pork **instead**.
不了，我寧可吃豬排。

insurance

n. 保險

🔊 *Track 1423*

😀 How much did you pay for your life **insurance**?
你花多少在你的壽險上面？

😊 10 million dollars.
一千萬元。

interaction

n. 互動；互相影響

🔊 *Track 1424*

😀 I feel great to have some **interaction** with you.
跟你互動讓我感覺很開心。

😊 Me too.
我也是。

a b c d e f g h i j k l m n o p q r s t u v w x y z

intimate
n. 知己
adj. 親密的
v. 暗示
🔊 *Track 1425*

She's an **intimate** friend of mine.
她是我一個很親密的朋友。

I know.
我知道。

這裡使用的是形容詞喔！

juvenile
n. 青少年；孩子
adj. 青少年的
🔊 *Track 1426*

The **juvenile** in our country needs to be well educated.
我們國家的青少年需要被良好的教育。

I agree.
我同意。

這裡使用的是名詞喔！

kid
n. 小孩
v. 開玩笑
🔊 *Track 1427*

Who is the **kid** playing in the yard?
那個在院子裡玩的小孩是誰？

He is Daniel.
他是丹尼爾。

這裡使用的是名詞喔！

kin
n. 親族；親戚
🔊 *Track 1428*

He is a **kin** of mine.
他是我的親戚。

No wonder you are so intimate.
難怪你們看起來這麼親密。

lady
n. 女士；淑女
🔊 *Track 1429*

Today is the **Lady**'s night of this restaurant.
今天是這間餐廳的淑女之夜。

We can get a 20% discount for all meal!
我們可以八折享用任何餐點。

leisure
n. 空閒
🔊 *Track 1430*

I need some **leisure** time to relax.
我需要點空閒時間來放鬆。

You looked so tired.
你看起來好累。

lie
v. 說謊
n. 謊言
🔊 *Track 1431*

Why did you **lie** to me?
你為什麼要騙我。

No, I didn't!
我沒有。

這裡使用的是動詞喔！

loan
n. 借貸
v. 借貸
🔊 *Track 1432*

🧑 He **loaned** me ten thousand dollars yesterday.
他昨天借我一萬元。

👩 What a generous person.
多麼慷慨的一個人呀。 這裡使用的是動詞喔！

---

luxurious
adj. 奢侈的；奢華的
🔊 *Track 1433*

🧑 The life of the rich is so **luxurious**.
有錢人的生活好奢侈。

👩 I'm so jealous of it.
我好嫉妒。

---

man
n. 成年男人
🔊 *Track 1434*

🧑 Every **man** should do the military service in our country.
我們國家的每個成年男子都應該要服兵役。

👩 That's a great test.
那是一個很大的考驗。

---

marriage
n. 婚姻
🔊 *Track 1435*

🧑 I've never thought of **marriage**.
我從來沒想過要結婚。

👩 Why? Marriage is a part of life!
為什麼？結婚是人生的一部份啊！

---

marry
v. 使結為夫妻；結婚
🔊 *Track 1436*

🧑 Will you **marry** me?
妳願意嫁給我嗎？

👩 Yes I do.
是的，我願意。

---

mate
n. 配偶；（夥計）
🔊 *Track 1437*

🧑 Do you have a **mate** now?
你現在有配偶嗎？

👩 No, I'm still single.
沒有，我還是單身。

---

mature
adj. 成熟的
v. 成熟
🔊 *Track 1438*

🧑 The apple looks delicious.
蘋果看起來好好吃。

👩 We should wait until it's **mature** enough to eat.
我們應該等到它熟透了再吃。

這裡使用的是形容詞喔！

a b c d e f g h i j k l m n o p q r s t u v w x y z

merry
adj. 快樂的

🔊 *Track 1439*

👦 The atmosphere is so **merry** here.
這邊的氣氛真開心。

👧 Yeah, I feel so happy.
嗯，我感到很快樂。

mild
adj. 溫和的

🔊 *Track 1440*

👦 The blue whale is so enormous!
藍鯨真的好大！

👧 But it's a **mild** animal.
但牠是個很溫和的動物。

mislead
v. 誤導

🔊 *Track 1441*

👦 Don't be **mislead** by the trap.
不要被陷阱所誤導。

👧 Okay, I'll be careful.
好的，我會很小心的。

mother
n. 母親；媽媽

🔊 *Track 1442*

👦 Tomorrow is **Mother**'s day.
明天是母親節。

👧 What have you bought for her?
你為她買了什麼？

mutual
adj. 相互的；共同的

🔊 *Track 1443*

👦 We have 200 **mutual** friends on Facebook.
我們在臉書上有兩百個共同好友。

👧 Wow! That's a lot!
哇！真多！

name
n. 名字；名義
v. 指名；命名

🔊 *Track 1444*

👦 What's your **name**?
妳叫什麼名字？

👧 My name is Terry.
我的名字是泰瑞。

這裡使用的是名詞喔！

necessity
n. 必需品；必要性

🔊 *Track 1445*

👦 You must think of the **necessity** before you buy things.
你一定要在買東西之前確認其必要性。

👧 Alright.
沒問題。

needy
adj. 貧窮的;貧困的

🔊 *Track 1446*

He is **needy**.
他很窮困。

Maybe we can help him.
也許我們可以幫他。

nephew
n. 姪子;外甥

🔊 *Track 1447*

My **nephew** is 2 meters tall.
我的外甥有 200 公分高。

Wow! That's really tall.
哇!那真的好高。

nickname
n. 綽號
v. (取)綽號

🔊 *Track 1448*

You must have a **nickname** in this team.
在我們的團隊裡你必須要有個綽號。

Let me think of one.
讓我想一個。

這裡使用的是名詞喔!

niece
n. 姪女;外甥女

🔊 *Track 1449*

My **niece** is a singer.
我的姪女是個歌手。

She must have a great voice.
她肯定擁有一個好嗓音。

nominate
v. 提名;指定

🔊 *Track 1450*

Mr. George was **nominated** the president candidate.
喬治先生被提名為總統候選人。

I'll vote for him.
我會投給他。

nonetheless
adv. 儘管如此;然而

🔊 *Track 1451*

You make a lot of money from your job.
你從工作上賺了很多錢。

Nonetheless, it's tiring.
儘管如此,卻很累。

notable
n. 名人;出眾的人(事物)

🔊 *Track 1452*

He's a **notable** person that I met.
他是我認識的一個了不起的人。

He's got brilliant ability.
他擁有傑出的能力。

nurture
v. 養育；培育

Track 1453

Our parents **nurtured** us and gave a lot to us.
我們的父母養育我們，也為我們付出很多。

So we should be thankful to them.
所以我們應該感激他們。

occasion
n. 事件；場合

Track 1454

This suit looks nice.
這件西裝看起來真不錯。

Yeah, it fits with all kinds of **occasions**.
對呀，它適合所有場合。

offspring
n. 子孫；後裔

Track 1455

We should protect the environment so that our **offspring** can enjoy the same resources.
我們應該要保護環境好讓我們的子孫能夠享有同樣的資源。

Let's start from recycle and reduce the trashes.
讓我們從回收和減少垃圾量開始吧。

oppress
v. 壓迫；威迫

Track 1456

I'm **oppressed** by the boss's attitude.
老闆的態度讓我感到壓迫。

Relax, don't be too nervous.
放鬆點，別太緊張了。

option
n. 選擇；取捨

Track 1457

Would you like coffee or tea?
你想要咖啡還是茶？

Is there another **option**?
還有其他選擇嗎？

orphan
n. 孤兒

Track 1458

The **orphan** lost his parents when he was 2 years old.
那位孤兒在兩歲的時候就失去了他的雙親。

I feel sad for him.
我為他感到難過。

outsider
n. 外人；門外漢

🔊 Track 1459

🧑 Don't tell this secret to the outsiders.
別告訴外人這個秘密。

👩 Okay, I won't.
好的，我不會。

own
adj. 自己的
pro. 自己（的）
v. 擁有

🔊 Track 1460

🧑 I've complete this job on my own.
我已經獨立完成這個工作了。

👩 Good for you.
做得好。

這裡使用的是代名詞喔！

parent(s)
n. 雙親；家長

🔊 Track 1461

🧑 Tomorrow is the parents' day of our school.
明天是我們學校的家長日。

👩 Will your parents attend?
你的家長會出席嗎？

payment
n. 支付；付款

🔊 Track 1462

🧑 You must make all the payments before you get the car.
你必須付清所有的帳款才能拿到車子。

👩 Can I use credit card here?
這邊可以使用信用卡嗎？

peer
n. 同儕；同輩

🔊 Track 1463

🧑 He's outstanding among his peers.
他在同儕間非常的出色。

👩 And he's a hard working kid.
而且他是個認真的小孩。

pension
n. 退休金

🔊 Track 1464

🧑 Someone stole my pension.
有人偷了我的退休金。

👩 What! Are you kidding me?
你在跟我開玩笑嗎？

possession
n. 擁有物；財產

🔊 Track 1465

🧑 Who does this beautiful yard belong to?
這個美麗的院子是誰的？

👩 This yard is a possession of Mr. Young.
這個院子是楊先生的財產。

postpone
v. 延後

Track 1466

😊 Linda, can you help me make a **postponement** of my flight?
琳達，妳可以幫我延後我的航班嗎？

😊 Sure, I'll do my best.
當然，我會盡我所能。

potential
n. 潛力
adj. 潛在的

Track 1467

😊 She's got the **potential** to be a great artist.
她有潛力成為很好的藝術家。

😊 I would say "Sky is her limit".
我會說：「天空才是她的極限。」

> 這裡使用的是名詞喔！

predecessor
n. 祖先；前輩

Track 1468

😊 Our **predecessor** worked hard so that we can enjoy a better life.
我們的祖先努力工作好讓我們能夠享受更好的生活。

😊 I always feel grateful when I think of what they'd done for us.
每次我想到他們為我們做了什麼我總是很感激。

price
n. 價格；代價

Track 1469

😊 This computer's **price** is 10 thousand dollars.
這台電腦的價值是一萬塊。

😊 Wow! What a bargain.
哇！多麼划算呀。

primary
adj. 主要的

Track 1470

😊 What's the **primary** ingredient of this dish?
這道菜的主要成份為何？

😊 It's made of flour.
是用麵粉做的。

privacy
n. 隱私

Track 1471

😊 I didn't mean to invade your **privacy**.
我不是有意要侵犯你的隱私。

😊 That's okay.
沒關係。

private
adj. 私密的

◀ *Track 1472*

My bedroom is a **private** place of mine.
我的房間是我個人的私密空間。

Mine too.
我的也是。

---

privilege
n. 特權

◀ *Track 1473*

Nobody has the **privilege** against the law.
在法律之下沒有人有特權。

With no exception?
沒有例外嗎？

---

probable
adj. 可能的

◀ *Track 1474*

Will it rain in the afternoon?
明天下午會下雨嗎？

It's **probable**.
有可能。

---

process
n. 過程

◀ *Track 1475*

I wonder what the **process** of making a car is.
我很好奇車子製造的過程到底是如何。

Maybe we should visit the factory.
也許我們應該去參觀工廠。

---

proof
n. 證據

◀ *Track 1476*

Do you have any **proof** to sue him?
你有任何證據控告他嗎？

Plenty.
還蠻多的。

---

protection
n. 保護

◀ *Track 1477*

Some parents give too much **protection** to their kids.
有些家長給予孩子太多的保護了。

And their child may not be happy at all.
他們的小孩可能根本就不快樂。

a b c d e f g h i j k l m n o p q r s t u v w x y z

protective
adj. 保護的；防護的

◀ *Track 1478*

😀 I trust the quality of this company's firewall.
我信任這間公司防火牆的品質。

😊 It's highly **protective**.
它有很高的防護。

reaction
n. 反應

◀ *Track 1479*

😀 It's interesting to see the chemical **reaction** between these two people.
觀察這兩個人的化學反應是很有趣的。

😊 Let's wait and see.
我們等著看吧。

reconcile
v. 調停；和解

◀ *Track 1480*

😀 Is everything fine between you and Jane?
你和珍之間發生了什麼事？

😊 We've **reconciled** and everything is well.
我們和好了，一切都很好。

receipt
n. 收據

◀ *Track 1481*

😀 Did you see my **receipt**?
你有看到我的收據嗎？

😊 What kind of receipt?
什麼樣的收據？

receiver
n. 收受者

◀ *Track 1482*

😀 Please help me check out what's wrong with my email, I can't send it.
幫我看看我的電子郵件出了什麼問題，我寄不出去。

😊 You forgot to write the **receiver**'s email address.
你忘記填寫收件者的電子郵件地址。

refuge
n. 避難（所）

◀ *Track 1483*

😀 Where should we hide when the earthquake comes?
當地震來臨時我們應該躲在哪裡？

😊 Maybe go downstairs to the **refuge** in the basement.
也許下樓到在地下室的避難所。

relationship
n. 關係

◀ *Track 1484*

What is your **relationship** with Ryan?
你跟萊恩是什麼關係？

Nothing.
沒什麼。

---

relative
n. 親戚

◀ *Track 1485*

Who's Eileen?
誰是艾琳？

She's a **relative** of mine.
她是我的一個親戚。

---

release
v. 解放；（公佈；發行）
n. 解放；（公佈；發行）

◀ *Track 1486*

The bomb **release** enormous energy on the ground.
炸彈釋放巨大的威力到地面上。

And it destroyed everything.
也毀滅了所有東西。

這裡使用的是動詞喔！

---

reliable
adj. 可靠的

◀ *Track 1487*

What do you think about Brian?
你覺得布萊恩這個人怎麼樣？

He's a **reliable** person.
他是個可靠的人。

---

relieve
v. 解除；減輕

◀ *Track 1488*

I'm so nervous now.
我現在好緊張。

Maybe you should **relieve** some of your pressure.
也許你應該減輕一些壓力。

---

religion
n. 宗教；信仰

◀ *Track 1489*

What's your **religion**?
你的信仰是什麼？

I don't have a specific one.
我沒有特定的信仰。

rely
v. 依賴

Track 1490

> You are the only person that I can **rely** on now.
> 你是我現在唯一可以依賴的人了。

> I'll try as hard as I can to help you.
> 我會盡我所能的幫你。

remind
v. 提醒

Track 1491

> Be polite John.
> 約翰，你要有禮貌。

> You **remind** me of my mother.
> 你好像我媽媽。

replace
v. 代替

Track 1492

> She's so important to our team.
> 她對我們團隊非常的重要。

> No one can **replace** her.
> 沒有人能取代她。

request
v. 要求
n. 要求

Track 1493

> You **requested** too much of me.
> 你對我要求太多了。

> I don't think so.
> 我不這麼認為。

這裡使用的是動詞喔！

resemble
v. 類似；（相像）

Track 1494

> These two cars **resemble** each other.
> 這兩部車長得好像。

> It's because they are products of the same company.
> 那是因為他們是同一家公司的產品。

respond
v. 回答
n. 回答

Track 1495

> I can't do this.
> 這我沒辦法做到。

> Is that your **respond**?
> 這就是你的回覆？

這裡使用的是名詞喔！

response
n. 回應;答覆

Track 1496

There's still no **response** from the school.
學校還是沒有給予任何回覆。

I guess we just have to wait.
我想我們只能夠等吧。

responsibility
n. 責任

Track 1497

Don't worry, I'll handle this.
別擔心,我會處理的。

You are a person with great **responsibility**.
你真是個有責任感的人。

reunion
n. 重聚;團圓

Track 1498

How long has it been since our last **reunion**?
自從我們上次團聚已經多久了?

I think it has been 5 years.
我想已經有五年了。

revenue
n. 收入

Track 1499

When your **revenue** can't afford your expense, you may run out of money.
當你入不敷出時,你會花光所有的錢。

That sounds terrible.
聽起來很糟糕。

rivalry
n. 對抗;競爭

Track 1500

The **rivalry** between these two teams is splendid.
這兩隊的競爭真是精采。

Both teams had the chance to win this game.
兩隊都有機會贏得這場比賽。

romantic
adj. 浪漫的

Track 1501

My boy friend is so **romantic**.
我男朋友好浪漫。

I'm a little bit envy of you.
我有點羨慕你。

saving(s)
n. 拯救；救助；存款

🔊 *Track 1502*

How much do we have in our bank account?
我們的銀行戶頭還剩多少錢？

Still plenty of **savings**.
還剩蠻多存款的。

seduce
v. 引誘；慫恿

🔊 *Track 1503*

The enemy **seduced** him into a trap.
敵人引誘他進入陷阱。

He was too careless.
他太不小心了。

self
n. 自己；自我

🔊 *Track 1504*

What's the spirit of basketball?
籃球的精神是什麼？

Playing as a team, not just fight by **self**.
以團隊去打球而非個人。

setting
n. 安置；背景

🔊 *Track 1505*

I love the **setting** of your furniture.
我喜歡你家具的擺設。

Thank you.
謝謝你。

sex
n. 性；性別

🔊 *Track 1506*

It's dangerous to have **sex** with strangers.
跟陌生人發生性關係是很危險的。

I agree.
我同意。

share
n. 一份；佔有（率）
v. 共享

🔊 *Track 1507*

I have a large **share** of the company's stock.
我有公司很大一部分的股票。

How much?
多少？

> 這裡使用的是名詞喔！

sibling
n. 兄弟姊妹

🔊 *Track 1508*

How many **siblings** do you have?
你有多少個兄弟姊妹？

Three in total.
總共三個。

silent
adj. 沉默的

Why are you so **silent** today?
你今天為何如此沉默？

I'm sick.
我生病了。

sincere
adj. 誠懇；真摯

Why did you believe her?
你為什麼要相信她？

Because she sounded **sincere**.
因為她聽起來很誠懇。

sober
adj. 清醒的

I'm drunk.
我喝醉了。

Drink some water and it will make you more **sober**.
喝點水會讓你更清醒。

soften
v. 使柔軟

How do they **soften** the meat?
他們是如何讓肉變得鬆軟的？

Maybe we should ask the chef.
也許我們應該問問主廚。

spectator
n. 觀眾；旁觀者

There's so many **spectators** around.
有好多觀眾在附近。

Don't be nervous, you are great.
別緊張，你很棒的。

spend
v. 花費；付錢
n. 花費

Don't **spend** too much money on shopping.
別花太多錢在購物上。

Got it.
知道了。

這裡使用的是動詞喔！

splendor

n. 燦爛；光輝

Track 1515

I was amazed by the **splendor** of the moon light.
我為那燦爛的月光所著迷。

Never did I know the moon can be this beautiful.
我從來不知道月亮可以如此美麗。

spouse

n. 配偶；夫妻

Track 1516

Please fill in your **spouse**'s name in this column.
請在這個欄位填入你配偶的名字。

No problem.
沒問題。

stepfather

n. 繼父；後父

Track 1517

Who's that old man over there?
那邊那位老人是誰？

Oh, he's my **stepfather**.
喔，他是我的繼父。

stock

n. 庫存；股票
v. 儲存

Track 1518

I earned a lot of money from buying **stocks**.
我買股票賺了很多錢。

Maybe you should teach me someday.
也許你可以找一天教我。

這裡使用的是名詞喔！

stranger

n. 陌生人

Track 1519

Don't hang out with **strangers**.
別跟陌生人出去。

Okay, I won't.
好的，我不會。

stray

n. 漂泊者；流浪；（流浪寵物）

Track 1520

There are so many **stray** dogs in the park.
公園裡有好多流浪狗。

Poor doggies.
可憐的狗狗。

stubborn
adj. 頑固的

🔊 *Track 1521*

Mr. Smith is the most **stubborn** person that I've ever met!
史密斯先生是我見過最頑固的人。

He doesn't listen to anybody's advice.
他不聽任何人的建議。

---

successor
n. 後繼者；繼承人

🔊 *Track 1522*

The boss is still finding the **successor** of his company.
老闆還在找公司的繼承者。

I think Eric would be a nice candidate.
我認為艾瑞克會是一個很棒的候選人。

---

supply
v. 供給
n. 供給

🔊 *Track 1523*

This place is running out of water.
這個地方缺水了。

we need to wait for the **supplies**.
我們需要等待補給。

> 這裡使用的是名詞喔！

---

sympathetic
n. 有同情心的

🔊 *Track 1524*

I feel **sympathetic** to their feelings.
我對他們的感受感到同情。

Me too.
我也是。

---

talkative
adj. 健談的

🔊 *Track 1525*

Tell me more about Vincent.
跟我多說點文森這個人的事吧。

He is a **talkative** boy.
他是個健談的男孩。

---

teenager
n. 青少年

🔊 *Track 1526*

What's your hobby when you are a **teenager**?
你青少年時期的興趣是什麼?

I loved to swim when I was young.
我年輕的時候很愛游泳。

tenant
n. 承租人

Track 1527

Are you a **tenant** of this apartment?
你是這個公寓的房客嗎?

NO, I own this whole building.
不,我擁有整棟房子。

thrifty
adj. 節儉的

Track 1528

My mother is a **thrifty** person.
我媽媽是一個節儉的人。

I think we should look up to her.
我認為我們應該尊敬她。

tolerance
n. 容忍

Track 1529

It's a virtue of having great **tolerance** on others.
能夠容忍他人是美德。

I agree with you.
我同意你的說法。

tomb
n. 墳墓;塚

Track 1530

The **tomb** of the greatest scientist of all time is at the next block.
有史以來最偉大的科學家的墳墓就在下一個街區。

Let's visit there.
我們去拜訪那裡吧。

true
adj. 真的;對的

Track 1531

Is it **true**?
這是真的嗎?

Certainly.
那當然。

twin
n. 雙胞胎

Track 1532

Nick and Andy are **twin** brothers.
尼克和安迪是雙胞胎兄弟。

It's fun when seeing them walking together.
看他們走在一起很好玩。

uncle
n. 叔叔

🔊 *Track 1533*

👦 **Uncle** Hank is coming tomorrow.
漢克叔叔明天要來。

👩 We should better clean this mess up.
我們最好把這裡清乾淨。

unfortunate
adj. 不幸的

🔊 *Track 1534*

👦 It's **unfortunate** for me to fail the test.
很不幸地，我沒有通過那個考試。

👩 Your mom will definitely be upset.
你媽肯定會很不高興。

value
n. 價值
v. 價值

🔊 *Track 1535*

👦 What's the **value** of friendship?
友誼的價值是多少？

👩 It's priceless.
那是無價的。

這裡使用的是名詞喔！

violence
n. 暴力

🔊 *Track 1536*

👦 We should say no to **violence**.
我們應該向暴力說不。

👩 You are right.
你是對的。

wedding
n. 婚禮；結婚

🔊 *Track 1537*

👦 I'm going to attend a **wedding** tomorrow.
我明天要出席一場婚禮。

👩 Who's wedding?
誰的婚禮？

widow
n. 寡婦

🔊 *Track 1538*

👦 The **widow** lives on her own.
那個寡婦獨自生活。

👩 How poor she is.
她是多麼可憐呀。

wife
n. 妻子

🔊 *Track 1539*

👦 Who's that charming girl over there?
那邊那個迷人的女孩是誰？

👩 Oh, that's my **wife** Betty.
喔，那是我的妻子貝蒂。

woo
v. 求婚；求愛

Track 1540

Steven is **wooing** my sister.
史蒂芬在追求我姐姐。

Really?
真的嗎？

young
adj. 年輕的；年幼的

Track 1541

Take care of your health when you are **young**.
年輕的時候就要照顧好你的身體。

Okay, I'll remember that.
我會記得的。

youth
n. 青年

Track 1542

The **youth** are always filled with energy.
年輕人總是富有滿滿的活力。

How I wish we were still that young.
我多麼希望我們也那樣年輕。

The youth are always filled with energy.

Part

08

各種狀況

各種狀況

要學就學最實用的英文單字，搭配最稀鬆平常的生活對話，馬上就知道外國人都是這樣用這個單字的喇！＊單字、對話分開錄音，學習目標更明確

aberrant
adj. 脫離常軌的

Track 1543

Recently, I got drunk almost everyday.
最近，我幾乎每天都喝醉。

Oh my God! Your life is so **aberrant**!
我的天啊！你的生活太脫離常軌了！

abhor
v. 憎惡

Track 1544

I **abhor** cockroaches, they are disgusting.
我非常討厭蟑螂，牠們都好噁心。

Nobody likes them.
沒有人喜歡牠們。

abstraction
n. 抽象；出神

Track 1545

I went to the Museum of Contemporary Art yesterday.
我昨天去了當代藝術博物館。

And do you get the **abstraction** of contemporary art?
那你了解當代藝術的抽象概念嗎？

accuracy
n. 正確；精密

Track 1546

Mary always makes mistakes on calculation.
瑪莉在算數時總是出錯。

But **accuracy** is very important when calculating.
但計算的正確度是非常重要的。

adjust
v. 調節；對準

Track 1547

The clock seems slow.
這個時鐘似乎慢了。

It is slow, we need to **adjust** it.
它是慢了，我們得把它調整回來。

appear
v. 出現；顯得

Track 1548

Amy **appears** ill at ease when she saw John.
當瑪莉看見湯姆時，她顯得很不自在。

That's because she likes John.
那是因為她喜歡湯姆。

artificial
adj. 人工的

Track 1549

How can these flowers be so beautiful!
這些花怎麼會如此美麗！

Because they are **artificial**.
因為這些是假花。

athletic
adj. 運動的；行動靈敏的

Track 1550

I like **athletic** boys.
我喜歡運動型的男生。

Me, too. But I don't like them when they're sweating.
我也是。但當他們流汗時我就不喜歡他們了。

attachment
n. 連接；附著

Track 1551

I just e-mailed you the information of the conference.
我剛剛把會議的資料用電子郵件寄給你。

Did you put the agenda in the **attachment**?
你有把議程表放在附件裡嗎？

attempt
v. 嘗試；企圖
n. 嘗試

Track 1552

They **attempt** to win the champion of this competition.
他們企圖在這個比賽中奪冠。

They are very ambitious.
他們很有野心。

這裡使用的是動詞喔！

attract
v. 吸引

Track 1553

Yeah, many guys are **attracted** by her smile.
對啊，許多男生都被她的笑容所吸引。

Lily is a charming girl.
莉莉是個迷人的女孩。

attractive

adj. 吸引人的；動人的

Track 1554

What do you want to eat for dinner? How about McDonald's?
你晚餐想吃什麼？麥當勞如何？

Sounds **attractive**!
聽起來很吸引人！

---

awkward

adj. 笨拙的；不熟練的；（尷尬的）

Track 1555

The scarf that you're weaving looks so ugly.
你織的圍巾看起來好醜。

I'm really **awkward** with handicraft.
我對手工藝真的很不熟練。

---

beautify

v. 美化

Track 1556

Our bathroom is in a mess.
我們的浴室真是一團亂。

Let's clean it up and **beautify** it.
我們來清理並美化它吧。

---

become

v. 變得；變成

Track 1557

She **became** a beauty after putting on a lot of make up.
她畫上很厚的妝後就成了美女。

Why do you say so? Is she ugly before putting on make up?
你為何這麼說？她化妝之前是很醜嗎？

---

big

adj. 大的

Track 1558

Your eyes are **big** and pretty.
你的眼睛好大而且好美。

Thank you. But it's a pity that I don't have a double-fold eyelid.
謝謝你。但很可惜我沒有雙眼皮。

---

black

n. 黑人；黑色
adj. 黑色的

Track 1559

I don't like the color **black**, it looks dirty.
我不喜歡黑色，它看起來髒髒的。

Really? But I think black is a noble color.
真的嗎？但我覺得黑色是很高貴的顏色。

這裡使用的是名詞喔！

---

blue
n. 藍色
adj. 藍色的

🔊 *Track 1560*

👦 The sky is so **blue**, so as my mood…
天空好藍，我的心情也是……

👧 Are you okay?
你還好嗎？

> 這裡使用的是形容詞喔！

bold
adj. 大膽的

🔊 *Track 1561*

👦 He asked Linda to marry him in front of the crowds.
他在大庭廣眾之下向琳達求婚。

👧 He is so **bold**! Did Linda say yes to him?
他好大膽！那琳達有答應他嗎？

boredom
n. 乏味

🔊 *Track 1562*

👦 Ted is a "**boredom** breaker", he always brought us laughter.
泰德是個「打破無聊的人」，他總是為我們帶來歡笑。

👧 That's why people love him.
這就是為什麼大家都愛他。

bound
v. 彈跳
n. 界限；範圍

🔊 *Track 1563*

👦 What is the **bound** of the midterm exam?
期中考的範圍是什麼？

👧 From chapter 1 to chapter 4.
從第一章到第四章。

> 這裡使用的是名詞喔！

bravery
n. 大膽；勇敢

🔊 *Track 1564*

👦 Tim was promoted.
提姆升職了。

👧 Because his boss appreciates his **bravery**.
因為他老闆很賞識他的勇敢。

broaden
v. 加寬；擴展

🔊 *Track 1565*

👦 Do you want to study abroad?
你想要出國留學嗎？

👧 Sure, I want to **broaden** my vision.
當然，我想要擴展我的視野。

brown

n. 褐色；棕色
adj. 褐色的；棕色的

The **brown** color of your hair is beautiful.
你褐色的頭髮真漂亮。

Thank you. I just dyed my hair last week.
謝謝你。我上禮拜才染的。

這裡使用的是形容詞喔！

browse

v. 瀏覽

Track 1567

What are you doing?
你在做什麼？

I'm **browsing** the web pages to find a job.
我正在瀏覽網頁找工作。

bulky

adj. 龐大的

Track 1568

Why do you bring such a **bulky** luggage?
你為什麼帶一個這麼龐大的行李？

Cause I'm going to America for three months.
因為我要去美國三個月。

calm

adj. 冷靜的
v. 使平靜

Track 1569

That guy is so unreasonable!
這傢伙簡直不可理喻！

Hey, stay **calm**. Don't ruin your mood for this kind of person.
嘿，保持冷靜。別因為這種人破壞了你的心情。

這裡使用的是形容詞喔！

capture

v. 捕捉；拍攝

Track 1570

I've **captured** more than 100 pictures.
我已經照了超過100張照片。

That's a lot!
那還真多！

carefree

adj. 無憂無慮的

Track 1571

I'm so tired with preparing the final exam.
我覺得準備期末考真的好累。

Hold on, we will be **carefree** after the test.
撐住，考完後我們就會無憂無慮了。

changeable
adj. 可變的

🧒 Can we update or modify our proposition latter?
我們之後還可以新增或修改我們的提案嗎？

👧 Yes, all the propositions in this meeting are **changeable**.
是的，今天開會所有的提案都是可以再改變的。

🔊 *Track 1572*

characteristic
n. 特徵

🧒 The **characteristic** of this girl is her big eyes.
這個女孩的特徵就是她的大眼睛。

👧 And her fair skin.
還有她白皙的皮膚。

🔊 *Track 1573*

characterize
v. 具有……特徵

🧒 Insects are **characterized** as six-feet.
昆蟲具有六隻腳的特徵。

👧 So spiders are not considered as insects.
所以蜘蛛被認為不是昆蟲。

🔊 *Track 1574*

cheerful
adj. 愉快的；興高采烈的

🧒 You look **cheerful**. What happened?
你看起來很愉快。發生什麼事了？

👧 A cute guy just asked me for a date.
有個帥哥剛剛約我出去。

🔊 *Track 1575*

circle
n. 圓形；圈子
v. 兜圈子；畫圈

🧒 We should discuss this problem first.
我們應該先討論這個問題。

👧 Alright. Then let's sit in a **circle** for discussion.
好。那我們圍坐成一圈來討論吧。

🔊 *Track 1576*

> 這裡使用的是名詞喔！

circular
adj. 圓形的；（環形的）

🧒 The **circular** cookies taste better.
這種圓形的餅乾比較好吃。

👧 I don't think so.
我不覺得。

🔊 *Track 1577*

coherent
adj. 連貫的；有條理的

All the ideas are mixed together.
所有的想法都混在一起了。

We need to make a **coherent** plan to combine these ideas.
我們必須做一個有條理的計畫來結合這些想法。

Track 1578

color
n. 顏色
v. 著色

What **colors** do you like?
你喜歡什麼顏色？

I like red 'cause red represents passion.
我喜歡紅色，因為紅色代表著熱情。

這裡使用的是名詞喔！

Track 1579

colorful
adj. 富有色彩的

The pictures in this book are so **colorful**.
這本書裡的圖片色彩都很豐富。

That's why it's good for kids.
這就是為什麼這本書很適合小孩子。

Track 1580

column
n. 圓柱；專欄；欄

He is a columnist for the gossip **column**.
他是八卦專欄的作家。

I love his articles!
我超愛他的文章！

Track 1581

combine
v. 聯合；結合

Brainstorming is a good way to solve the problems.
集思廣益是解決問題的好方法。

The power is great when people **combine** their ideas together.
當人們把想法結合起來時，力量就會很大。

Track 1582

conceive
v. 構想；構思；（受孕）

Is that you who **conceived** this idea?
是你構思出這個想法的嗎？

Yes, I've put in a lot of effort into it.
是的，我在上面做了很多努力。

Track 1583

concentrate
v. 集中

Track 1584

👦 Did you **concentrate** on you study before the test?

你考試前有專心讀書嗎？

👧 Yes, I did. I really don't know why I still failed this test.

是的，我有。我真的不知道為什麼這次考試我還是不及格。

concentration
n. 集中；專心

Track 1585

👦 If you want to get a good grade on the exams, **concentration** is prerequisite.

如果你想要在考試拿到好成績，專心是必要的。

👧 That's true.

這是真的。

concept
n. 概念

Track 1586

👦 My **concept** of math is really poor.

我對數學的概念真的很差。

👧 At least your English is good.

至少你的英文很好。

consist
v. 組成；構成

Track 1587

👦 Our team **consists** of many outstanding people.

我們團隊是由許多優秀的人所組成的。

👧 I believe that you will win this competition.

我相信你們會贏得這次的比賽。

exhibit
v. 展示

Track 1588

👦 The museum is now **exhibiting** the paintings of Monet.

博物館現在正在展出莫內的畫。

👧 Really? Then let's go see it after school.

真的嗎？那我們下課後一起去看吧！

exotic
adj. 外來的；異國的

Track 1589

👦 This restaurant we went yesterday is full of **exotic** elements.

我們昨天去的餐廳充滿異國的元素。

👧 What is the name of the restaurant?

那家餐廳的名字是什麼？

extend
v. 延長;(適用於)

🔊 *Track 1590*

👦 I would like to **extend** my trip in France.
我想要延長我在法國的旅程。

👧 When will you come back?
你何時要回來?

extraordinary
adj. 特別的;(非凡的)

🔊 *Track 1591*

👦 She is such an **extraordinary** girl.
她是一個很特別的女孩。

👧 It is said that a lot of guys are pursuing her.
聽說很多男生在追求她。

extreme
adj. 極度的
n. 極端

🔊 *Track 1592*

👦 Your words gave me an **extreme** courage.
你的話給我很大的鼓勵。

👧 Your welcome.
不客氣。

這裡使用的是形容詞喔!

facial
adj. 臉部的;表面的

🔊 *Track 1593*

👦 His **facial** expression is so funny.
他的表情很滑稽。

👧 That's because his face looks funny.
因為他的臉本來就看起來很滑稽。

fantastic
adj. 想像中的;古怪的

🔊 *Track 1594*

👦 Kids always have many **fantastic** ideas.
孩子們總有許多稀奇古怪的想法。

👧 Yeah, sometimes their ideas are really surprising.
對啊,有時候他們的想法很令人驚訝。

fantasy
n. 空想;異想;幻想

🔊 *Track 1595*

👦 Stop having **fantasies**! You should be more realistic.
停止幻想!你應該要實際一點。

👧 I don't think my ideas are fantasies. Actually I think they're all practical.
我不覺得我的想法是空想。事實上我認為這些想法都是可行的。

feature

n. 特徵；特色
v. 以……為特色

🔊 *Track 1596*

😊 Being polite is a key **feature** of Tom.
禮貌是湯姆的特色。

😊 So teachers all like him a lot.
所以老師都很喜歡他。

這裡使用的是名詞喔！

finish

v. 完成；結束
n. 結束

🔊 *Track 1597*

😊 When do you take a shower?
你都何時洗澡？

😊 Usually, after I **finish** my homework.
通常我都在做完功課後去洗澡。

這裡使用的是動詞喔！

focus

n. 焦點；焦距
v. 聚焦；專注

🔊 *Track 1598*

😊 Hey, that girl is hot!
嘿！那個女孩好辣！

😊 You are digressing from our topic. Please **focus** on our discussion.
你離題了。請專注於我們的討論。

這裡使用的是動詞喔！

follow

v. 跟隨；遵循；聽得懂

🔊 *Track 1599*

😊 Do you know how to get to the train station?
你知道怎麼到火車站嗎？

😊 I know, just **follow** me.
我知道，跟我走就對了。

formal

adj. 正式的；有禮的

🔊 *Track 1600*

😊 Why do you dress up?
為什麼你打扮得如此正式？

😊 Because I'm attending a **formal** party tonight.
因為我今晚要參加一個正式的晚會。

format

n. 格式；版式

🔊 *Track 1601*

😊 Your **format** of essay is wrong, please correct it.
你的論文格式錯了，請修正。

😊 Okay, I'll correct it immediately.
好的，我會立刻修正。

foster
v. 養育；收養；培養
adj. 寄養的

🔊 *Track 1602*

👦 What triggers you to learn music?
是什麼引發你去學音樂？

👩 Playing piano has **fostered** my interest in music.
彈鋼琴培養了我對音樂的興趣。

> 這裡使用的是動詞喔！

fragile
adj. 脆的；易碎的

🔊 *Track 1603*

👦 There are some fragile stuff in the box, please be careful.
箱子裡有一些易碎物品，請小心。

👩 **Fragile** stuff? What are those?
易碎物品？是什麼？

fragment
n. 破片；碎片

🔊 *Track 1604*

👦 Lisa just broke a glass, so **fragments** are all over the floor.
麗莎剛剛打破了杯子，所以地板上到處都是碎片。

👩 Then please clean up the floor as soon as possible.
那請盡快將地板清理乾淨。

frame
n. 框架
v. 構築；為……裝框

🔊 *Track 1605*

👦 The **frame** of your article is great.
你的文章架構很好。

👩 Thank you.
謝謝你。

> 這裡使用的是名詞喔！

fraud
n. 欺騙；詐欺（罪）

🔊 *Track 1606*

👦 More and more Internet **frauds** appear recently.
最近越來越多網路詐騙出現。

👩 I know, I was once an Internet fraud victim.
我知道，我也曾經是網路詐騙受害者。

freak
n. 怪胎；異想天開

🔊 *Track 1607*

👦 I like to mix ketchup and jelly together.
我喜歡把番茄醬和果醬混在一起。

👩 You are really a **freak**!
你真是個怪胎！

free

adj. 自由的；免費的；空閒的
v. 釋放

🔊 *Track 1608*

👧 Are you **free** tonight?
你今晚有空嗎？

🧑 No. I have to do my homework.
沒空。我得做我的作業。

這裡使用的是形容詞喔！

general

adj. 大體的；一般的
n. 將軍

🔊 *Track 1609*

👧 What do you do on weekends?
你週末都在做些什麼？

🧑 In **general**, I go to yoga class every weekend.
一般來說，我週末都去上瑜珈課。

這裡使用的是形容詞喔！

gesture

n. 手勢；姿勢；（表示）
v. （比）手勢

🔊 *Track 1610*

👧 What does your **gesture** mean?
你的手勢是什麼意思？

🧑 That means I'm hungry.
那代表我很餓。

這裡使用的是名詞喔！

gift

n. 禮物；天賦

🔊 *Track 1611*

🧑 My boyfriend didn't give me a **gift** on my birthday. I was so angry.
我男朋友在我生日當天沒有送我禮物。我好生氣。

👦 Oh my god! Did he forget your birthday?
我的天啊！他是忘了你的生日嗎？

gigantic

adj. 巨人般的；巨大的

🔊 *Track 1612*

👦 These boxes are so heavy, I need someone to help.
這些箱子實在太重了，我需要有人來幫我。

🧑 You can ask Kevin for help. He has **gigantic** strength.
你可以請凱文幫你。他的力氣很大。

glorious

adj. 著名的；榮耀的

🔊 *Track 1613*

🧑 Our basketball team is going to attend a sports game.
我們的籃球隊要去參加一個體育比賽。

🧑 Wish you win a **glorious** victory.
祝你們可以贏得榮耀的勝利。

gold
n. 黃金
adj. 金的

Track 1614

😀 The **gold** shoes on the shelf are pretty.
架上的那雙金色鞋子很美。

😊 But they are expensive.
但它們很貴。

這裡使用的是形容詞喔！

gorgeous
adj. 炫麗的；極好的

Track 1615

😀 You look **gorgeous**.
你看起來很棒。

😊 Thank you, I'm going to a premiere.
謝謝你，我正要去電影首映會。

gray/grey
n. 灰色
adj. 灰色的

Track 1616

😀 Your eyes are **gray**!
你的眼睛是灰色的。

😊 Because I wear colored contact lenses.
因為我帶有顏色的隱形眼鏡。

這裡使用的是形容詞喔！

green
adj. 綠色的
n. 綠色

Track 1617

😀 The color **green** is good for our eyes.
綠色對我們的眼睛很好。

😊 That's why the black board is green.
所以黑板才會用綠色的。

這裡使用的是名詞喔！

handful
n. 一把；少數

Track 1618

😀 The conference invited at least 50 people, but only a **handful** came.
這個會議邀請了至少50個人，但只有少數人來。

😊 Why?
為什麼？

handwriting
n. 手寫；筆跡

Track 1619

😀 This signature is Obama's **handwriting**.
這是歐巴馬的手寫簽名。

😊 How did you get this?
你怎麼拿到的？

hard
adj. 硬的；難的

Track 1620

It's **hard** to make a speech in front of the crowds.
在大眾前面説話很難。

So you need to practice.
所以你需要練習。

harden
v. 使硬化；變硬

Track 1621

Don't **harden** your heart against him.
別對他硬心腸。

But he really broke my heart before.
但他之前真的傷了我的心。

harmony
n. 一致；和諧

Track 1622

I really love our team.
我真的很愛我們的團隊。

Yeah, our team's atmosphere is always in **harmony**.
對啊，我們團隊的氣氛總是很和諧。

high
adj. 高的；（高級的）
adv. 高的

Track 1623

The building is so tall.
這棟建築好高。

Yeah, it has 20 stories **high**.
對啊，它有二十層樓高。

這裡使用的是形容詞喔！

hollow
adj. 中空的；空的

Track 1624

This chocolate cake looks so delicious.
這塊巧克力蛋糕看起來好美味。

But the chocolate cake is **hollow**.
但這塊巧克力蛋糕是中空的。

huge
adj. 龐大的；巨大

Track 1625

You looked tired. Why?
你看起來很累。為什麼？

Because I have a **huge** pile of documents to deal with.
因為我有一大堆文件要處理。

imaginary
adj. 想像的；虛構的

Track 1626

👦 This historical story is excellent!
這個歷史故事很精彩！

👧 But many characters are **imaginary**.
但許多角色都是虛構的。

imitate
v. 仿效；效法

Track 1627

👦 Meow…Meow…
喵……喵……

👧 Wow! You **imitate** cats very well!
哇！你模仿貓咪模仿地很好！

imitation
n. 模仿；仿造品

Track 1628

👦 How can you paint so well?
你是如何畫的這麼好的？

👧 I learned painting from **imitation**.
我從模仿中學習畫畫。

implicit
adj. 含蓄的；不表明的

Track 1629

👦 I don't understand what Katy is talking about.
我不了解凱蒂在説什麼。

👧 Because her words are too **implicit**.
因為她的話太含蓄了。

inner
adj. 內部的；內心的

Track 1630

👦 My reason tells me that I should keep on working, but my mind says that I want to quit.
我的理智告訴我，我應該繼續工作，但我的心卻告訴我，我想辭職。

👧 I think you should follow your **inner** voice.
我覺得你應該聽從你內心的聲音。

innovative
adj. 創新的

Track 1631

👦 I don't have **innovative** ideas.
我沒有創新的想法。

👧 You can go out and relax to find more ideas.
你可以出去放鬆，去找更多點子。

irritable
adj. 暴躁的；易怒的

🔊 *Track 1632*

👦 I can't stand that woman anymore!
我再也無法忍受那個女人了！

👧 You are too **irritable**.
你太容易生氣了。

key
adj. 主要的；關鍵的
n. 答案；鑰匙

🔊 *Track 1633*

👦 What is the **key** point of this article?
這個文章的關鍵重點是什麼？

👧 I don't think there's any point in this article.
我不認為這篇文章有任何重點。

這裡使用的是形容詞喔！

large
adj. 大的；大量的

🔊 *Track 1634*

👦 This bowl is too **large**.
這個碗實在太大了。

👧 Then you can take the smaller one.
那你可以拿比較小的那個。

layer
n. 層
v. 層疊

🔊 *Track 1635*

👦 Photoshop processes pictures with the concept of **layer**.
Photoshop 處理圖片時使用圖層的概念。

👧 It sounds very hard to learn.
聽起來非常難學。

這裡使用的是名詞喔！

lean
v. 傾斜；倚靠

🔊 *Track 1636*

👦 Look at that guy **leaning** on the desk. He's so cute.
看那個靠在書桌上的男生。他好可愛。

👧 I don't like that kind of type at all.
我一點也不喜歡這種型的。

let
v. 讓

🔊 *Track 1637*

👦 God! **Let** me pass the final exam, please!
上帝啊！拜託讓我通過期末考吧！

👧 You should beg your teacher, not God.
你應該求的是你的老師，而不是上帝。

lighten
v. 變亮；減輕

◀︎ *Track 1638*

It's too dark here. Can you **lighten** up?
這裡太暗了。你可以讓這裡變亮一點嗎？

I'll turn on more lights, wait a minute.
我打開更多燈，等一下。

likely
adj. 可能的
adv. 可能地

◀︎ *Track 1639*

It's **likely** to rain later.
等一下可能會下雨。

Oh no! I don't have an umbrella!
喔不！我沒有帶雨傘！

這裡使用的是形容詞喔！

limitation
n. 限制

◀︎ *Track 1640*

Why can't I upload my video to Facebook?
為什麼我無法把我的影片上傳到臉書？

Because Facebook has a **limitation** of 1G for uploading a video.
因為臉書對上傳影片有 1G 的限制。

line
n. 線；線條

◀︎ *Track 1641*

I can't draw a **line** very straight.
我無法畫一條很直的線。

You can use a ruler.
你可以用尺。

list
n. 清單
v. 列舉

◀︎ *Track 1642*

I'm going to the supermarket later.
我待會兒要去超市。

Then make a **list** of what you want to buy first.
那先擬一個購物清單吧。

這裡使用的是名詞喔！

logo
n. 商標；標誌

◀︎ *Track 1643*

I like the **logo** of this brand.
我喜歡這個品牌的商標。

And it's easy to remember, too.
而且它很容易記住。

lousy
adj. 卑鄙的；討厭的

Track 1644

I don't like Mandy. She is so lousy.
我不喜歡蔓蒂。她好討厭。

Me neither.
我也不喜歡。

lower
v. 降低

Track 1645

Please lower your voice in the library.
在圖書館請降低音量。

Okay, I'll remember that.
好，我會記住的。

magnify
v. 擴大；放大

Track 1646

Those pictures are pretty.
這些照片都很美。

But if you magnified these pictures, you will find that their definition is very low.
但如果你把這些照片放大，你會發現他們的解析度都很低。

makeup
n. 結構；化妝；（化妝品）

Track 1647

That girl is beautiful.
那個女生很漂亮。

I think that's because she puts on a lot of makeup.
我覺得是因為她妝化得很厚。

margin
n. 邊緣

Track 1648

Can you borrow me your notes?
可以借我你的筆記嗎？

Sure. But I wrote all the notes in the margin of the book's pages.
沒問題。但我把筆記都寫在書頁的邊緣。

masterpiece
n. 傑作；名著

Track 1649

What are you reading?
你在讀什麼？

I'm reading a masterpiece of an economic master.
我在讀一本經濟大師寫的名著。

midst

n. 中央;中間

Track 1650

Where's your book?
你的書在哪?

It's in the **midst** of the book shelf.
在書架的中間。

mimic

n. 模仿者
v. 模仿

Track 1651

This actor performs well in the drama.
這個演員在戲劇中表現得很好。

Yes, he is a good **mimic**.
對,他是個很棒的模仿者。

> 這裡使用的是名詞喔!

minimize

v. 減到最小

Track 1652

Oops! I made a mistake in the task!
哦喔!我在工作中出了一個錯!

Don't worry. Let's fix it and **minimize** the damage.
別擔心。我們一起修正它,然後把傷害降到最低。

miraculous

adj. 神奇的

Track 1653

I can't believe that we won the champion!
我不敢相信我們竟然贏得冠軍!

Yeah, it's **miraculous**.
對啊,真是神奇!

missing

adj. 失蹤的;缺少的

Track 1654

There is a page **missing** from the book which I borrowed from the library.
我從圖書館借回來的書少了一頁。

Is the content on that page important to you?
那一頁的內容對你重要嗎?

mode

n. 款式;方法

Track 1655

Have you switched your cell phone into silent **mode**? The class has started already.
你把手機調到靜音模式了嗎?已經開始上課了。

Oh! Thanks for reminding me.
噢!謝謝提醒。

modernize
v. 現代化

Track 1656

Look at my new smart phone.
看我新的智慧型手機。

Wow, you are **modernized** with such a popular device.
哇，你有了這麼流行的裝置後變得現代化了。

---

mold
v. 塑造
n. 模具；黴菌

Track 1657

They are so much alike as if they are being cast in the same **mold**.
他們好像同一個模子刻的。

Yeah, because they're twins.
對啊，因為他們是雙胞胎。

這裡使用的是名詞喔！

---

monotonous
adj. 單調的

Track 1658

What do you think about my painting?
你覺得我的畫如何？

It's too **monotonous**.
太單調了。

---

mournful
adj. 令人悲痛的

Track 1659

That movie is so **mournful**.
這部電影好令人悲傷。

Yeah, I cried when I watched this movie.
對啊，我看這部電影時哭了。

---

must
v. 必須；必定
n. 必須（的事物）

Track 1660

It's 7:25 already!
已經七點二十五分了！

We **must** hurry, or we might be late for school!
我們必須快一點，否則上學就要遲到了！

這裡使用的是助動詞喔！

---

near
adj. 近的；近親的；親密的
prep. 近的
adv. 近的

Track 1661

Where's the post office?
郵局在哪？

It's **near** the park.
在公園附近。

這裡使用的是介系詞喔！

need

n. 需要；必要
v. 需要

Track 1662

I **need** some help.
我需要幫忙。

Let me help then.
讓我來幫你吧！

這裡使用的是動詞喔！

negative

adj. 否定的；消極的

Track 1663

Does Sally have a boyfriend yet?
莎莉交男朋友了沒？

I think the answer is **negative**.
我想答案是否定的。

never

adv. 從來沒有；決不；永不

Track 1664

I **never** give up easily.
我從不輕易放棄。

I wish I could be like you, I always give up easily.
我真希望可以像你一樣，我總是很容易就放棄了。

new

adj. 新的

Track 1665

Look at my **new** skirt! Is it pretty?
看我的新裙子！它好看嗎？

Yes, it looks good on you.
是的，你穿起來很好看。

nod

v. 點頭

Track 1666

How did you answer his question?
你如何回答他的問題的？

I just **nodded** to show that I know without saying anything.
我只是點頭表示我知道了，而沒有說任何話。

oblong

n. 長方形；（橢圓形）

Track 1667

That book is square not **oblong**.
這本書是正方形而不是長方形的。

That's weird.
那真奇怪。

offensive

adj. 令人不快的；冒犯的

◀ *Track 1668*

You are so fat.
你真的好胖。

Your words are really **offensive**.
你的話很令人不愉快。

other

det. 其他的；另外的

◀ *Track 1669*

Do you have any **other** things that you want to do?
你還有其他事情想做嗎？

No. Let's go home.
不。我們回家吧。

outline

n. 外形；輪廓

◀ *Track 1670*

What are you doing?
你在做什麼？

I'm writing the **outline** of my report.
我在寫我報告的大綱。

over

prep. 在……上方；遍及；超過

adv. 在……上方；（越過）

◀ *Track 1671*

I **over** slept this morning.
我今早睡過頭。

Were you late for work?
你工作有遲到嗎？

這裡使用的是副詞喔！

overhead

adj. 頭上的；上方的

adv. 頭上的；上方的

◀ *Track 1672*

Where are my glasses? I can't find them.
我的眼鏡在哪？我找不到它。

They're on the **overhead** shelf.
在你頭上的架子。

這裡使用的是形容詞喔！

painful

adj. 痛苦的

◀ *Track 1673*

It's painful to study hard.
用功讀書好痛苦。

Once you are working, you will find out that working is more **painful**.
一旦你工作後，你會發現工作更痛苦。

pale
adj. 蒼白的

🔊 *Track 1674*

😀 You looked **pale**. What happened?
你看起來很蒼白。發生什麼事了？

😊 I got a headache.
我頭痛。

panic
n. 驚恐
v. 驚恐；（慌張）

🔊 *Track 1675*

😀 It's an earthquake!
是地震！

😊 Don't **panic**! Calm down!
別慌張！冷靜！

> 這裡使用的是動詞喔！

part
n. 部分
adv. 部分地
v. 分開

🔊 *Track 1676*

😀 I've finished the first **part**.
我剛完成第一部分。

😊 And the hardest **part** is just about to begin.
最難的部分才正要開始。

> 這裡使用的是名詞喔！

particular
adj. 特別的；（特定的）

🔊 *Track 1677*

😀 Though everyone thinks that he is excellent, I think he is nothing more than just lucky.
雖然每個人都認為他很優秀，但我覺得他只不過是幸運。

😊 Your thoughts are really **particular**.
你的想法真的很特別。

pattern
n. 模型；圖樣

🔊 *Track 1678*

😀 I don't like the **pattern** on this dress.
我不喜歡這件洋裝上的圖案。

😊 Why? I think it's pretty.
為什麼？我覺得很漂亮啊。

peculiar
adj. 獨特的；奇怪的

🔊 *Track 1679*

😀 He looked at me with a very **peculiar** expression.
他用很奇怪的表情看我。

😊 Why?
為什麼？

各種狀況

a b c d e f g h i j k l m n o p q r s t u v w x y z

peer
v. 凝視
n. 同輩

Track 1680

😀 Are you **peering** at that guy?
你在看那個男生嗎？

😊 Well, I think he's cute.
嗯，我覺得他很可愛。

> 這裡使用的是動詞喔！

perfection
n. 完美

Track 1681

😀 I can't stand anything without **perfection**.
我無法忍受任何不完美的事。

😊 Then I believe that anyone who works with you can't stand you.
那我相信任何跟你共事的人都無法忍受你。

perhaps
adv. 也許；可能

Track 1682

😀 I can't fit in my old clothes anymore.
我穿不下我以前的衣服了。

😊 **Perhaps** you need to go on a diet.
也許你該節食了。

perspective
n. 透視；觀點

Track 1683

😀 What is your **perspective** on this issue?
你對這個議題的觀點是什麼？

😊 I think we should quit that event.
我認為我們應該退出這個活動。

persuasion
n. 說服

Track 1684

😀 He is really good at **persuasion**.
他真的很會說服別人。

😊 That's why he works as a salesman.
這就是為什麼他做業務員。

persuasive
adj. 有說服力的

Track 1685

😀 That advertisement is really **persuasive**.
那支廣告好有說服力。

😊 So do you want to buy their products?
所以你想買他們的產品嗎？

319

pink
adj. 粉紅的
n. 粉紅色

Track 1686

My favorite color is **pink**.
我最喜歡的顏色是粉紅色。

I can tell that, because you have everything in pink.
看得出來，你所有的東西都是粉紅色的。

這裡使用的是名詞喔！

plan
v. 計畫；安排
n. 計畫

Track 1687

What's your **plan** for the summer vacation?
你暑假的計劃是什麼？

I'm going to take a part time job.
我要打工。

這裡使用的是名詞喔！

polish
v. 擦亮；潤飾

Track 1688

I have to **polish** my windows, they're dirty.
我得把窗戶擦亮，他們好髒。

Do you need some help?
你需要幫忙嗎？

poor
adj. 貧窮的；可憐的；差的
n. 貧民

Track 1689

I don't have any money this month, I'm **poor**.
我這個月沒有錢了，我好窮。

Where did you spend all your money?
你把錢都花到哪去了？

這裡使用的是形容詞喔！

popularity
n. 名望；流行

Track 1690

Do you play golf?
你會打高爾夫嗎？

Yes, golf has gained **popularity** in our country.
會，高爾夫在我們國家已經流行起來了。

portray
v. 描繪

Track 1691

The author **portrays** his father as a miserable character.
那個作家把他父親描寫成一個悲慘的角色。

I think he is just using his father to play up.
我覺得他只是利用他父親在炒作。

possible
adj. 可能的

🧑 Let's deal with this **problem** together.
讓我們一起來處理這問題吧。

👩 Okay. First of all, we need to find out all the possible solutions.
好。首先,我們需要找出所有可能的解決方案。

🔊 *Track 1692*

proper
adj. 適當的

🧑 What's the **proper** dress for the concert?
去音樂會的適當穿著是什麼?

👩 I think you can dress in a suit.
我覺得你可以穿西裝。

🔊 *Track 1693*

prove
v. 證明;證實

🧑 I don't agree with your opinion.
我不同意你的意見。

👩 It's okay. Time will **prove** that I am right.
沒關係。時間會證明我是對的。

🔊 *Track 1694*

publish
v. 出版

🧑 When will the book be **published**?
這本書何時會出版?

👩 I'm not sure.
我不確定。

🔊 *Track 1695*

pure
adj. 純粹的

🧑 I want to buy a dog with **pure** blood.
我想買一隻純種狗。

👩 I suggest that you should adopt one if you want to raise a dog.
如果你想養狗的話,我建議你去領養一隻。

🔊 *Track 1696*

purple
n. 紫色
adj. 紫色的

🧑 **Purple** is a noble color in ancient China.
紫色在中國古代是高貴的顏色。

👩 Really? I thought that it's yellow!
真的嗎?我以為是黃色。

這裡使用的是名詞喔!

🔊 *Track 1697*

purpose
n. 目的；意圖

🔊Track 1698

😊 Before doing a research, you should find out the **purpose** of your research.
在做一個研究之前，你必須找出你研究的目的。

😊 I know.
我知道。

quite
adv. 完全地；相當；頗

🔊Track 1699

😊 You looked **quite** different than before.
你看起來和以前完全不一樣。

😊 Of course, I lost 10 kilos during last year.
當然，去年我瘦了10公斤。

reckless
adj. 魯莽的

🔊Track 1700

😊 I regret yelling at her.
我真後悔對她大吼。

😊 You are too **reckless**.
你太魯莽了。

redundant
adj. 過剩的；冗長的

🔊Track 1701

😊 The movie is too **redundant**.
這部電影實在太冗長了。

😊 That's why I fell asleep during the movie.
所以我在看電影時睡著了。

refine
v. 精練；陶冶

🔊Track 1702

😊 Reading good books helps to **refine** our speech.
讀一些好書有助於使我們的言談更優雅。

😊 And reading is especially important for kids.
而且閱讀對小孩特別重要。

reflective
adj. 反射的

🔊Track 1703

😊 Why do we draw back our hand immediately when we are burned?
為什麼我們被燙到時會立刻把手縮回來？

😊 It's a natural **reflective** motion to protect ourselves.
這是我們保護自己的自然反射動作。

resemblance
n. 類似；（相似）

◀ *Track 1704*

> The children have a great **resemblance** to their parents.
> 孩子們和他們的父母親十分相像。

> Especially the daughter.
> 特別是女兒。

reasonable
adj. 合理的

◀ *Track 1705*

> The government is going to announce a law that prohibits people to smoke in the parks.
> 政府即將頒布法令禁止人們在公園抽菸。

> That sounds **reasonable**.
> 這聽起來很合理。

rectangle
n. 長方形

◀ *Track 1706*

> What are we going to do with these papers?
> 我們要怎麼處理這些紙？

> Let's cut these papers into neat **rectangles** for reuse.
> 一起把這些紙裁成整齊的長方形以便重新利用。

regret
v. 後悔；遺憾
n. 遺憾

◀ *Track 1707*

> I told you not to be so impulsive.
> 我早告訴過你別這麼衝動。

> I **regret** that I didn't take your advice.
> 我好後悔我沒聽你的建議。

`這裡使用的是動詞喔！`

reveal
v. 顯示；揭示
n. 揭示

◀ *Track 1708*

> The computer **reveals** that you need to update your software.
> 電腦顯示你應該更新你的軟體了。

> I know, but I want to postpone the update for I'm busy right now.
> 我知道，但我現在很忙，所以我想要把更新延期。

`這裡使用的是動詞喔！`

reverse
v. 顛倒
adj. 顛倒的

◀ *Track 1709*

> Where is the notification on this paper?
> 這張紙上的注意事項在哪？

> It's on the **reverse** side of this paper.
> 在這張紙的背面。

`這裡使用的是形容詞喔！`

round

adj. 圓的；球形的
n. 一輪
prep. 圍繞；附近
adv. 圍繞；附近

🔊 *Track 1710*

The apple is as **round** as a ball.
這顆蘋果圓的像一顆球一樣。

Yeah, so it's expensive.
對啊，所以它很貴。

這裡使用的是形容詞喔！

---

same

pron. 同樣的
adv. 同樣的
adj. 同樣的

🔊 *Track 1711*

I have the **same** clothes as you're wearing today!
你今天穿的這件衣服我也有一件。

Really? What a coincidence!
真的？好巧！

這裡使用的是形容詞喔！

---

satisfactory

adj. 令人滿意的

🔊 *Track 1712*

This handicraft is **satisfactory**.
這件手工作品很令人滿意。

Of course, I made it for the whole week.
當然，我做了整個禮拜。

---

sector

n. 扇形；區

🔊 *Track 1713*

Here is the private **sector** of the store.
這裡是店裡的私人區域。

So the customers are not allowed to get in.
所以顧客不能進來。

---

seem

v. 似乎

🔊 *Track 1714*

It **seems** that you are tired today.
你今天似乎很累。

Yeah, I didn't sleep till 3:00 last night.
對啊，我昨天晚上三點才睡。

---

severe

adj. 嚴厲的；（嚴重的）

🔊 *Track 1715*

She has a **severe** father.
她有個很嚴厲的父親。

No wonder she's always well-behaved.
難怪她總是很乖。

shadow

n. 陰暗之處；影子

◀ *Track 1716*

Why is she sitting alone in the **shadow**?
她為什麼一個人坐在陰暗的角落？

She seems in a bad mood.
她似乎心情不好。

shallow

adj. 淺的；膚淺的

◀ *Track 1717*

I really can't agree with his opinion.
我實在無法同意他的意見。

His perspectives are always very **shallow**.
他的觀點總是很膚淺。

short

adj. 短的；不足的

◀ *Track 1718*

Should I have my hair cut?
我應該去剪頭髮嗎？

Yes, I think **short** hair is much more suitable for you.
對，我覺得短髮比較適合你。

shrink

v. 收縮；退縮

◀ *Track 1719*

Are you the kind of person who is shy with strangers?
你是那種怕生的人嗎？

Yes, I am. I always **shrink** from strangers.
是的，我是。我看到陌生人就會退縮。

side

n. 邊；旁邊；側面

◀ *Track 1720*

Where's my notebook?
我的筆記本在哪？

It's just right by your **side**.
就在你旁邊。

similar

adj. 相似的；類似的

◀ *Track 1721*

Your skirt is so **similar** to mine.
你的裙子和我的好像。

Really? Where did you buy it?
真的？你在哪裡買的？

simply

adv. 簡單地；樸實地

🔊 Track 1722

🗣 Can you cook?
你會做菜嗎？

🗣 I can **simply** cook fried rice.
我只會做炒飯。

sketch

n. 素描；草圖；概略
v. 素描

🔊 Track 1723

🗣 What is this?
這是什麼？

🗣 It's a **sketch** of my painting.
這是我畫畫的草圖。

這裡使用的是名詞喔！

slender

adj. 苗條的

🔊 Track 1724

🗣 What do you think of the jeans?
你覺得這條牛仔褲如何？

🗣 You look **slender** in them.
你穿上後看起來很苗條。

slim

adj. 苗條的

🔊 Track 1725

🗣 I want to go on a diet.
我想要節食。

🗣 What? You are **slim** already!
什麼？你已經很苗條了！

smash

v. 粉碎；打破；（猛擊）

🔊 Track 1726

🗣 He is getting drunk.
他開始醉了。

🗣 Yeah, and he will start to **smash** things if he got more drunk.
對，而且如果他再醉一點的話，他就會開始砸東西了。

smooth

adj. 平滑的

🔊 Track 1727

🗣 Your skin is so **smooth**. How did you do that?
你的皮膚好光滑。你怎麼辦到的？

🗣 I use skin milk everyday.
我每天擦乳液。

soft
adj. 軟的；柔和的

◀Track 1728

😊 Your bed is **soft**.
你的床好軟。

😊 I know. You can sleep on my bed if you want.
我知道。如果你想的話，你可以在我床上休息一下。

sophisticated
adj. 世故的；精緻的

◀Track 1729

😊 Sophie is **sophisticated**.
蘇菲好世故。

😊 Once you start to work, you will find that being sophisticated is necessary.
一旦你開始工作，你就會發現世故是必要的。

sorrowful
adj. 哀痛的；悲傷的

◀Track 1730

😊 Why do you look so **sorrowful**?
你為什麼看起來這麼悲傷？

😊 Because my dog died yesterday.
因為我的狗昨天死了。

sort
n. 種類
v. 分類

◀Track 1731

😊 What **sort** of clothing style do you like?
你喜歡哪種穿著類型？

😊 I like casual clothes.
我喜歡休閒的衣服。

這裡使用的是名詞喔！

square
adj. 公正的；方正的
v. 平方
n. 正方形

◀Track 1732

😊 I can't believe that my boss blames all the faults on me!
我不敢相信我老闆把所有的錯都怪到我頭上！

😊 He is indeed not **square** enough.
他的確有點不夠公正。

這裡使用的是形容詞喔！

straight
adj. 筆直的；正直的
adv. 直接地

◀Track 1733

😊 Your nose is **straight**.
你的鼻子很挺直。

😊 Yeah, I'm satisfied with my nose shape.
對啊，我很滿意我的鼻形。

這裡使用的是形容詞喔！

structural
adj. 結構上的

Track 1734

The **structural** of the two articles are the same.
這兩篇文章的結構一樣。

So do I still have to read both these two articles?
所以我這兩篇都必須讀嗎？

superiority
n. 優越（性）；卓越

Track 1735

She has the **superiority** in learning English because she has been studying abroad for three years.
因為她曾出國讀書三年，所以她有學習英語上的優勢。

No wonder her English is so good.
難怪她的英文這麼好。

suppress
v. 壓抑；制止

Track 1736

Many bad news are **suppressed** by government.
政府通常把許多壞消息壓下來。

That's why the media didn't report the news of flu.
這就是為什麼媒體沒有報導流感的新聞。

surface
n. 表面

Track 1737

He seems a nice guy.
他似乎是個好人。

That's because you just look at the **surface**.
那是因為你只看到表面。

symbol
n. 象徵；標誌

Track 1738

Red is a beautiful color.
紅色是很漂亮的顏色。

And it's a **symbol** of passion, too.
而且它是熱情的象徵。

symbolize
v. 象徵

Track 1739

The dove **symbolizes** peace.
鴿子象徵和平。

So the dove appears in many international events.
所以鴿子常常出現在許多國際的活動中。

take
v. 抓住;拾起;量出;吸引;(搭乘;帶)

Track 1740

I feel so nervous about the interview.
我對於要去面試感到很緊張。

Take it easy! Trust yourself, you can make it.
放輕鬆!相信自己,你可以做到的。

thrill
v. 興奮;緊張
n. 激動

thrilled
adj. 非常高興

Track 1741

"Saw 6" is really good and exciting.
《奪魂鋸6》真是好看又刺激。

I'm always **thrilled** while watching this kind of movie.
我每次看這種電影都非常高興。

tiny
adj. 極小的

Track 1742

The writings on the book is too **tiny**.
這本書字體太小了。

You need a magnifying glass.
你需要一支放大鏡。

total
adj. 全部的
n. 全部
v. 總計為

Track 1743

How much are these?
這些多少錢?

The **total** is 159 dollars.
總共159元。

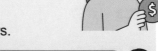

這裡使用的是名詞喔!

transform
v. 改變

Track 1744

Try to **transform** your life, or you will be crushed by pressure.
試著改變你的生活,不然你會被壓力壓垮。

What shall I do?
我該怎麼做?

triangle
n. 三角形

Track 1745

Son, look! Sandwiches are **triangles** and toasts are squares.
兒子，看！三明治是三角形的，吐司是正方形的。

Mommy, I understand.
媽咪，我懂了。

tremendous
adj. 巨大的；驚人的

Track 1746

Wow! This building is so **tremendous**.
哇！這棟大樓好巨大。

I think so, too.
我也這麼覺得。

upset
adj. 使心煩
v. 顛覆；使心煩

Track 1747

Math makes me very **upset**.
數學使我很心煩

But it's fun for me.
但對我來説很有趣。

這裡使用的是形容詞喔！

underline
v. （畫）底線
n. 底線

Track 1748

What are the points of this book?
這本書的重點在哪？

The points are those sentences with **underlines**.
重點在有畫底線的部分。

這裡使用的是名詞喔！

visual
adj. 視覺的

Track 1749

This design is so special.
這個設計好特別。

Yeah, it's also called a kind of **visual** design.
對啊，這也被叫做一種視覺設計。

widen
v. 使……變寬；增廣

Track 1750

Why do you want to go abroad?
你為什麼想出國？

Because I want to **widen** my vision.
因為我想增廣視野。

woe

n. 悲哀；悲痛

Track 1751

You look sad. Tell me about your **woes**.
你看起來很傷心。告訴我你的苦惱。

Well… I don't know how to say it.
嗯……我不知道該怎麼說。

wrong

adj. 壞的；錯的
adv. 錯的
n. 錯誤
v. 冤枉

Track 1752

Where are you? You are late!
你在哪？你遲到了！

Sorry, I've taken the **wrong** way.
對不起，我走錯路了。

這裡使用的是形容詞喔！

原來如此 系列 E266

零基礎自學王：英文單字 零勉強、免死背！
考大學、多益、出國旅遊與生活，絕對必備！

8大情境╳常用單字╳實境對話，全面提升英文能力！

作　者	張慈庭英語研發團隊 著
社　長	王毓芳
顧　問	曾文旭
編輯統籌	耿文國、黃璽宇
主　編	吳靜宜
執行主編	潘妍潔
執行編輯	吳芸蓁、吳欣蓉、范筱翎
美術編輯	王桂芳、張嘉容
封面設計	阿作
法律顧問	北辰著作權事務所　蕭雄淋律師、幸秋妙律師

初　版	2023年07月
出　版	捷徑文化出版事業有限公司
電　話	（02）2752-5618
傳　真	（02）2752-5619

定　價	新台幣380元／港幣127元
產品內容	1書

總 經 銷	采舍國際有限公司
地　址	235新北市中和區中山路二段366巷10號3樓
電　話	（02）8245-8786
傳　真	（02）8245-8718

港澳地區經銷商	和平圖書有限公司
地　址	香港柴灣嘉業街12號百樂門大廈17樓
電　話	（852）2804-6687
傳　真	（852）2804-6409

本書圖片由Freepik提供

國家圖書館出版品預行編目資料

零基礎自學王：英文單字零勉強、免死背！考大學、多益、出國旅遊與生活，絕對必備！／張慈庭英語研發團隊著. -- 初版. -- 臺北市：捷徑文化出版事業有限公司, 2023.07
面；　公分. -- (原來如此；E266)
ISBN 978-626-7116-34-0(平裝)

1. CST: 英語　2. CST: 詞彙

805.12　　　　　　　　　112007478